"You ████████████████████████████████ **ered.**

"Then ██████████████ a little battle of wills before us, does it not?"

Suddenly, and so swiftly that she gasped, he reached down and pulled her into the saddle in front of him. One arm closed around her midriff and in a trice she was imprisoned like a bird in a cage. She squirmed and fought to wrestle free, but she could hardly breathe, let alone move.

Gwennan twisted to look into his face and only just curbed the impulse to spit into it. "Don't you *trust* me, Rolant Guyarde?"

With his free hand, he replaced his helmet, securing it under his chin with deft fingers. The cold steel of the nose blade sent a shudder through her.

"No, I don't trust you at all. But at least you are using my name, although a more correct form of address would be Sir Rolant."

Gwennan's skin shuddered as his chain mail dug into her shoulders. Even worse was the strong length of his thighs clasped like iron against hers, the warmth of his hips as they cradled her bottom in a shockingly intimate manner.

And there was nothing at all she could do about it. She had no form of either defense or attack, only her pride and her hate. But as for calling him, this man who was her enemy, sir or any other title? No, no and never! She'd rather die first.

Author Note

In the two decades following the Norman Conquest of England in 1066, ambitious Marcher lords made rapid inroads into the neighboring land of Wales. Despite fierce opposition from native Welsh rulers, the northern coastal swath and the fertile southern lowlands were quickly annexed. But the remote and barren uplands became the bastions of a long and passionate resistance. The fictitious llys of Carn Egryn is one such haven, bordered by mountains to the east and the sea to the west, and held by a proud Welsh princess who is determined to defend her home and her family at all costs. I live not far from the Dysynni valley and I look out at the Cadair Idris mountain range every day from my window. The wild beauty, turbulent skies and rich history of this region have always inspired me, and so it was the perfect setting for this, my second book.

LISSA MORGAN

—

An Alliance with His Enemy Princess

ISBN-13: 978-1-335-72364-2

An Alliance with His Enemy Princess

Recycling programs
for this product may
not exist in your area.

For questions and comments about the quality of this book,
please contact us at CustomerService@Harlequin.com.

Harlequin Enterprises ULC
22 Adelaide St. West, 41st Floor
Toronto, Ontario M5H 4E3, Canada
www.Harlequin.com

Printed in U.S.A.

Lissa Morgan hails from Wales but has traveled far and wide over the years, usually in pursuit of the next new job. She has always pursued her love of history, too, taking in as many castles, abbeys, hill forts and museums as possible along the way. She once worked as a costume tour guide at Hampton Court Palace, where she donned her sumptuous Tudor gowns in Catherine of Aragon's dressing rooms! Now happily back home, Lissa lives between the mountains and the sea in rugged North West Wales, where she works in academia and web design. She has also recently returned to her first great literary love, historical romantic fiction, not just reading it now but, amazingly, writing it, too! Visit her at www.lissamorgan.com, Facebook.com/lissamorganhistoricalromance or Twitter.com/lissamorganauth.

Books by Lissa Morgan

The Welsh Lord's Convenient Bride
An Alliance with His Enemy Princess

Look out for more books from Lissa Morgan coming soon.

Visit the Author Profile page at Harlequin.com.

With gratitude for the friendships
made along the way.

Chapter One

Wales, 1091

'We are ambushed!'

Gwennan screamed a warning. Hauling on Tarian's reins, she turned the great stallion on his haunches to meet the Normans who came swarming down upon them. Between one curse and the next, the quiet valley they'd been riding through became filled with the thunder of hooves, the yelling of men and the clash of steel on steel.

Her heart raging, she rushed into the thick of the fighting, swinging her sword high and bringing it down hard on the raised shield of a Norman knight. She ducked beneath his slashing parry and, as his courser plunged, thrust her point deep into a gap in the chainmail under his armpit. He fell from the saddle, but she didn't even glance at him as she drove Tarian on into the midst of the enemy ranks.

But even as another Norman perished under her sword—Rhys's sword, and a blazing talisman of Welsh freedom—Gwennan knew this battle was lost. Too many

Welshmen already lay dead or dying around her and it was useless to fight on. They were outnumbered three to one at least and, caught as they were on open ground, it would only be a matter of time before her little band was overwhelmed completely.

She parried another attack, swinging away from the arcing weapon, and with all her might dragged her sword across the back of the Norman's neck. As he crashed to the ground she called the order to retreat, to regroup at their hidden camp, high on the slopes of the Dysynni Mountains, to live to fight another day.

And then a blow like a falling boulder hit the back of her head. A flash of white light blinded her and everything went black.

Rolant guided his horse through the bodies of the warriors on the ground. Most were dead, and the one or two that were merely injured were being swiftly dispatched by his foot soldiers. None would be left to live. It sickened him that life, even the lives of these truculent yet courageous Welshmen, was so cheaply held.

But to show mercy, to spare an enemy, only meant having to face them again another day. And the resistance of the inhabitants of this wild, mountainous district—admirable though it was—had been a thorn in the side of his overlord for too long already.

A horse standing with its head low, just where the trees began, caught his eye. Its dark, iron-grey coat gleamed like a burnished shield, and an unusually light-coloured mane and tail flowed like silken silver.

A beautiful steed and an unexpected prize! Who would have thought such an animal to belong to a Welsh barbarian? No doubt it was a Norman animal, the property of a nobleman, either won in battle or, more likely, stolen from its rightful owner in one of the audacious raids that these people were so skilled at.

Dismounting, Rolant tethered his gelding to a bush and approached the grey stallion. It flung its head up and eyed him viciously, ears flat and nostrils flared in warning. Its reins were broken and trailed over its neck to the ground. The end of one was in the hands of a boy, who was lying face-down, a dented helmet partly covering his young head.

It didn't take long to assess the situation. The magnificent horse, the dead Welsh warrior lying a yard or so away, and this his page, or squire perhaps, faithful to his master even in death.

Rolant glanced at the dead man. The sightless eyes were staring upwards and there was a deep and bloody gash where his throat had been. No need to linger there. The warrior had already gone to meet his creator. So instead he knelt down next to the boy. Removing what was left of the helmet, he discovered a lump the size of a lark's egg beneath the chestnut-brown hair that fell to the nape of a slender neck.

But the skull was intact, and there was little blood, so carefully he turned him over. If this young one lived, he'd spare him for his loyalty as much as his youth. If he were too badly hurt, then a swift and painless death would save him from the scavenging wolves that haunted these remote places.

The face was even younger than he'd expected, smooth and pale, the lips full, the closed eyelashes long and soft. There was no other wound apparent but from the dent in the bronze helmet. He surmised the boy had been merely stunned by a glancing blow from a weapon and might yet live.

Rolant put a hand over the heart, feeling for a beat of life, and found...*breasts?* He snatched his hand away in surprise. Surely he was mistaken? He explored further and, as much as his mind refused such a thing, the male in him knew there was no mistake. Beneath the well-worn brown tunic, his fingers traced and recognised the small mounds of a young woman's breasts. And, below the left one, a strong and steady heartbeat.

He lifted his eyes to the face, and as he stared, bemused, the lashes fluttered open. This time it wasn't just surprise that struck Rolant, but shock too—and a startling stab of lust. For they were beautiful eyes, large and wide and the colour of dark honey, and so unexpected that his breath caught.

Dazed and questioning, those eyes stared up at him for a long moment, struggling to focus, and then the lips parted. *'T-Tarian! Lle mae Tarian?'*

Rolant didn't understand the Welsh. Was Tarian a name? The name of the dead warrior, perhaps? He shook his head but she'd already slipped back into oblivion. Sitting back on his haunches, he cursed his luck. What the devil was he supposed to do with a girl—and a lovely one at that?

'Ho! Rolant!' Giles de Fresnay rode into sight. 'Why are you idling there, man? We must be after those miserable Welsh cowards while there is still daylight. There's no one left alive here now, anyway.'

Rolant looked up at his comrade, noting the dripping crimson edge of the sword in the man's hand. Giles was as bloodthirsty a soldier as he'd ever known and he didn't like him. He liked him even less as the man's eyes lit with cunning on the unconscious form lying on the ground.

'What have you got there? A boy, by God! Is he dead?'

'No, not dead.' Rolant made his mind up. If he hesitated, Giles's blade would be poised in a flash to slit the girl's throat from ear to ear, adding to his greedy tally of Welsh dead. 'The boy lives and seems to have been only stunned,' he said, his voice a warning. 'And, since I am without either page or squire, I mean to take him for my own—the horse too,' he added, jerking his chin in the direction of the grey stallion.

Spoils of war were hotly contested, fought over as bitterly as the battle itself, but as leader he had precedence. None of them would dare lay claim to the animal before him, but neither would any one of them spare an ounce of compassion for the girl on the ground. A girl that he had to ensure remained a boy as far as his men were concerned—at least until he could decide what best to do with her.

'A noble beast.' Giles's grey eyes narrowed as they flickered to the horse and back again, his mouth curling with undisguised envy. 'Though more fit for a king than a bachelor knight!'

Both of them had been honoured by the new King in the late rebellion, when the sons of the Conqueror had argued over who should have Normandy and who England. De Fresnay was equal to Rolant in status, but subordinate in rank—something that Rolant had soon discovered stuck in the man's gut. It only partly accounted for the rivalry between them that simmered constantly, just below the surface.

It was a rivalry he didn't need on this expedition into Wales. And a command that he'd accepted eagerly at first. But day by day it sat less and less comfortably on his shoulders. Conquest was one thing; the extinction of an entire race was quite another.

'As for the boy...you'll have your work cut out for you, Rolant. If you take my advice, you'll slay the wretch here and now.' Giles spat on the ground. 'These people are savages—uncivilised. I wouldn't trust my throat with any of them.'

Rolant ignored him and reached for the grey stallion's reins, looping them over the pommel of his saddle. Then, lifting up the girl, he put her astride his gelding, carefully leaning her forward on its neck so she wouldn't fall off.

As he prepared to mount behind her, the glint of a sword lying nearby caught his eye. It lay half hidden in the grass, as if flung from a stricken hand, and he crossed to pick it up.

The carving on the hilt looked ancient and mysterious, the gleaming blade not newly forged but seeming to belong to some bygone age. Rolant slipped it into his belt. No need to let such a fine weapon go to waste either.

When he turned again, Giles had ridden up alongside his courser. Leaning down, he took the girl by the hair and wrenched her head up.

'A pretty boy and no mistake.' Roughly, he let the head drop back again, malice twisting his mouth. 'Make sure he warms only your *ale*, Rolant, and not your *bed* as well! If you can train him at all, that is.'

'When I want advice, de Fresnay, I'll ask for it.' Any doubts he might have had as to the wisdom of taking the girl with them vanished. He was a warrior, not a murderer, and if he left her here she would perish if not by the swords of his men then by others who would come in their wake. Of that there was no doubt.

'Now, get the men to burying these dead—Norman *and* Welsh,' he added. 'We'll not leave any for the wolves.'

With a smirk, the man rode away, and Rolant clenched his teeth. No one dared say it to his face, but he knew what they called him behind his back, de Fresnay and his crew. How they ridiculed him for his chastity. *Virgin, monk, catamite.*

None of those descriptions applied, but he wasn't going to rise to their bait and explain himself. As violent a body of men as he'd ever commanded, how would any of them understand the shame of losing your name and your honour? Having your home and your family stripped from you in one fell blow? Your heart and trust severed as swiftly and as callously as man's head from his body?

As *his* head should have been, since *he'd* been the instrument of his own disgrace, the death of his brother and the devastation of his family. So what did that make him at the end of the day?

Rolant mounted his gelding and, with the reins in one hand, supported the girl with his free arm. She was like a sleeping, fragile bird in the crook of his elbow, and as he glanced down at her face something stirred again in his gut.

Something he banished at once, even as the bile of his own dishonour remained like a bitter aftertaste in his mouth. No, it wasn't a vow of chastity or devotion he'd taken that day five years ago, when they'd buried his brother John, but a lesson he would never forget.

Love was a blindfold that could lead a man to wreak

unwitting desolation that could never be undone. Pity the poor wretch who ever put it over his eyes—as he'd done, and willingly—and was left to live with the consequences of his blindness.

Gwennan was having a nightmare—a waking nightmare, for she knew she didn't sleep. The torment that assailed her didn't bring the peace of sleep with it at all. Instead, her skull seemed to have split wide open, and her body was racked with a heaving, bone-shuddering nausea such as she'd never known.

In her dream, she felt hands upon her. Gentle hands that turned her onto her side, held her head as bitter vomit gushed up from her stomach, wiped her mouth and nose clean.

And she heard a voice, too, that murmured words she didn't understand but somehow made the nightmare less real, less frightening—until finally it stopped altogether and oblivion came and sucked her down into its dark and blissful depths.

Rolant ordered the campfires to be doused now that the meat to break their fast was cooked. Taking his ration, he returned to his place, where the girl still slept. She'd kept him awake for hours during the night, as she'd swung from a deep state of unconsciousness to half-waking bouts of vomiting until there could be nothing left inside her.

He'd done his best to ease the retching, wiped the slime from her mouth and even managed to get some drops of water between her cracked lips. And when he'd gone to get his meat he'd tied her upright to the wagon wheel, so that should she vomit again at least she wouldn't choke.

Other than that, there was nothing else he could do. It was the blow to her head, he knew. Not severe enough to kill, but hard enough to shock the body into violent reaction. It would pass, and hopefully pass soon. He couldn't keep his men encamped here in the midst of enemy territory any longer just for the sake of what they believed to be a worthless Welsh boy. All of them wondered, though none asked, why he was taking such trouble over a prisoner who, in their shared opinion, should be put out of his misery.

Not for the first time, Rolant rued the fact that he'd ever looked into those compelling honey-glazed eyes. Would it have been better, after all, to have left the girl where she was to take her chances?

He shook his head, silently answering his own question.

All his better instincts, such as they were, had told him not to abandon her as he'd abandoned John. Perhaps it was *because* he'd abandoned his brother that he couldn't leave her behind. Either way, it was too late to regret his act of compassion, but it meant she was now both his captive and his responsibility.

He swallowed a mouthful of ale and, taking his knife from his belt, began to cut the roast boar's flesh into strips. As he worked, he eyed the sleeping figure slumped before him and asked himself different questions—which were equally hard to find answers for. What was the reason for those clothes and that shoulder-length hair? Was she dressed thus out of necessity or deception? And what was *her* part in the small band of Welsh resistance they'd encountered yesterday?

Because no man took a girl as his page, or squire, and exposed her to the dangers of war—not even here in this strange and savage country.

Gwennan tried to open her eyes, but the pain behind them made the effort too much, so she gave up. Forcing her mind to work instead, she assessed her body, trying to discover what was causing the ache in her arms and shoulders, the stiffness in her legs.

Her neck ached too, as if her head were too heavy to hold, and the tingling in her fingers told her that her hands were bound in front of her. Slowly, it dawned on her that she was sitting on the ground, leaning against something hard.

Around her were sounds and smells—some familiar, some strange—all of them laden with peril. The smoke of dying fires, the stamp of horses' hooves, the noise of men eating, the mutter of conversation from here and there…not in Welsh but in the Norman tongue. And, nearest of all, the rhythmic rasp of stone on steel as a weapon was sharpened.

Quick fear flooded all the way through her and her body jerked instinctively. Something cut into her stomach and she shuddered inside as she realised what it was. A rope, tied snugly around her waist, binding her fast to what could only be the wheel of a cart.

'I know you're awake, so you might as well open your eyes.'

Gwennan's blood froze and her heart started to hammer in her breast. The voice had spoken in English but it was accented with Norman French too, like the others, which meant the enemy was all around her. Panic rose up in her throat and, gritting her teeth to silence the scream that rose with it, she braced herself for the thrust of the knife between her ribs which was surely to come.

'Or you can pretend to be asleep and stay hungry. It's up to you.'

As he spoke Gwennan's belly rumbled loud, even through the fear that had set her limbs quivering. It had been a long time since she'd eaten, though she couldn't remember how long. Hours? Days?

Then the memory of the blow on her head surged back, making her feel as if her skull had shattered all over again as the pieces finally came together.

She was alive—for now—and she was a prisoner of the Normans who had ambushed them. Her fate was sealed, but pray God the rest of her men had got away to safety.

The noise of sharpening ceased and was replaced by the clunk of metal against wood. The smell of roasted meat drifted into Gwennan's nostrils and her mouth began to water. She pressed her lips firmly together, trying to stem the tremble of her lips that betrayed the fear inside, but the sound of teeth ripping into flesh followed by satisfied chewing was too much.

Finally forcing her eyes open, she saw, sitting cross-legged in front of her, a giant of a man. A chainmail hauberk covered a vast chest, and his head was bare to reveal thick black hair cut short in the Norman style.

'That's more like it.' Spearing a small chunk of meat on the point of his knife, he held it to her mouth. 'Eat.'

Oh, how she wanted to refuse—or, better still, take it and spit it back out, right into his face. But, to her horror, her mouth grabbed at it and she swallowed it with hardly a chew. He speared another small chunk, which went swiftly the way of the first. More followed, all of which she devoured like some starved creature. Then he put the meat aside and lifted a cup of cool ale to her mouth.

'Drink.'

Gwennan drank, feeling the ale flow like healing nectar down her parched throat.

From beneath her lowered lashes, she studied her captor carefully. After all, one had to know one's enemy in order to defeat him.

His fingers around the cup were long and strong, and an old scar running along the back of his right hand told her he was a soldier, not a servant. But his magnificent body and sharp alertness had told her that already.

'Not too much. Your stomach is still raw from the purging.' After a few more precious sips, the cup was removed from her lips. 'The wound on your skull is not too bad, although you were stunned by it.'

Purging? Gwennan ran her tongue around her mouth, over her teeth, tasting amid the meat and ale the remnants of nausea. So it hadn't been a nightmare after all. And if the vomiting had been real, had the hands and the voice been real too? And had they been *this* man's hands and voice? This cursed Norman invader's?

She closed her eyes again and, leaning her head back, winced as the sore place at the back of her skull proved she had indeed been stunned. But vigour and warmth began to seep into her body. If he was feeding her, satisfying her thirst, he clearly didn't intend to kill her. So…why was she still alive?

The sound of sharpening recommenced, the rhythm grating and irritating to her ears. Swiftly her mind raced around her body again, looking for other wounds, finding none. Apart from the ache in her head and the numbness of her limbs she was whole, but tethered securely to a wagon wheel!

'Open your eyes.'

The command was as soft as before, and yet it suggested compliance or suffering the consequences. So Gwennan obeyed and looked into a young face rather than old, although he looked to have had more summers than she did—at least five and twenty.

She saw a square chin, a full mouth, straight nose, a wide brow above green long-lashed eyes. Then, lower, she saw broad shoulders, a lean, tough body, and the muscles of the forearms flexing as he sharpened his weapon.

And not *his* weapon either, but hers! Rhys's sword—Cleddyf Gobaith. The blade of hope, blessed and invincible. The weapon that was destined to vanquish their foes and win their freedom. And now this accursed Norman had it!

Clenching her teeth, she tested her bonds again as cold anger finally eclipsed helpless fear. But the ropes were tied too securely and impossible to break loose.

His head tilted slightly, catching the first dappled rays of sun just as they broke through the canopy of the trees. 'Do you speak English?'

Gwennan glared at him. She knew the language well enough and she needed answers. 'Where is my horse?'

'*Your* horse?'

She licked her lips, found them dry and cracked, but her voice was strong and steady. 'Where is he?'

The Norman said nothing as he put down the piece of flint and placed Cleddyf Gobaith across his thighs. Her eyes flickered down to the burnished steel and then back to his, and a shock ran all the way through her. Even in the deceptive light of dawn, they gleamed as bright and as green as the lake at Talyllyn in high summer.

'You mean your master's horse, do you not? He's well, but he's *my* horse now—as is this fine sword too.' He ran a fingertip over its keen edge. 'Your master is dead and has no need of either. Or of you.'

Gwennan's heart jolted. Not since Rhys had a man looked at her as this Norman was looking at her now. With a frank and assessing stare that seemed to pass through her skin and delve deep inside her.

No other man had dared intrude on her love, her loyalty, or her grief for her dead husband as she carried on his fight to drive the enemy out and take back their homeland. So how did the eyes of this man—a man who *was* the enemy—dare to stare so boldly?

She tore her gaze away and looked over his shoulder to the camp beyond. Thirty or so men, half a dozen of them knights, the rest foot soldiers. Not a full army, just an advance guard—or a scouting party, perhaps, leading the way into the heart of her lands. She could see Tarian now, tethered with all the other horses at the far side of the forest clearing.

'What is your name, boy?' The Norman leaned in and, taking her chin, turned her face back towards him. 'You have one, I assume?'

His touch was strong, yet strangely gentle. But at least he'd confirmed that her sex was as yet undiscovered. She was still fully clothed, but her helmet was gone, and it must have been he who removed it. *Diolch i Dduw* he'd not removed any more!

With her shoulder-length hair and attire of tunic and woollen *socasau*, Gwennan knew she passed easily for the boy she pretended to be, even if she could do nothing about the soft skin of her face. A face that warmed uncomfortably as he waited for an answer.

'G...Gerallt.'

She'd lied to him. If he found out who she truly was she'd be killed on the spot—as her husband had been. Or tossed into a dungeon to rot and rage—like her parents.

'Gerallt.' He repeated the name. 'And where do you hail from...Gerallt?'

The emphasis in his voice sent a ripple of discomfort along her nerves, and the next lie came far less steadily than the first. 'C-Caernarfon.'

Gwennan's heart began to thud as his fingers still held her jaw with that soft yet firm force, compelling her to meet his scrutinising stare. If he discovered her true sex, even if her identity remained undiscovered, she was lost. For everyone in Wales, and in Saxon England too, knew what treatment women received at the hands of these Norman devils.

She would be raped, violated—and not just by this man, but by others of his party too. Then her nose would be slit for a harlot and—if she was lucky, and if they were merciful—her throat slit too. To be left alive after such brutality and shame was no life at all for any woman.

'And what are you doing in these parts so far from home...Gerallt of Caernarfon?'

He turned her face slightly to one side and then the other, his eyes peeling away her skin as he studied her like some sort of new species of creature he'd discovered.

'Fighting you Norman dogs—what else?' she spat.

His mouth stretched into a slow smile. 'Courageous words from naught but a child...'

'I'm not a child! Free my hands and return my weapon to me and I'll prove that to you!'

This time he didn't just smile, he laughed. Not a cruel laugh, but one that dismissed her challenge like an annoying insect buzzing around his head.

'Not today, my fiery young Welshman.'

He took hold of the rope that bound her to the wheel. Gwennan shuddered as his knuckles pressed into her midriff, steeling herself for the death thrust that was surely coming. But with a deft stroke he cut her bonds and then, getting to his feet with quick grace, slipped Cleddyf Gobaith into his belt.

'I am in need of a page, and since your master is dead, you will serve me in that office.'

Gwennan stared up at him, her mouth dropping open, as behind him the camp began to break up. Serve this Norman *cythrawl*? Words of contempt and refusal burned on the tip of her tongue, but she had no chance to say them as he bent and hauled her to her feet.

Her legs throbbed as the blood flowed back into them, and if he hadn't been holding her she might have fallen down. Nausea churned again in her belly, and she grabbed his shoulders to steady herself.

The strength of him was overpowering, and the height of him towered over her. He was taller even than he'd appeared when he'd been sitting on the ground. And, to her shame, Gwennan felt her cheeks turn as hot as fire.

'Are you faint still?' he asked, a frown creasing his brow.

She shook her head. 'No... But you can hardly expect me to spring to my feet like a hare from cover when I've been tied to a cartwheel for hours on end!'

For a moment he glared down at her, a battle between irritation and concern seeming to shimmer in his eyes. Then he muttered something in his own language, and the next moment she was up and in his arms, as helpless as a sack of corn.

Laughter rang out all around as he dumped her into the wagon, beside the supplies it bore. Then, as a final insult, he ruffled her hair.

'I'm sorry I had to tie you up. But I have to keep you tethered for a little while longer in case you try and run—as I suspect you would at the first chance you got.'

He looked deep into her eyes, and his startling green gaze was far too keen. And then he had the audacity, the irreverence, to smile at her!

'Because something tells me you don't care at all for the idea of being my page—do you, Gerallt of Caernarfon?'

Fuming, Gwennan watched him stride away, buckling on his helmet and pulling on his gauntlets, Cleddyf Gobaith glinting at his hip. A man held Tarian ready for him and he hitched his shield to the saddle and swung himself up onto the stallion's back.

Tarian reared high into the air, neck arching and hooves pawing. A lesser horseman would have been off again straight away. But this man—clearly the leader here—leaned forward, his balance perfect, and with a word and a touch of his heels brought him down again.

He laughed and slapped the stallion's neck—not in punishment but in careless appreciation. It was the action of a man who knew and respected an animal of quality and mettle even while he mastered it.

The Normans moved out of the woodland clearing, their leader in front, heading away from the rising sun, and deeper into the Dysynni lands—*her* lands. Gwennan bumped along behind them in the wagon, grinding her teeth at the indignity of it. She was the daughter of Cynddylan Fawr—a princess of Wales! The last of the Royal House of Dysynni and keeper of the blessed sword of hope!

And when she was free again, and that sword was flaming once more in her hand, she'd make sure that nameless, arrogant, green-eyed Norman would be the first to die by it.

Chapter Two

It was noon when they reached the river, the sun bright and the day clear and hot. Despite that, the rains of the previous weeks had left the waters high here at the ford of the Dyfi. Gwennan lifted herself up on her elbows and craned her neck to look over the side of the wagon.

Up ahead, the Norman leader was frowning down at the mud-coloured flow of water below the bank. She couldn't hear what he said to the man beside him, but as the two turned their heads to glance upstream it was clear they were weighing up the risks of crossing here.

She ducked down again and, rolling onto her back, stared up at the sky. If the Normans turned upstream, to look for a shallower ford, at least they'd be going in the opposite direction to her fortress, Carn Egryn. But it would also take her further away from home and make rescue more difficult.

Her Welshmen had been following all morning, keeping out of sight among the trees that cloaked the hillsides. But she knew they were there from the occasional glint of the sun off a bridle bit or the crown of a bronze helmet. The Normans were completely oblivious to the fact that they were being shadowed, more fool them!

A different sort of shadow loomed up to block out the sun and Gwennan looked up at her captor, towering high above her on Tarian's back. He dropped the reins and, removing his conical helmet, rested it on the pommel in front of him. Then he raked the gloved fingers of both hands through his hair.

The black strands gleamed like pitch. Beads of moisture stood out on his brow and there were lines of tension around his mouth as he spoke. 'The river is too deep to wade through safely here. Do you know of another crossing place nearby?'

Gwennan curled her fingers into her palms, making the cord around her wrists chafe at her skin. 'If I did, do you think I would tell you?'

A wry smile hovered briefly, but his gaze was troubled, distracted. 'No, but I thought I'd ask anyway.'

With the sun behind him his features were dark and his gaze darker still beneath the fall of hair as he leaned forward in his saddle. Pain twisted inside her as the sun caught the hilt of Rhys's sword and blinded her.

'Then you were wasting your breath, Norman!'

His eyes flashed with the easy humour that she'd glimpsed there more than once. Quick and warm, and hinting at a generous soul, it somehow made her hate him even more.

'My name is Rolant Guyarde.'

'I care little what your name is! You're all the same to us—invaders and oppressors and murderers, all of you!'

'Hardly a fit manner for a page to speak to his master, Gerallt.'

Gwennan turned her head away, biting her lip in fury

as he gathered up Tarian's reins again. 'You'll never be master of me,' she muttered.

'Then it seems we have a little battle of wills before us, does it not?'

Suddenly, and so swiftly that she gasped, he reached down and pulled her into the saddle in front of him. One arm closed around her midriff, and in a trice she was imprisoned like a bird in a cage. She squirmed and fought to wrestle free, but she could hardly breathe let alone move.

'Beth uffern!' She hissed between her teeth as the Norman's breath stirred her hair and his jaw touched the top of her head. 'Wh—what are you doing?'

'Keeping you where I can see you.'

Gwennan twisted to look at his face and only just curbed the impulse to spit into it. 'Don't you *trust* me, Rolant Guyarde?'

With his free hand he replaced his helmet, securing it under his chin with deft fingers. The cold steel of the nose blade sent a shudder through her, as it transformed his countenance from almost friendly to closed and forbidding.

'No, I don't trust you at all. But at least you are using my name, and that is a step in the right direction. Although a more correct form of address would be Sir Rolant.'

Gwennan's skin shrank away from the chainmail that dug into her shoulders. But even worse was the strong length of his thighs clasped like iron against hers…the warmth of his hips that cradled her bottom in a shockingly intimate manner.

And there was nothing at all she could do about it. She had no form of either defence or attack, only her pride and her hate. But as for calling him *Sir*, or any other title—this man who was her inferior as well as her enemy—no, no, and never! She'd rather die first.

'*Dos i'r diafol*, Norman dog!'

Rolant bit back a smile. He didn't have to understand the Welsh to know its meaning. If all her race were as spirited and stubborn as this girl was proving to be, no wonder they were so unconquerable.

He shifted her weight so that she was more secure in the saddle. Her body went rigid as he tightened his arm, and beneath the slight swell of her breasts he could feel her heart racing.

Urging the stallion up alongside Giles de Fresnay, he made his decision. 'We'll cross here.'

His captain tilted his head. 'Is that wise, Rolant?'

Rolant looked down at the swollen river. 'We're already delayed in getting these supplies to Carn Egryn. The Earl's garrison is in dire need, and I won't waste more time looking for another fording place. We'll risk it.'

Giles nodded, but his shrewd eyes flickered briefly to the girl and back again. 'Very well. Though for myself, I'd sooner cross further upstream.'

Rolant ignored the challenge. It *was* risky, but he'd face that risk alone before exposing the rest of his men to any danger. 'Remain here. I'll go first,' he said.

He nudged the stallion down the muddy slope of the bank and into the swirling waters. The river reached to its belly and the animal—bold as it was—baulked and snorted, and he had to force it onwards with heel and voice.

They were midstream when the girl clutched at his

sleeve and turned her head, her eyes urgent. 'What are you doing? The river is treacherous here, you fool!'

As she spoke, the horse slithered and its hooves sank deeper. He felt the water rising higher until it gushed icy cold into his boots. He jerked to a halt and, dipping his head, placed his lips next to the girl's ear.

'So, Gerallt of Caernarfon, do we go on—or do we go back? You know this river. Advise me.'

Her skin was cold against his mouth, her body shivering as the water swirled around their legs, though the sun overhead shone relentlessly. Rolant felt his feet begin to freeze and the sweat between his shoulder blades bit like beads of ice. Despite the peril, a smile rose to his lips.

'Or perhaps you'd be more than content to see me drown, even if that means you go under with me?'

There was still no answer and, banishing his smile, he gauged the distance to the far bank. She'd been right when she'd called him a fool, for it was indeed folly to cross here. He might be heedless of danger, and of death, but there were his men to consider, and the horses too. And the wagon that carried corn, ale and salt, as well as coin—precious supplies that were sorely needed at their destination.

They would have to find a safer crossing.

Setting his heels to the stallion's flanks, he turned him back the way they'd come. But its hooves sank even deeper and the animal began to plunge, sending water spraying upwards to soak him and the girl too.

'Wait!' Her fingers dug into his forearm again. 'There is a wide bed of pebbles a few yards upstream. Make for that before you drown us all!'

Rolant looked where she did but saw nothing. 'Where?'

Her bound hands lifted and she pointed. 'Do you see those ripples? That is where the water runs over the pebbles. You can't go straight there because of the quicksand midstream. You must go at an angle, over the ridge of pebbles.'

He didn't wait to hear any more but urged the horse onwards to the place she'd indicated. Sure enough, within a few paces the stallion's hooves struck stone and the water dropped a foot or so around them. Rolant didn't call to his men to follow just yet, however. For who was to say the girl wasn't leading him into further danger? Right into the quicksand and not away from it?

'I hope you're not lying to me,' he muttered into the chestnut hair as they made for the opposite bank, keeping a diagonal path as she'd advised. 'Because if you are, then we're both doomed.'

'I spoke the truth!' The honey eyes cast him a brief but withering glance. 'I would never let Tarian drown.'

Their way across was easier now, the river shallower, the ground surer, although the current still tried its utmost to drag them downstream. In no time at all they were up and over the bank onto solid ground again.

Rolant beckoned his men to follow, instructing them to take exactly the same route he had. And as he watched the wagon in its slow progress across the river something oozed into his awareness like the water that had oozed into his boots.

The girl in front of him was shivering so much he could hear her teeth chattering. She was also sitting right in his lap. And suddenly, far from feeling cold himself, his blood turned to fire in his veins.

Rolant shifted and put a gap between them, although he could do nothing as yet about the growing hardness inside his hose. To cover it, he drew his cloak forward, wrapping it around her as well—not that it would warm her much since it was wet too.

At once, she pushed the cloak from her, but he drew it forward again. This time, with an audible sigh, she let it lie, though her heart was beating fast beneath his arm. And once more he wondered... How had she ever thought her disguise would fool him—or fool *any* man?

Because she might be dressed as a boy, for reasons he had yet to discover, but she was a woman. And as his loins burned Rolant discovered *he* was still a man of flesh and blood after all.

'While I appreciate you'd happily see *me* drown...' he said, and even his voice betrayed him, though mercifully she might take its quiver for a shiver. 'Do you care more for a horse than you do for yourself, Gerallt?'

There was the slightest shrug of her shoulders against his chest and his blood boiled hotter still.

As de Fresnay rode up the bank, for once his captain's sarcasm was a timely intervention.

'Your little page got his feet wet after all, Rolant!'

Rolant met the other man's eyes, marking how they stared and speculated. His lust cooled as quickly as it had heated, leaving a chill in his heart. It would only be a matter of time before Giles, and the rest of them too, discovered the girl's true sex. And when they did...

Fighting men in the field—driven by bloodlust, and far from home and the company of women—were capable of terrible things. Sometimes such men could forget they were human. He'd only have to drop his guard once, be distracted or absent, and she'd be like a fawn surrounded by hungry wolves.

'As did we all.'

He gathered up the stallion's reins. He would have to be vigilant—keep her close to him always. But since he was also a man—and a man who'd been without female company for five years—not too close.

'The sun tells me it is past noontide,' he said to de Fresnay. 'Send scouts ahead to find a place for us to camp. We'll get dry and take food before we go further.'

Gwennan was used to hardship. She'd lived the life of a fugitive, along with her men, for more than a year now. But at least that had been on *her* terms. Now, to be a prisoner and tethered, cold and damp, to a wagon wheel was too much to bear. As was the constant attention of her captor, who appeared determined not to take his eyes off her for a moment.

He was sitting on a fallen tree trunk, not two yards away. After pulling off his boots and tipping the water out, he began to rub the wet hose that covered his feet and calves with a cloth.

Around the camp, some of his men were doing the same, while others prepared food and saw to the horses. The thick covering of trees that encircled them was quiet, undisturbed by birdsong, hiding her Welshmen.

'Of course, as my page, *you* should be doing me this service—should you not, Gerallt?'

The Norman glanced up at her from under his brows. He'd taken off his helmet and stripped the chainmail from his upper body, though he hadn't removed any other garments. Even so, the sight of him in his linen shirt and hose was unsettling in a way Gwennan didn't want to examine.

She'd seen naked male flesh before—she'd been a wife and now, living wild with her followers, how could she not have done? Yet this man's body, even though fully clothed, made her uncomfortably aware in a way theirs didn't.

'You'll wait a long time before that happens,' she retorted. 'If I don't kill you first, that is.'

His eyes narrowed and a slow blush crept into her cheeks as his gaze travelled down her body to rest on her legs. Then he rose, his height darkening the sky, and came to stand before her.

'Then mayhap you need a lesson.'

Fear jumped into Gwennan's throat. If he meant to kill her, deeming her too much trouble to keep alive, then she'd die as her husband had done. Helpless, but with courage and dignity, resisting until the last ounce of breath left his body on a bitter curse against his enemy. *Her* enemy too—and embodied now in this man.

'A lesson from *you*?' she sneered up at him, feeling her neck crick from the angle she had to adopt to meet his eyes. 'You won't teach me anything I don't already know—so do your worst, Norman dog.'

A laugh broke from him, but instead of drawing his knife from his belt, he took up the cloth he'd been using to dry himself. A moment later he was down on his haunches in front of her and pulling off *her* boots.

Instinctively, Gwennan kicked out, but his hands were like fetters around her ankles, deflecting her attack as he removed first one boot then the other. Shaking the water out of them, he laid them to one side.

'Now, take note, my little page—for it's clear you must have been a poor servant to your last master, whoever he was.'

And then, to her horror, he began to rub her feet vigorously, making them smart into warmth as if a torch had been set to her toes. With her back against the wheel and her hands tethered she could do nothing to prevent him as he dried first her feet and then her calves, and then moved upwards to her knees—and beyond.

'Stop!'

His hands stilled at once and an eyebrow arched. 'Surely you don't prefer to remain wet and cold…Gerallt?'

There was something in his voice that made her feel naked, even though he hadn't actually touched her bare flesh at all. 'Yes.'

'Truly?'

'I mean…it is of no consequence.'

'It is of consequence to me.' His gaze raked over her face. 'I don't take a servant one day and expect him— or allow him—to die of a chill the next.'

Servant! Gwennan stared into his eyes and found the expression in them both curious and knowing. Did he suspect she was not what she pretended to be? After all, his hands had been on her body while she'd been unconscious, and then again when they'd crossed the river.

Even though she'd held her breath as best she could, his arm had cushioned her breasts like a binding. And now, if he was allowed to continue his way up her legs, all pretence would be gone and he'd know everything.

Swiftly, she jerked a leg free and, planting her foot square in the centre of his chest, shoved with all her might. But he was swifter, his reactions quicker than she'd anticipated. Strong fingers closed over her foot and, balanced though he was on his haunches, he didn't even sway, let alone go sprawling backwards as she'd intended.

'And what did you hope to achieve by that?'

'What do you think?'

'Escape?' His eyes danced down at her more with amusement than anger. 'No, I think not.'

Once more Gwennan pushed her foot hard against his chest, but it was to no avail whatsoever. She might just as well try and move a mountain.

'You are hurting me!' she bit out, words her only weapon now.

He wasn't hurting her at all—in fact, his long fingers cradled rather than entrapped her foot. Even so, they relaxed a little, though he didn't relinquish his grasp entirely.

'Forgive me. I intended no hurt.'

Forgive? That was a word she'd never heard from a Norman before. One she hadn't imagined these merciless conquerors even capable of uttering. She searched his face for irony, sarcasm—guile, even. But saw only contrition.

'If I release your foot, do you promise not to kick me again?'

Gwennan shook her head. This made no sense. *He* made no sense. Any other man—any other enemy— would have struck her for that. In fact, they would have killed her long since. Why wasn't *this* one acting as all the rest would?

'I will promise you nothing,' she spat at him, her mind a whirl of confusion and doubt.

Because his lack of cruelty, his moderation, even consideration, surely must be some kind of ploy—a trick for reasons she could not fathom.

He smiled. 'Tell me, Gerallt. Were you so intractable towards your last master? Or is it just me you hate?'

How could she even begin to answer that? For the last year her life had been nothing but hate for the Normans. Her days and her nights driven by revenge. Every thought focussed on regaining her lands and her house, freeing her parents from captivity, protecting her people.

Gwennan lifted her chin higher. She'd sacrificed too much in this quest, learned hard and dreadful lessons. She had found ways of staying alive, and—terribly—of taking lives. She'd honed her hatred to a fine point and she mustn't weaken now—not ever. Not even in the presence of kindness, if that was what it really was.

'I hate you all equally. Although right at this moment—you especially!'

Beneath her foot—still planted in the centre of his chest—she could feel his heartbeat, the strength of his muscles and sinews, the hard bone of his breast.

'I hope, given time, that you will lose that hate—if you know what is wise and what is not.'

Her own heart was beating hard too. Because, in the eyes that held hers—as securely and inescapably as his hands held her body—she saw assessment. A man's experienced and instinctive assessment of a woman. Had she been both blind and stupid to think she'd fooled him? Had he seen through her disguise right from the start?

'Then your hope is gravely misplaced!' Gwennan bit out as panic rose up in her throat. Deny her womanhood all she might—even to herself—but he only had to order her stripped of her clothes to reveal her disguise.

She jerked her foot free and this time, to her surprise, he let it go.

He sat back, his forearms resting on his knees, his expression pensive. 'Is it, Gerallt? I wonder…'

All at once, her body betrayed her. Her breasts suddenly ached, her belly seemed to melt, and her lips began to remember things they'd long forgotten. Things she didn't want to remember.

At that moment a man approached with food and ale. With a final blazing stare, deep into her eyes, her captor got nimbly to his feet. Then he frowned and spoke brusquely to his man.

'Fetch another portion for the boy—ale also.'

The repast was brought and, although he'd not taken his own yet, Guyarde dropped to one knee in front of her and took out his dagger. His eyes nailed hers sharper than any point as he cut the cords that bound her.

'You can't eat with your hands tied.'

Gwennan glanced down at the faint bruises on her wrists and resisted the urge to rub at them. God forbid she'd give this Norman the pleasure of seeing her pain. But when she looked up again it wasn't pleasure she saw in his eyes but something more akin to remorse.

'I regret the bruises. If you will give me your promise not to try and escape, you may be left unbound from now on.'

She flexed her fingers, found them too weak and too slow to snatch that dagger from his hand and thrust it into his heart. But her tongue was still fluid, still free, still able to wound. 'I've already told you. I'll promise you nothing!'

'That was before, was it not?'

Before what? Before their strange talk that had confused rather than clarified? Before his hands on her had perhaps confirmed to him what he already suspected? Before his burning eyes had stripped away her disguise in one smooth, shrewd glance?

Fear began to trickle along her veins, and yet thus far Guyarde had displayed none of the callous brutality she'd witnessed in others of his kind—when they'd taken her parents away, killed her brothers and her husband. When they'd deprived her of her home and made her an outlaw in her own realm.

'Nothing has changed,' Gwennan hissed at him.

And it was true. Even if this man hadn't done those things himself, he represented everything she fought against. Everything she *had* to fight against if she was to reclaim what was rightfully hers.

'I will resist you with my dying breath if I have to.'

'I have no doubt of that.' He slid the dagger back into his belt. 'But for now, eat and quench your thirst.'

As they ate, Guyarde's eyes bored into hers from his seat on a log. Gwennan stared straight back from her wagon wheel. Neither even blinked as, between them, invisible questions flowed. Questions that would soon be asked and ones she would have to answer with silent resistance.

She had to escape before that happened. This Norman confused her with his manner, disarmed her with his kindness, so he presented far greater dangers than those met in open battle. Then, girded with sword and steel, prepared to kill or be killed, she felt no confusion. Then, she forgot kindness, forgot the woman she'd once been, the innocent soul she'd had to shed when she'd donned her armour.

But now she lacked the weapons to combat this man so different from the others. His quiet intensity—a force she'd never encountered before—dented her inner armour without striking a blow. Pierced right inside her to the shield that lay over her heart and made a dent there too—small but sharp. Making both her disguise and her defence more necessary than ever.

Chapter Three

Their brief respite was soon over. As the Normans made ready to move on, Gwennan tested the strength of her arms and legs, and then cleared her throat.

'I need to…to ease myself.'

She'd averted her eyes as some of the men had relieved themselves up against a tree, while others, requiring more privacy, had taken themselves a short distance away and squatted behind a bush. The Norman leader had done neither, and now he looked down at her with a calculating eye.

'That presents us with a little problem, does it not?'

Gwennan held his stare with a boldness she was far from feeling. 'Why? Do you think I'll run?'

'I'm certain of it.' His mouth curved. 'So, just to make sure you don't, I'll come with you.'

She'd prepared herself for that. There were two choices—let him come with her and hope her men, hidden and waiting in the woods, were ready to cut him down. Or try and persuade him to let her go alone, then slip away into the trees. The latter held the less risk, although it was unlikely he'd allow her out of his sight.

The moments dragged on and still Gwennan hesitated. Finally he shook his head, and with a shrug started to get to his feet. It was only then that she reached out and took the sword, curling her fingers around its blade, feeling the edge cut into her skin.

Blood spotted her hands but she clung on tight. Closing her eyes, she placed her lips against the precious metal and felt her heart tear itself in two.

'I...I swear.'

When she opened her eyes again Guyarde was looking at her curiously. Not as if he didn't believe her but—strangely—as if he did. She pushed herself up from the ground and walked away into the trees, not looking back.

There was no need to look back. Now that she'd sworn by Cleddyf Gobaith she would return. She could never—would never—betray either the sword or her husband's memory. Not even to kill a Norman.

Not for the first time, Rolant glanced at the sullen figure riding at his side. When he'd allowed her to go alone to see to her bodily needs, he'd half expected her to take to her heels and disappear into the trees. A part of him had even hoped she would, and so relieve him of the burden of protecting her, while another part had reminded him—swiftly and brutally—that he hadn't been there to protect John either, and John had died.

Just as this girl might die, should he fail to protect her now as he'd failed to protect his brother.

But deep down he'd known she would keep her word. He'd known it from the moment she'd gripped the sword so hard that she'd drawn blood. He'd seen it in the way her eyes had clouded with anguish, felt it in the trem-

ble of her breath on his hand as she'd placed her lips
on the gleaming hilt.

The stallion beneath him started at something in the
undergrowth. Something unseen and yet there all the
same—like the invisible presence of danger that had
been trailing them all day. It was as if the very air carried a silent warning, audible only to those who knew
what to listen for.

He turned to the girl. 'How many renegades are in
these parts?'

'There *are* no renegades in this land—only Welshmen.'

'And Welsh women?'

The honey-coloured eyes flashed. 'And Welsh women!'

Rolant noticed the sway of her hips in the saddle, the
shape of her leg beneath its woollen stocking. He'd put
her on his own bay courser and she handled the horse
with a skill worthy of any knight. But her hands on the
reins were still too soft, too small, to be those of a man.

'And would these Welsh women be maid or married?' he pursued.

'What would that matter to you?' Her head turned
away. 'You Normans kill man, woman and child without a thought.'

'You have a very low opinion of us.'

'It is not an opinion but a well-known truth. Even
here in Wales we know what the Conqueror did to the
Saxons in the north of England. And he and his earls
are doing the same now to us. I've seen their greed and
their cruelty with my own eyes, time and again.'

Rolant studied her profile—the haughty line of her
jaw, the fine curve of her cheek, the soft lips. How many
summers did she have? Nineteen? Twenty? Not much

more, certainly, and she came from no common stock either. Her pride, as well as her voice and her manner, betrayed her as someone higher born than that.

'You speak with an old tongue for one so young.'

'In war, even babes grow up quickly and too soon.' She tossed her head and the chestnut locks glinted with strands of fiery red. 'And the old, instead of being revered and respected, are hauled off to prison or slaughtered like animals that have no further use nor worth.'

The words were bitter, but Rolant could hardly disagree with them. He'd seen it himself, in the short time he'd been in the service of Robert of Rhuddlan. The brutality with which the nobles of the March acquired yet more land, yet more wealth, yet more power at the cost of the Welsh they displaced, disinherited or destroyed.

And he was charged to do the same, even though that charge weighed heavily on his conscience the further they advanced into Wales. There were ways and means to conquer a country, and they didn't need to be the ones she spoke of. Or the methods Giles de Fresnay favoured, he added silently, on a sigh, as the man trotted up on his right.

'The light is fading, Rolant, and I don't like this terrain.'

Rolant scanned the hillsides around them, dark in shadow as the sun sank lower on the horizon. 'No, this valley is too convenient for ambush. We'll ride on a while further before we make camp.'

Giles nodded, his gaze sliding across to the girl. 'I begin to believe you might tame your new page, after all.'

Rolant's stomach clenched at the cunning in the other man's eyes. Did de Fresnay suspect his page was nothing of the sort? The man might be a brute, but he wasn't blind or a fool either, and the more distance he could keep between his captain and his captive the better.

He nodded ahead of them. 'Take two men and look for a suitable camping place. We'll not reach Carn Egryn before nightfall, that is certain.'

As the three men rode off, the girl turned to him, her tongue suddenly fluent. 'So you *are* heading for Carn Egryn?'

Rolant saw her eyes alight with a keen eagerness he hadn't seen there thus far. What interest did she have in Carn Egryn?

'We are taking supplies there,' he confirmed. 'And we are to relieve the garrison. Perhaps you have heard those lands are now the property of Earl Robert of Rhuddlan?'

Her face went white. 'Robert of Rhuddlan!' The three words came as if spat with disgust from her mouth.

Rolant frowned. 'You know him?'

She turned her head away. 'I know *of* him only too well.' There was a short beat of silence before she spoke again. 'Then you are his man?'

He nodded. 'I am—though only newly in his service.'

'How long?'

The question was an unexpected one, but at least she was conversing with him now, not doing her best to ignore him.

'Not yet three full months. Until Eastertide I was campaigning with King William in Normandy. Now I have been sent to claim Carn Egryn to hold in knight's fee for the Earl of Rhuddlan.'

Her mouth trembled when she responded, though

her words were like ice. 'You'd have done better to stay in Normandy and not come here to serve that devil!'

Rolant searched her face, saw the searing hatred that drew the soft skin tightly across the bones. 'I take it you have no love for the Earl?'

Her eyes snapped back to his and the answer to that was crystal-clear even before her words confirmed it. 'I detest him.'

Just then the glint of sun on something hard and sharp, high on the hillside beyond, caught Rolant's eye. The hairs at the back of his neck rose and he turned in his saddle, looking all around him. But there was nothing to be seen, only sensed.

It was strangely quiet. The hills were too thickly covered with trees and the valley echoed too softly with hoofbeats and the creak of harness. There was no birdsong except the eerie call of a hawk high in the sky, while the river alongside murmured low and ominous. And as he turned back to the girl Rolant felt himself riding on a knife-edge, not solid ground.

'Has the Earl done you or your family some harm?'

He bit his tongue, but too late. And the harm *he'd* done *his* family seemed to tumble down upon him from the looming hillsides. He who in trying to do the right thing had brought his family nothing but death and grief, and himself a disgrace that he would carry to his grave.

Rolant cleared his throat, feeling his brow bead with sweat inside his helmet as his past squeezed like a vice around his head and his heart.

'Or some injustice?' he added, as if Rhuddlan's ill deeds might deflect his mind from his own crime.

But she made no response, her profile set like stone,

her mouth a line of contempt. All at once another face wove into his imagination—one which had also set like stone and become harsh with scorn where it had once been soft, tender...loving.

But Adeliza would never sit a horse astride like that, or curse like a man, or get her hands bloody. Although, as he'd discovered, she was more than adept at dealing the most lethal of wounds, all the more shocking because they were unforeseen.

Rolant's hands jerked on the reins, causing the stallion to fling up its head. He lived with his brother's dead face day and night, but it wasn't often now that his mind conjured up Adeliza's face, or the last humiliating day that had made his dishonour complete. So why was he thinking of it now?

He dragged his mind back to more imminent concerns, driving the past away, focussing on the present dangers that every instinct told him lurked ever closer with every mile they rode.

'I am not well acquainted with the Earl,' he said, 'but I might be able to speak with him, perhaps, on your behalf, if there is a wrong to be righted.'

The honey eyes met his as she answered, although there was no sweetness in her tone. 'Why would you do that, Rolant Guyarde? You who, like all your kind, slay those who stand in your way and steal lands from their rightful owners in the name of conquest!'

Rolant's palms grew moist within their leather gauntlets as her words drove like a blade into his bowels. It was an accusation impossible to gainsay, even if he himself had done far less slaying and stealing than some of his countrymen.

'We are not all as bad as you would have us.'

'Are you not? Yet actions speak louder than any words.' She put out a hand and stroked her mount's neck, her eyes glancing briefly upwards to where the sinking sun just touched the crest of the mountains. 'Granted you have treated me kindly, whereas another might not. I suppose I should thank you for that, at least, if for nothing else.'

Then she smiled suddenly, almost coyly. It was the first time he'd ever seen her smile thus, and it was that incongruity that alerted him to her deception. He saw the way her fingers had gathered her reins, how she sat straighter in the saddle, her spine stiffening.

Rolant tensed too, his nerves primed, as he reached for his sword, his head suddenly and starkly cleared of the debris that had begun to fog his thoughts and suck him down into the abyss of his guilt.

But it was already too late.

A flight of arrows flew from the sky just as Giles, with the two men-at-arms he'd sent ahead, came galloping back towards them as if the hounds of hell were in pursuit of them. His captain shouted a warning, but almost at the same time he fell from the saddle, an arrow piercing his back.

Rolant yelled to his men to take cover, but even as the words left his mouth he felt himself lifted into the air. It happened swiftly, and yet so slowly, and he could do nothing to prevent the low but effective tactic.

The girl had leaned down from her horse, placed her foot under his stirrup and, bracing her body, hoisted him sideways and out of the saddle. At the same time she'd wrenched the reins from his hands and he was left unhorsed and helpless.

Before he'd even hit the ground she'd vaulted from

his gelding and onto the back of the grey stallion. Then she was galloping away, crouched low over its neck, under cover of a hail of arrows.

By the time Rolant had leapt to his feet, winded but unscathed, it was all over. His men, who'd scattered in confusion, were regrouping. There were one or two wounded among them, and a horse was dead on the ground. Giles de Fresnay was dead too, but at least the baggage cart and its precious cargo was intact.

There was no sign now of the Welsh who'd attacked them, or of the girl. It was as if they'd never been there at all—like phantoms come out of a mist and then simply melting away again.

But as he cursed his own stupidity and set about re-establishing some sort of order Rolant could almost feel her, somewhere high on that hillside, watching him, laughing at him, mocking him.

Just as Adeliza had.

The sun had long since disappeared into the west and darkness had come down. There was a sliver of moon low in the eastern sky. Gwennan crouched in the undergrowth and waited as the Normans made camp for the night. Rolant Guyarde's voice carried to her ears as he posted guards around the clearing, saw to it that every precaution was in place. Not that it would do him any good.

He was a fool if he thought she'd let him keep the sword. And even if he *had* treated her decently while she'd been his captive that counted for naught. Now she knew whose man he was, she owed him nothing but her hate. Even if he'd not been in the Earl's service a year ago, when devastation had come to change her whole life, it made no difference. He was her enemy now even more so than before.

She waited an age, it seemed, until the camp had settled. Then she crept closer, inch by slow inch, her eyes and ears vigilant, every sense heightened. All the men were asleep in little groups around the fires they'd lit, apart from the four guards who had been posted on the fringes of the forest clearing.

But their bodies drooped and their heads nodded, for it had been a long march that day. They were lax, and it would be easy for her small force to dispatch them if necessary. Besides which, their weary eyes would be turned outwards—not inwards to where their comrades lay in exhausted slumber.

Gwennan closed her fingers around the hilt of the dagger at her waist. No doubt they supposed she and her Welshmen to be far away now, not surrounding them in the trees. The last thing they would expect was an attack.

Slowly, hardly daring to breathe, she crawled on her hands and knees between the sleeping Normans. The quiet crackle of banked-down fires mingled with the sound of snoring from here and there. Low but frequent moans came from someone doubtless wounded in the rescue rout earlier.

Gwennan stilled as the wounded man gave another groan, louder this time. Hopefully, he was too far gone in delirium to be any threat, though he might wake his companions if he became too restless. She must make haste.

Moving forward, until she was right next to her target, she drew her dagger.

Like his men, the Norman leader was sleeping soundly,

on his back, his sword arm resting outside the blanket rather than inside it. His profile, lit by the fire beyond, was almost serene, his brow unlined, the sharply cut bones of cheek and jaw smooth instead of harsh. His lips, slightly parted, were full and generous, not cruel as they should have been, and there was a gentleness about his mouth only hinted at in daytime.

Gwennan stared at him. Why did he appear so unlike the other Normans? Why had he not exposed her? And why did he make her think not of greed or cruelty or violence but of far more tender things? Things she had forced herself to forget.

Then through his lips came a soft sigh, a troubled sound, as if his dream was not a happy one. Her hand lifted, its fingers curious to trace their sensual curve, as if they might speak of his sad dream. She almost touched him, curious to remember what the mouth of a man felt like. Then the hoot of an owl came—it wasn't really an owl—and his eyelashes flickered.

Gwennan held her breath, her dagger ready should he wake. He didn't stir, but the call brought her hurtling back to her senses. This man—beautiful in the moonlight—was by day a soldier, a conqueror and a killer, and he wasn't different at all. Like every other Norman, he was here to take her land, steal her birthright, enslave her people.

Dragging her eyes away from his face, she stretched her hand out for the sword. A little glow of triumph warmed her heart as her fingers closed once more around its golden hilt.

'So you've come back, Gerallt.'

Her hand and her heart froze as one. In the same instant long, strong fingers came down to cover hers.

Guyarde was wide-awake now, his eyes dark yet keen. Quick as a flash, Gwennan brought the point of her dagger to his throat and a slow smile touched his mouth.

'Well, my errant page.' The words were no more than a murmur. 'So you are going to kill me after all!'

She tensed for the counter attack, but he made no move to defend himself. He lay still, staring up at her, his eyes questioning, even amused. He didn't even call out, or try to overpower her, he just…waited, smiling and completely at her mercy.

Gwennan bit her lip, tasted blood. Why couldn't she push her dagger deep? All she had to do was lean her weight on it and he'd be dead. She'd killed men before, in the desperate throes of battle, when it was kill or be killed.

But never like this. Not in cold blood.

Once upon a time, in another lifetime altogether, she'd never have killed at all, but fate had forced the blade cruelly into her hand. Or did she hesitate because this Norman *was* different, even if she didn't understand that difference.

He seemed to sense her conundrum. 'You hesitate. Why? Isn't that why you came back? To be rid of me?'

Gritting her teeth, Gwennan gripped the dagger tighter. Her hand started to shake and a spot of blood appeared on his skin where the point grazed. But he didn't even flinch, let alone show any fear, just went on holding her with his eyes as inescapably as those bonds of hemp had done.

Time dragged out, every moment she wavered lessening her opportunity to flee and increasing the risk of the camp waking. Yet still she couldn't drive the blade home and make an end of him.

'Or mayhap you don't hate me as much as you think you do...*Gerallt?*'

So quickly that Gwennan didn't have time to react— let alone refute that—he moved. And suddenly she was pressed beneath him. His body—lean though it was— was heavy on hers, and his hands, large, rough-palmed yet gentle, pinned her arms to the ground and rendered her dagger useless.

She started to struggle but stilled at once. A tussle would wake the entire camp and she'd be back where she started—a prisoner once more. Sucking in a breath, she forced herself to lie quiet. But her heart began to hammer against her ribs and a slow panic started to build inside her.

'Now perhaps you will tell me who you really are?' In the darkness, his eyes gleamed intently. 'You are clearly not a killer. Neither are you a squire or a page any more than you are a man. So why are you hiding in those clothes, I wonder?'

Gwennan couldn't breathe, couldn't even think. She could only feel shocking things that she'd never expected—or wanted—to feel again. The weight of a man's body on hers, his warm breath fanning her face, his male scent filling her mind.

This man's body, *this* man's breath, *this* man's scent! This man she should hate—*did* hate with all her heart.

Why, then, did he stir her senses so and penetrate her defences so easily? Not with weapons of steel—but with something else far more fatal.

'And neither are you a common whore or a camp follower.'

His face was only inches above hers, so close that she felt the words on her skin.

'If you were, I might be tempted to discover what you look like beneath those humble clothes by removing them.'

Gwennan twisted her head to the side, her eyes searching for Cleddyf Gobaith and her heart sinking. The sword lay so near that she could almost touch it, yet still too far out of reach. And then his hand came up, palmed her cheek and turned her gaze back to his again.

'But I am not that sort of man. Neither would I insult a lady in that manner. For you *are* a lady, are you not?'

His mouth was nearly touching hers, almost caressing her lips. His taut limbs were quivering and there was an unmistakable hardness in the loins that pressed against her thighs. Then his eyes narrowed and his quiet question was like an accusation.

'*Why* did you come back, for God's sake?'

'For the sword!' she bit out at last, her limbs beginning to quiver too, as something worse than fear took possession of her.

'The sword?' The moon had slipped behind a cloud but in the firelight Gwennan saw him frown. 'It's a handsome weapon, I grant, but why would you risk being captured again just for that?'

Fury welled up inside her. 'Because it's mine!'

Somewhere in the camp a cough sounded and a man grunted. Another turned over in his blanket and then settled again. As one, she and Guyarde tensed. Held their breaths. Held each other's eyes.

'Then why didn't you simply ask me for it?'

Gwennan gave a little push of her body—a useless attempt to throw him off, she knew full well. 'And if I had would you have returned it to me, a *Welsh renegade*?'

'I might yet if you tell me who you really are and what is behind all this subterfuge.'

There was no threat in his words. The threat came rather from within, as her fury flared and then went out like a snuffed candle. In its place, something tugged low in her abdomen and her heart kicked in her breast. To her horror, her lips parted, as if her tongue was imagining the taste of his even as her mind forbade it.

Would his kiss be as soft as his eyes or as hard as his loins? Would it be as tender as his voice or passionate and savage? Would it capture her all over again, with no need this time for bonds of rope?

Gwennan turned her head to one side again, squeezing her eyes tightly shut against temptation. Again he turned her face back, trailing his fingers slowly down her cheek as if softly seeking. But his breath was harsh, not soft, and his voice was ragged with what she recognised as lust.

'Tell me who you are!'

His question and his touch were her salvation. For it meant his guard was down, just as hers had been. But she was the quicker to recover. And the fool, in stroking her cheek like that, in desiring her with his body, in wanting to know *her* and not just her secret, had released her hand. Not the one with the dagger, but she could use the other just as well.

Her mind her own again, Gwennan felt stealthily over the ground until her fingers found what she needed: a small but jagged rock. And there were no thoughts of kissing in her mind now as she spat her answer into his face.

'I am Gwennan *ferch* Cynddylan Fawr, the rightful ruler of these lands. And I'll tell you something else,

Rolant Guyarde. You'll never set foot in Carn Egryn. Because the next time we meet I *will* kill you!'

Then, quicker even than the blink of shock he gave, Gwennan brought the rock down on his cheekbone with all her might. He grunted and jerked his head backwards. His body recoiled and his grasp on her loosened. She knew she hadn't hit him hard enough to knock him senseless. But he was unbalanced long enough for her to wrench herself free.

As she wriggled like an adder out from under him a shout went up from one of the guards and the whole camp woke to alarm.

Gwennan didn't stop or look back. Leaping to her feet, she grabbed Cleddyf Gobaith and ran for her life into the trees.

Chapter Four

Rolant drew rein and, signalling to his men to halt, stared at the fortress in the middle distance. Perched on a crag that rose out of the green valley, the small wooden-walled enclosure looked lonely and deserted. Yet it shouldn't be. Robert of Rhuddlan's garrison were in possession—so why was no one coming down the hill to greet them at sight of their approach?

He scanned the countryside around. The forest had been long cut back, to clear some lowland for pasture and crops, and at the foot of the hill a small hamlet of wattle and mud dwellings nestled. As he looked, a figure appeared out of one of the huts. It stared for an instant in their direction, then darted into another hut, like a weasel seeking a safer bolthole.

A ripple of unease crawled down Rolant's spine as Alan Fitz Osbert, his second in command now that Giles de Fresnay was dead, moved up alongside.

'It's too quiet, Rolant. I don't like it.'

'Neither do I,' he replied. 'The garrison must see us, so where are they?'

The man shrugged. 'Asleep still?'

'At this hour?' Rolant glanced upwards. The sun was halfway to its highest point, the blue sky almost cloudless. 'Even if they have become lax of a morning, there should still be a watch on the wall. And the gates shouldn't be wide open like that.'

'No, they should not. It smells all wrong to me.' Fitz Osbert rubbed his nose thoughtfully. 'What do you intend to do?'

Rolant considered a moment longer, then made his mind up. He'd lost too many men already in this venture and he didn't intend to lose any more. An uncouth and violent crew they might be, but he was their leader and their lives were his responsibility.

'Wait here with the men, Alan. I'll take two with me and go and see what's amiss.'

He pushed his helmet firmer down on his head, feeling the cuff of his gauntlet scraping the cut on his cheekbone. It was still raw from the blow with the rock the girl had dealt him four nights ago. But she'd dealt him an even more staggering blow when she'd revealed her true identity.

Gwennan, daughter of Cynddylan Fawr, the dispossessed local ruler who had been languishing for the last year, along with his poor wife, in Robert of Rhuddlan's dungeons. No wonder the girl hated him!

Two men on his heels, Rolant ascended the track that wound up the small hill. Nerves taut, he passed through the gates and halted in the middle of an empty compound. The silence was ominous, and the rustic buildings clustered around the main hall looked utterly deserted.

'What in God's name is afoot?' he muttered, more to himself than to his companions.

There was livestock—pigs, goats and horses too—in pens against the far wall. Hens pecked and clucked, and two scrawny dogs that looked more like wolves ran barking at them. Hackles up and eyes gleaming yellow, the pair circled menacingly, growling through bared fangs. But of human life there was no sign, living or dead.

'Ho!' Rolant called out. 'Is anyone here? Show yourselves!'

His order was answered at once from two directions. A horse whinnied, and too late he recognised the iron-grey stallion with the light mane and tail. At the same time the gates slammed shut with an echo that shattered the silence all around. Men came swarming from nowhere, like ants out of their hillocks, and before Rolant even had time to draw his sword, he and his soldiers were surrounded.

'*Henffych*, Rolant Guyarde! We've been expecting you.'

And there she was, striding towards him through ranks of Welshmen. Gwennan *ferch* Cynddylan. She looked the same as the last time he'd seen her. Still in male attire, with the sun glinting off her smooth chestnut head, the sword she'd taken back from him swinging at her hip.

'The tables have turned have they not, Norman?'

Rolant swung his leg over his horse's neck and slid to the ground. As he landed lightly on his feet his hand moved to the hilt of his weapon, even though he knew it was useless to try and fight his way out.

'I wouldn't draw your sword, if I were you.' She came to stand in front of him, tilting her head to meet his eyes, her own flashing with triumph. 'You'd be lucky if you even got it clear of the scabbard before my men cut you to pieces.'

Rolant stared down at her, and for the life of him didn't know whether to be outraged or awed. She was so slight that a gust of wind might blow her away. Yet, as she'd said, the tables had indeed been turned.

He drew off his helmet and her eyes flickered to the wound on his cheek. For a brief instant the look of triumph faded to something else, though he doubted it was remorse.

'That will leave a scar, I fear.' There was no remorse in her tone either. 'But at least you can count it as a war wound and save your valour a little.'

Rolant looked around the compound. Plenty of Welsh warriors, with their evil-looking knives ready to slit his belly wide open. But there was not a Norman in sight, neither living or dead, and no trace that any had ever been there.

'Where is the garrison?' he demanded, bringing his eyes back to hers.

Dwarfed by the ranks of men behind her, she still managed to tower above all of them. Or was it because he knew her royal status now that she seemed every inch a queen?

'As you see, it is not here.'

Her gaze was like hard frost. No sign now of the softness he'd glimpsed there briefly the night she'd returned for her sword. When he'd been foolish enough to look at her too deeply in the moonlight, his body afire over hers on the warm earth.

It was just as well she'd hit him when she had and knocked some sense into his head. Because such eyes could fool a man in broad daylight, with no need of a silvery moon to help tie the blindfold.

She *had* fooled him! As he'd been fooled once before—to his cost and the sorrow of those he loved. But he wouldn't let his guard drop a second time.

'Then where are the soldiers?' he demanded. 'Are you claiming to have ousted them? A score and more of battle-hardened Normans?'

Gwennan fought the temptation to look again at the gash on his cheek. It wasn't too deep, but although cleaned it hadn't been properly treated. And the surrounding bruise stretched in a black and yellow stain from temple to eye socket.

There was no room for contrition, however, nor compassion. 'Yes, that is what I am claiming—since it is fact,' she replied. 'They didn't put up much of a fight and were only too willing to return my home to me.'

His brows arched. 'So how did you breach the walls, just you and a handful of warriors?'

Gwennan shrugged. 'We had a little inside help from a woman they'd coerced into washing and cooking for them—among other things.'

She swallowed back her disgust on Nest's behalf. No man, Norman or otherwise, would force the woman against her will ever again. She'd made Nest her maidservant, and in doing so had placed her firmly under her personal protection. To touch her now would be to touch the Princess herself.

'She unbarred the gates to us by night and, as you can see, my forces are much increased since we last met in battle.'

Guyarde cursed under his breath and she saw him

clench his hand inside his gauntlet. For a fleeting moment Gwennan almost felt sorry for him. It would have galled her too to be so easily outwitted.

'Don't berate them *too* much, Guyarde,' she said, infusing a note of mockery into the words. Why should she care if his pride was as injured as his face? 'They were sick, and in no condition to withstand us. Your supplies were too long in coming, and naturally the people of the village wouldn't spare their food to sustain a garrison, even such a small one—although it was taken from them anyway.'

His gaze smouldered, dark and turbulent, as if he was holding himself in check. And once again the height, the strength, the reined-in power, seemed to set him apart from all the other men around her—even the biggest and most fierce of her Welshmen.

'What have you done with the survivors—or did you leave none alive?'

'We are not butchers!' she replied, tossing her head as the insult scorched her cheeks. 'We buried those few that were killed or dead of disease.'

'In consecrated ground, I hope?'

'Or course! We are not barbarians either! They lie, seven in all, behind the church.'

To spare Nest's honour, she didn't add that two of those killed had perished by the executor's knife, their throats slit as punishment for their brutal crime.

'The rest have been allowed to return whence they came and warned not to come back.'

Guyarde folded his arms and his shoulders lifted, broad and wide, as he drew a deep breath. Arms and shoulders that, more than once when she'd been at his mercy, could have snapped her bones as easily as they would a twig.

Yet they hadn't. They'd rescued her, fed her and kept her alive. And neither had he done what the garrison had done to Nest, nor let any of his men molest her either. *Why?*

'And once they'd gone you set a trap for me?' he said.

She pushed away the puzzles that had no place in her thoughts. 'You yourself told me you were coming to take possession of Carn Egryn, did you not? Now it has taken possession of *you*.'

A muscle flexed in his jaw, along which now ran the faint shadow of a beard, emphasising the sharpness of bone. 'Then what are your terms?'

'Terms?' Gwennan laughed. 'There are no *terms*, Rolant Guyarde—at least none that will appeal to you. But for a start you will deliver your wagon of supplies to us. Since my ranks are increasing daily, I need them more than you do.'

His focus shifted beyond her to his surroundings, assessing her manpower, the extent of their weapons, as if weighing the odds in his mind. And once again she was reminded of the lake of Talyllyn, its deep and treacherous waters that could drag the unwary helplessly down below its surface.

And when his eyes came back to hers, green and vital, he seemed still unvanquished, despite his predicament. 'You know I won't agree to that.'

'You have no choice.'

Gwennan folded her arms and below her tunic felt the thudding of her heart, as if she had already placed a foot into those waters.

'We have heard that you put your dead and wounded

on a ship at Aberdyfi, and that ship is now bound for Caernarfon. Which means you have scarce more than twenty men left at your disposal.'

'You are well informed, Princess.'

She drew herself taller, though she still fell far short of his towering height. Was that why she still felt at a disadvantage? Or was it the disturbing memory of his arm around her as they'd forded the waters at the Dyfi? Of the unsettling way his breath and hers had danced in the firelight when he'd pressed his body over hers in the dark?

Gwennan banished those lingering memories from her mind. 'Very well informed. And your remaining men have been on the march for days—to the coast and then back into the mountains. They are in no state to fight.'

His lashes flickered, long and black against the greenness of his eyes. The air seemed to crackle overhead, as if a storm was rolling in from the sea far distant. Her men began to shift impatiently, eager for a fight, and Gwennan felt tension tighten across her forehead.

'Then we will take our leave.' At last he dipped his head in grudging agreement. 'But rest assured we will be back.'

Gwennan had no doubts about his intention. After all, hadn't he come here in the first place to take possession of her lands? Take them for his own, just as he'd taken her as his page? Well, that was an arrogance he would soon regret.

'Once we get the supplies your men may go, but they will leave their weapons and horses behind,' she said.

'And they can tell Robert of Rhuddlan that the *llys* of Carn Egryn is returned to its rightful owner.'

'I'll deliver that message to him personally, since it is I he will hold to account for this—and rightly so.'

Gwennan shook her head. 'You misunderstand me. Your *men* may leave, but *you* will remain here. I'm hardly going to let a valuable hostage go free when Robert of Rhuddlan would pay handsomely to get you back.'

She gestured to her Uncle Meuryn, who stood at her side as always, and took from him the roll of parchment she'd dictated that morning, after her scouts had spotted the Normans' approach.

A boon begot a boon, after all. She'd shown mercy to the enemy this day, and now it was the Earl's turn to be merciful—if he even knew what mercy was.

'Your men will take with them this message to the Earl. You may leave when I receive his answer—and only then if it is a favourable one.'

Those were reasonable terms, were they not? She'd spared his men's lives, as he'd spared her life when he could so easily have taken it. They were quits and she owned him nothing. He was simply her bargaining tool now—the only one she had.

'And how high a price are you putting on my head, Princess?'

'It's not *money* I want from your master, Guyarde! I am demanding the release of my parents, and I mean to get that demand satisfied.'

'And if you don't my life will be forfeit?'

She nodded. 'As is just.'

The green eyes narrowed and Gwennan saw something move in their depths, like a strong current disturbing deep waters.

'Very well, since there is clearly no alternative, I will remain as hostage for your parents' safe return.'

The sun slid out from behind a cloud and glinted on his hair as he turned to speak in French to the nearest of his men. Gwennan listened, understanding little, her eyes flickering against her will to the wound on his cheek—and quickly away again as he looked back to her.

'But I have some conditions of my own.'

'Which are…?'

'That my men be allowed to keep part of the supplies, sufficient to see them as far as Caernarfon. They may be your enemy, but they are loyal soldiers and deserve to be treated as such.'

Gwennan bit her lip. It galled her to concede anything to these Normans, but how could she refuse to be charitable? Men on foot through hostile lands had little hope of reaching their destination. At least with food and drink they had a chance, which was why she'd allowed the Earl's piteous garrison sustenance, despite the arguments of her Welshmen to the contrary.

And now they began to argue again, baying for Guyarde's blood and that of the depleted force that waited outside the walls. Too long under Norman domination, they were eager for battle—not bargaining.

If this had been a clash of swords, *she* would have craved blood too, but in a just cause and on equal terms. But this was not a battle, and the terms were not equal. She wasn't like the enemy, even if some of her countrymen might stoop as low. Warrior she might be—*had* to be—but she wasn't a murderer.

'I agree,' she replied, after a moment longer in consideration. 'Three days' ration for each man, since Caernarfon is not more than twenty leagues from here. But they will leave their horses, weapons and armour.'

The dark head inclined, although his face was grim as he watched his two comrades leave, taking her message with them. And as half a dozen of her Welshmen gathered outside the gates to receive the wagon and its booty she knew there remained only one last piece of revenge to enjoy.

Gwennan held out her hand, gratified to see it was as steady as a rock, even if inside she was trembling with a strange sort of exhilaration. 'Give me your sword.'

There was a moment's hesitation, then Guyarde unbuckled the scabbard from his belt and handed it to her. The leather was warm from the heat of his body but the metal hilt was unadorned. It was not a beautiful weapon, like Cleddyf Gobaith, just a soldier's blade, plain and serviceable.

She looked up from the sword into his face. There was no fear there, just a curious expression of challenge and acceptance, as if he dared her to do her worst. And, flustered without knowing why, Gwennan let him think she would do just that.

'On your knees, Norman.'

This time something stirred in that green-gold gaze. Men got down on their knees for three reasons—to pray, to be honoured, or to be beheaded. Was he wondering which it would be?

'If you are going to use that blade on me, Princess, then I will receive it standing on my feet.'

'I am waiting.' Gwennan pointed a finger at the ground, her voice quivering and her heart thudding against her ribs.

Her men jeered as the moments dragged out and the

sun beat mercilessly down. Guyarde stared at her, unafraid, proud, with his dignity intact, too haughty even now to be humiliated.

She swallowed, her throat suddenly dry. Would he comply? Or refuse? And if he did refuse… *Gras annwyl*—what then? Would she have to kill him after all? Take his life when he'd spared hers? Do what she should have done four nights ago?

But things were clearer by light of day, were they not? Not muddled and murky as they were in the dark. By day, rays of sunlight didn't dazzle and confuse in the way firelight flickering over a sleeping man's face did. Blue skies didn't blind one's eyes and drug one's mind the way treacherous moonlight did.

'I said on your knees!'

Gwennan repeated the command, loud enough for all to hear, no quiver in her tone now, only ultimatum. And finally, as if he didn't care one way or the other, he lowered himself to the ground.

Rolant stared at the weapon in front of him but hardly saw it. Instead, his eyes looked back to another time when he'd knelt like this, stones digging into his knees, the sun hot on the back of his neck. Waiting for the sword to fall—willing it to do so and deal him the punishment he deserved. A life for a life. His for John's.

Death at least was clean when it was a man's due, whereas disgrace and dishonour were bloody stains on his soul. A canker in a living heart that would never heal until it was cut out completely and that heart was thrown to the crows.

Before him, the Princess looked like an avenging angel, her gaze burning bright, her cheeks flushed. So be it. One executioner was much like another. Let her lop his head off there and then and have done. She would at least free him of his torment on earth, even if that would throw him into a worse torment in Hell.

Yet some part of his mind knew she wouldn't kill him. Not when she'd just taken him hostage. Even if she'd vowed vehemently to do so the last time they'd met. And sure enough, instead of arcing high and falling in a *coup de grâce*, the sword was held up in front of his face.

'Swear on this cross that you won't try and escape.'

Rolant almost groaned out loud with disappointment. His father had shown mercy and spared him, and now she was sparing him too. Purgatory was not somewhere a man wished to remain indefinitely, yet at the same time he could have laughed as she proceeded to flay him with his own lash. Perhaps he'd lost his wits along with his liberty!

'And if I choose not to swear?' he said, goading her to use that sword even now.

'Then you will be kept in a strong room night and day, instead of enjoying the freedom of the *llys*.' She placed both hands on the sword and steadied it in its wavering. 'It is your choice, so make it quickly.'

Another choice. Like the one he'd had to make five years ago that had led to John's death and severed him from his family. Like the choice he'd made four nights ago when he'd allowed Gwennan to disappear into the trees instead of ordering his men in pursuit.

Would he ever make a right choice?

'Then I will swear,' Rolant replied, and touched his lips briefly to the sword. 'But only so much as you swore to me. My oath will be as binding as yours proved to be.'

Her brow furrowed. 'What do you mean?'

'You *did* escape, did you not?'

Her gasp broke through the silence like a blade through buttermilk. 'I… Well, yes, but that was a different circumstance!'

Not waiting for her permission, Rolant rose up from the ground. 'Perhaps it was, Princess Gwennan, but either way you have my oath, to trust or distrust as you please.'

She flushed. 'You will address me properly. Arglwyddes Gwennan is my title.' Her lips curled in scorn. 'After all, did you not advise me to call you Sir Rolant?'

'Yet you never did, did you?' Rolant tried the Welsh on his tongue. 'Arglwyddes Gwennan.'

A guffaw broke out from the man at her side, a seasoned warrior by his manner as well as his appearance. He muttered something in their native tongue and the Princess laughed, though without mirth, as she translated for him.

'Meuryn ap Hywel here thinks you'll never master our language no matter how long you are with us.'

Rolant smiled too, with even less mirth, and looked from the one to the other. 'Is that a challenge, Arglwyddes Gwennan?'

This time he had the word almost perfect, and he saw her smile transformed into a scowl. The same one he'd seen many times when she'd been just Gerallt to him. If he'd known then who she really was, would he have handed her over to the Earl, as his duty and oath of allegiance demanded? Perhaps it was just as well he'd never know.

The sound of the wagon entering the compound came to his ears. Rolant watched the Welshmen swooping like hawks on the supplies, carrying them into one of the low buildings, primitive, yet sturdily built in oak, like all the others within the compound.

The Earl's grain, salt, ale, weapons and coin. Robert of Rhuddlan would not be pleased. His garrison dislodged, the *llys* back in Welsh hands, vital supplies lost and his commander a captive.

And that commander was not even to be granted a swift death to save him the burden of yet more dishonour on his guilty soul. Not a good day by any standards!

And as Rolant looked again at the victorious glow on the Princess's face he doubted it would end there. To have the daughter of Cynddylan Fawr back in power meant a strengthening of resistance in these parts—a resistance he'd been sent here to stamp out. And even if he had no stomach for it he'd failed before he'd even begun.

As if she read his thoughts, Gwennan spoke, and her smile was nothing less than radiant. 'Your expedition hasn't gone quite as planned, has it, Rolant Guyarde? No matter—for you will play no more part in it.'

She gestured two of her men forward, handing one of them his sword. 'And now we will require your armour and your horse too—both of which we will put to better use. But as I do not require a page, and we do not tether men like goats to wagon wheels, you will be treated according to your standing while you are within my walls.'

The word cut, swift and deep. He *had* no standing— or at least not the one he'd grown up believing was his. He'd forfeited that and everything that went with it, and not even his recent elevation to knight, bestowed upon him by the King himself, could erase that earlier tarnishing.

Rolant gritted his teeth as he was stripped down to his hose and linen shirt, his armour and his honour taken from him. Disgrace filled his nose and his mouth, leaving him struggling to breathe. But unlike five years ago, when his soul had gone to the grave with John, this time at least his heart would remain untouched and intact.

Gwennan watched her men divest Guyarde of his armour. Pallor had seeped into his cheeks, leaving the bones of his face harsh and prominent. But his eyes seemed to look inwards, to somewhere far away, without even a blink against the sunlight.

She'd seen him without armour before, when they'd camped in the forest. Now its removal by force seemed only to emphasise his stature. His shoulders looked even broader without it, his stance even taller, his body even stronger.

Yet the faint pulse that jerked quietly at the corner of his jaw betrayed that disturbing and expressionless stare. Hinted that there was something deep within him that he couldn't quite disguise. Something that her men wouldn't see even if they looked.

But she, having seen him take many forms over the last days, couldn't help but see it. And as she tried to interpret it she felt a pang of empathy surge up from the hollow of her stomach, stealing her satisfaction, spoiling her triumph.

And from the bottom of her heart came a sense of recognition. As if that stark countenance before her was a blinding mirror held up in front of her soul. A mirror that showed her a reflection not of the person she'd become—had had to become over the last year—but of the woman she'd once been.

The woman who had also once been divested of her clothes, but not by the hands of others. She herself had been the one to remove them—the gowns, the kirtles and the veils—and put on a tunic instead. She herself had laid down her breviary and her needlework and taken up the sword and the shield in their place.

And now, for the first time in all those months, as Gwennan looked into Rolant Guyarde's naked face she remembered that woman who had ceased to exist. Not just in the eyes of her people, who had accepted her choices and followed her cause, but in her own eyes and heart too.

She spun away quickly from the searing memories and the yearning that rose up behind them. It was futile to mourn the past and the things that were lost, the happiness and the love. All those things were dead and gone and would never come back.

'It is growing dusk,' she said to her uncle, her tone curt. Her fingers curled around Cleddyf Gobaith's golden hilt—not to draw it, but to fix her memory once again upon why she carried it and what she'd sworn by it. 'Have Sir Rolant escorted to the strong room and bring him meat and ale.'

Without another word she strode away to the hall. Tomorrow he would be allowed the freedom of her *llys*, as she'd promised, but not tonight. To sit with him at table this evening and wonder and remember would be impossible.

And she must never be tempted to ask if he suffered below the hard outer skin, or what it was he'd lost, or if he mourned it still. And she must never be compelled to expose either her own aching loss, her own unbearable grief, her own silent mourning in return.

Because that would be as foolish as handing a knife to her enemy and showing him exactly where to thrust it.

Chapter Five

On his pallet, hands behind his head, Rolant stared sleeplessly up at the stars. Or at least at the one solitary star he could see through the small window. He'd occupied this room for three long nights now and was already tired of looking at it.

Was this one the North Star? Or Venus? Without any others to place it alongside, he had no way of knowing, no hope of getting his bearings. And he needed to get his bearings, fixed and straight, for he was becoming lost amidst these wild Welsh mountains, with their tang of heather and gorse. Summer scents filled the air and stirred his senses as if an elixir, and not pure night air, drifted into the room.

But it was Gwennan, not the star, that glittered bright before his vision. Gwennan who, in one stroke, had gone from captive to captor, page to nemesis!

He turned over on his side, his conscience prickling. Even if he hadn't been in the Earl's service a year ago, he was still—as she'd said—Robert of Rhuddlan's man. Little wonder, then, that she blamed him for the fate that had befallen her parents.

He prayed to God that Robert would agree to the exchange—his freedom for that of King Cynddylan and his wife. At least that would make some small restitution for her loss. But if not…how could he witness her pain, her loss, without remembering his own?

The sound of a horn broke the stillness of the night, carrying eerily on the air and shattering his thoughts. The blood-curdling horn of the Norsemen. A long distance away, but its terrifying note sounded as clear as a bell.

His scalp tingling, Rolant leapt up and looked out of the window. It faced the back of the compound, so he could see nothing, but sounds of erupting activity came clearly to his ears.

The crackle and hiss of torches being fired. The hurried harnessing of horses. The rasp of steel and chain. Men running, shouting. Dogs barking. A commotion that raged loud and then—like a swiftly dissipating storm—became silence again.

Too silent…

He took hold of one of the bars on the window, testing it. Nailed firmly enough, like all its mates, but it wouldn't take much effort to break it none the less. Although the window itself was too small for a man to climb through.

Rolant drove his fist into the wooden wall and clenched his teeth at the resulting jolt of pain. Inactivity was the worst of torments. A soldier needed action, a quest, and danger to combat. Because without those distractions he got to thinking about things better left well alone.

Like the past that couldn't be changed, no matter how much he would give to change it—his own life included.

Once, when faced with the choice to fight on one side or the other, he'd chosen neither—and lived the long years since with the consequences. Now, when he ached for the distraction of action, and for the absolution that might come with his death in battle, as John had died, it seemed he wasn't even to be offered a choice.

Flinging himself back down on his pallet, Rolant looked up at the window again. The star had gone behind a cloud but his brother's youthful face—so vital and irrepressible in life and then so still and as grey as ash in death—burned there instead. He blinked it away, but immediately Gwennan's face rose up to take its place, the sad sheen that sometimes glazed her eyes raking across his vision like a jagged knife.

And the hours crept with agonising slowness towards the dawn.

Gwennan stood on the parapet until the red sky of fire on the western horizon melted into the pink-grey of daybreak. Below in the compound her men had stood ready all through the night, their swords, spears and shields prepared to meet whatever danger was coming.

She'd brought all the villagers safely within the compound too. None of them—not even the children—had slept, but had waited in dread and prayer. And now, as the sunrise began to crest the mountain ridges, the danger faded as if it had never been.

Soon after Terce, her scouts returned with the news that the Norsemen had attacked the settlement at Tywyn on the coast, firing the little monastery there and killing its inhabitants, or carrying them away to sea and into slavery.

As Gwennan watched the villagers return to their

homes she issued orders to her uncle. The walls would need to be reinforced with a second palisade outside the first, the ditch dug deeper and wider, the gates built higher. It would take time, but they must have defences as impregnable as possible and the sooner they began the better.

It was not long after Meuryn had left, with the sounds of chopping and sawing, digging and exertion filling the air around them, that Gwennan heard a footfall on the ladder. A light step, but it came as loud as a herald, and she knew at once who it was.

'What happened in the night?'

She kept her eyes on the horizon, where the settlement on the coast must still be smouldering even though she couldn't see the smoke.

'Llychlynwyr attacked Tywyn in the night. Did you not hear the horn, Rolant Guyarde?'

'*Llychlynwyr?*'

'Vikings,' she translated, still not turning to look at him, in case those strange shadows she'd glimpsed in his eyes three days ago might still linger there. 'They are raiding our coastal settlements again.'

There was a beat of silence before he spoke again, reminding her of what she already knew. 'If the Norsemen are on your western flank, and the Normans to the east and north, then you are even more vulnerable here now.'

Gwennan spun round to face him. 'I don't need *you* to tell me that!'

He was so tall, standing there in front of her, and the imposing strength of him filled her whole vision. Like her, he wore just a tunic and hose, for the morning was too warm for a cloak. But his blue and grey colours looked far finer in the sunlight than her rustic garb.

Moreover, his garments seemed to fit his body exactly as they should, whereas her clothing suddenly didn't belong on her body at all. It felt alien and uncomfortable, chafing her skin like salt being rubbed into invisible scars.

Exactly as it had when she'd first put it on, or clothes like it, a year ago. When she'd left behind her womanhood and taken up the weapons and garb of a man.

'How did you come up here anyway?'

She put a hand on the parapet wall, drawing support from its solid oak. Her palm still remembered the blisters that had formed as she'd learned to use a sword, even though Cleddyf Gobaith was now an indelible part of her.

'You should not be up on the ramparts at all. Like the gateway, they are barred to you.'

He shrugged. 'By the ladder—as no doubt you did yourself.'

'What I meant was did nobody stop you?'

'Everyone is evidently too busy.' His gaze bored down into hers, green-gold as the sun's rays fell full on his face. 'But the work they are doing is a little too late.'

Gwennan jerked her chin up at his annoyingly astute opinion. 'Better late than not at all! Besides which, we have not needed such defences before.'

'Before we came?'

She tried to focus on the feel of the wood beneath her hand—not on the way the sunlight caught his black hair and made it shine too brilliantly.

'We have fought for years against the Vikings, and against our Welsh neighbours too, who are greedy to enlarge their lands at the expense of ours. But those battles were fought on equal terms.'

'And now the fight is unequal?'

'Yes.' How were his thoughts able to pursue hers like a hound on the scent? Fleet, sure, relentless? 'You Normans come with new weapons, new tactics—a different sort of warfare that we have not faced before.'

Even without sword or chainmail, nor the conical helmet with its forbidding nose blade, he still looked every inch a conqueror as he stared down at her.

'But we will resist and repulse you,' Gwennan added, her accusation becoming defence. 'No matter how many times they...*you*...come.'

You. Them. Who *was* the enemy? He was, of course, and yet he was also her guest, and thus far had kept his word not to escape—although many times over the last three days she'd caught herself half wishing that he would!

She turned and walked briskly away to commence a circuit of the four-square parapet wall that enclosed Carn Egryn. But behind her his footsteps followed— and, worse, his voice caught her up as easily as his long and easy strides did.

'In that case, building a second palisade outside of this one is a good measure. But cover it with hides to prevent fire.'

Gwennan spun round and all but bumped into him. This time the sun was in *her* face, and his had the advantage of subtle shadow. Instantly she took a step backwards, but there was nowhere to go without looking as if she was running away.

Although that was exactly what she wanted to do. Because all at once her defences were every bit as inadequate as those of her fortress.

'That work is already in hand!' she bit out.

'And the ditch is not wide enough or deep enough. It would be easily breached in a concentrated attack.' He turned to gesture outwards, strong muscles flexing beneath the sleeve of his tunic. 'But I see that too is in hand...' he added with a smile.

A smile that was gone an instant later.

His brows drew together as he pointed to the parapet floor beneath them. 'The Norman garrison ought to have seen to these boards while they were here. They are rotten in places and need replacing.'

He stamped a foot to test one of the planks and suddenly the length broke free of its rusty nails. Swivelling on its joist, it shot upwards to hit him in the stomach.

It was so unexpected, and so funny, that Gwennan's hands flew to her mouth. A mad urge to giggle bubbled up in her throat and she pressed her lips tightly together to prevent it coming out.

Then, instead of laughter, a sort of awe filled her mouth and seeped into her heart. When had she laughed last...aloud and with abandon? Or even felt the desire to laugh simply out of the sheer joy of being alive? So long ago that she couldn't remember. But God forbid she should laugh now, in front of him!

However, Rolant Guyarde apparently had no such restraint. After a second or two of shock, and a deep intake of air to recover the breath that had been knocked out of him, he threw his head back and laughed out loud. A hearty and resonating sound that echoed above the noise of the work going on around them.

'And that, *Arglwyddes*...' He looked at her and rubbed his stomach, pressing the plank firmly back down with his heel. 'Proves my point, I think.'

Gwennan folded her arms across her chest as the sun

burned hotter overhead, searing through her clothes until they seemed to cling to her skin. Out of nowhere came the memory of the blessed looseness of a kirtle that never clung, no matter how warm the day.

She shook her head, banishing the futile memories, the regret and the hidden longings. Such clothes had no place on her body now, no matter how much she wished they did.

'Do you see anything here that might be worthy in your observation, Sir Rolant?'

I do.' He nodded slowly, his gaze never leaving hers. 'I see a strategic high point that has been well chosen for defence. I see the landscape cleared of forest, so no enemy can creep up undetected. I see walls built of good solid oak and strong gates that will be hard to break.'

His voice dropped lower. His eyes had lost their twinkle and his face was deadly serious now.

'I see warriors with hearts of fire and a leader possessing the most courage I've ever witnessed in anyone—man *or* woman.'

Gwennan's heart filled like a well. Swiftly she turned away, fixing her focus outwards, over her lands, her *maerdref*, and the horizon that simmered too blue, too clear.

'Why do you say that?'

Surely he wasn't feeling *pity* for her? Trying to comfort her with small mercies? That would be as insulting as it was humiliating.

'Are you mocking me?'

He took a step nearer. 'Do you find it so very hard to accept praise? Or is it praise from the mouth of a Norman you cannot stomach?'

The soft, yet hurtful remark brought a lump into

Gwennan's throat. Was she so ungracious? Had her hate made her blind and deaf as well as distrustful? And, worse, could he read her body as accurately as he seemed to read her mind?

A body that was even now reaching out towards him despite all her efforts to prevent it.

'I would prefer to hear nothing at all from your mouth.'

'Even so, I will give you a warning—one that you should both hear and heed.'

He moved closer and her breath caught.

'Even if the Earl agrees to your demand of an exchange—and there is no certainty of that—it will not end there but only delay the inevitable.'

Gwennan gripped the parapet wall again, but this time it gave her no support. 'Do you doubt, then, that your overlord wants your safe return to him?'

'I know how much he wants these lands.'

She felt his eyes boring into the nape of her neck, as if into the bone below, stirring the blood beneath her skin.

'If he can get both, all the better, but I can guess at which he would prioritise.'

The sun was high over the mountain now, and while it still bathed them in warmth, it was as if his warning suddenly painted the whole landscape midnight-black. Gwennan could almost see the Earl of Rhuddlan's iron-gloved hand sweeping over her land until all of it was once more sealed tightly inside his mailed fist.

Rolant spoke again, his voice brutally blunt, his presence far too near. 'Your Welshmen are full of fight and courage, but they lack suitable armour, their weapons are old, their methods of combat outdated.'

Gwennan tried to shake her head in denial, but her

heart shook instead with the truth of what he'd said. 'The mountains will shield us as they always have.'

'There are ways around mountains, or over them, and they did not shield you last time.'

She sensed his gaze follow hers to the western horizon as he continued.

'You are very close to the coast here. Not only Vikings but Normans too can come by ship, with men and supplies and machines of war. It is only a matter of time before this place falls again into the Earl's hands.'

'Into *your* hands, you mean?' Gwennan hissed through clenched teeth, attacking him and defending herself at the same time. 'Your advice is strange indeed, considering you are one of those who would try to take my *llys* from me.'

'I am and I would. But I would rather it be an equal contest and not as easy as taking a toy from a babe.'

He turned to look at her and she felt his gaze like a flame on her skin.

'And when the time comes your courage will not make up for faulty strategy and inadequate defences.'

Gwennan stared at the mountains that stretched to infinity. The same mountains that he had predicted—rightly—would not protect her. But why had he predicted at all? What should he care about her vulnerabilities?

'Is that why you have come up here, Rolant Guyarde? To gloat over my failings?'

She spun to face him, meeting her enemy head-on, as she always had. Except she'd never met an enemy like this one before. One who used words like weapons, skilfully designed to trick their way into her heart without even piercing the skin!

'Or do you give me these warnings in order to save your conscience when the time comes and not even my courage will be enough?'

Rolant flinched inwardly as her words hit him far harder than the loose plank had done. Was that what he was doing, in truth? Preparing himself—as well as Gwennan—so that when the time came and she had to submit to his overlord his conscience would be clear?

'My conscience is my own affair,' he replied, his defence tasting sour on his tongue. 'And my advice is freely given for you to take or leave, as you choose.'

'But you are only telling me what I already know!'

Rolant shook his head. 'You know it, yes, but you seemed determined not to see the reality of it—or else you are too stubborn to look.'

She cast him a venomous glare and issued an unintelligible curse before turning her back on him. Swiftly, he grabbed her wrist, stopping her from walking away from the truth.

'I have no wish to see you strung up from a gallows, *Arglwyddes*, which might well be your fate should you continue to resist.'

She gasped and recoiled. Her face paled and she seemed turned to stone under his hand. Even so, Rolant felt the racing of her pulse, felt his own pulse race just as rapidly, both beats merging into a frantic sort of harmony as her mouth curved with contempt.

'On the contrary. I imagine both you and the Earl of Rhuddlan would be overjoyed!'

The sweat that had broken out between his shoulder blades turned cold at the prospect. 'I can't speak for him, but as for me… It's not quite as simple as that any more.'

It hadn't been simple since the moment she'd revealed her identity to him in the forest. Now it had become too complicated for clear thought, less still precise definition.

Words like captor and captive, host and hostage, Welsh and Norman…all had seemed to lose significance over the last days. Now other words threatened to obscure, even usurp, the whole meaning of the term *enemy*.

'It is perfectly simple, Sir Rolant. Your overlord won't be satisfied until we are *all* dead.'

Her chin was tilted up, but despite the bravado she was shaking—so much so that even the ends of her hair trembled.

'And I am not your imaginary page any longer, so let go of me at once!'

Rolant stared down to where his fingers still encircled her wrist. The cuff of her tunic was frayed, and the gold thread was worn where it covered the fragile blue-veined skin.

But it was the bitten fingernails—like those of a work-worn serf or a child who worried perpetually—that made him step back as if lightning had struck him.

Gwennan was no serf or child. She was a woman—royal, proud, courageous, beautiful…desirable. When she'd been his captive in the forest…when she'd been his page…he'd touched her as he'd pleased. And he'd given her no alternative but to grit her teeth and bear the liberty.

Now—and not just because she was a princess and

not a page—he had no place touching her at all. Because now he wanted very much to touch her…and more.

'Forgive me,' he said with a low bow, severing the connection of their eyes, bringing to an end a moment that should never have been. 'I am fully aware of your status and mean no insult.'

Gwennan rubbed the flesh where his fingers had been, even though it didn't hurt at all. Just like in the forest, when he'd held her foot and to break free she'd kicked out at him and accused him of hurting her.

The truth was he'd never hurt her—not physically. Nor insulted her either…only in jest. But nevertheless his words had cut time and again right through her skin. Whether words of warning or challenge, or—like now—words too confusing to interpret, they had all cleaved deeper than they should.

When had he begun to encroach into her mind? When had he gone from hostage to…what? Not guest, nor even enemy any more. Rolant Guyarde's presence in her *llys*—in her life—had gone beyond all those neat and manageable descriptions.

'Do not venture up onto the parapet again,' she said, aghast at the way her voice trembled…not with fear, but with something quite different.

He shook his head. 'If the Norsemen come you will need every man, and I would rather help you fight them off than lie in my room, waiting until they break though and cut my throat, having first cut yours—or even worse.'

Gwennan swallowed. 'You seem to worry excessively about my health, Sir Rolant. You needn't, I assure you, since I need no protector.'

His eyes narrowed as the sun fell full on his face again. 'Perhaps you don't.' It was as if the sunlight, instead of dazzling him, had reflected his vision towards her. 'Or perhaps you need one more than you think.'

The planking seemed to shift under her feet—and not because of rotten wood or rusting nails. 'What do you mean by that?'

'How long do you think you can hold out here? A woman in a man's clothing leading a few ill-equipped warriors?'

Gwennan blinked as the comment hit her as soundly as if he'd struck her across the face. The impact left her reeling and shock drove the breath from her lungs.

'I can hardly ride and fight in skirts!'

'Is that why you shun them, then? Why you wear your hair short and conceal your shape?'

The green gaze bored intently down upon her.

'Or do you doubt your men would follow you if you appeared before them in kirtle and coif?'

He stepped closer, once more closing the gap she'd put between them, and his unrelenting accusation pared the skin from her bones as cleanly as if he'd used a knife.

'Or perhaps you are hiding behind those clothes you wear?'

'Hiding?' Gwennan flung her head high but even she recognised the defensive tilt of the gesture, the retort that came too quickly, too heated. 'I've nothing to hide from—and my men will follow me for as long as I ask them to!'

She clenched her hands into fists to stop them pummelling that broad chest, as she longed so badly to do.

'I wasn't *born* in these clothes, nor with a sword in

my hand. Nor was I raised a boy like my brothers. But a year ago, when God took them, he spared *me* to fight another day. And I will go on fighting until I safeguard my home and free my parents.'

She didn't pound at his chest but, to her horror, her finger lifted and poked him hard, midway between his collarbone and his belly. But she was gone far beyond restraint now.

'Then and only then will I put on a coif and kirtle, Rolant Guyarde, and not before!'

And with that declaration Gwennan turned away and marched on around the parapet, expecting every plank to give way beneath her. Because he might just as well have ripped the very earth from under her with his perception.

She walked quickly, her breathing hard and fast, dreading the sound of his footsteps behind her, the feel of his touch on her arm. But this time he didn't follow and, rounding the corner, she leaned into the welcome concealing shadow of the tower.

Placing her palms over her stomach, Gwennan slowed her breath and willed the tremoring inside her to stop. But it wouldn't, and neither would her limbs stop their quivering.

She wasn't a fool, and neither was she a naive virgin, too innocent to wonder why her skin shivered and her heart pounded.

It wasn't delayed reaction to his remark about her being hanged, or worse. It wasn't even his challenging words about her clothes that had all but left her bare. It was the invisible marks of his touch on her wrist, the imprint of his strong yet tender fingers upon her that had stripped her, body and soul, right down to her bones.

O nefoedd! Pray God her hostage would be gone soon and she'd never have to encounter him again unless in battle, when he'd be just one more Norman, one more enemy among many…faceless, soulless, heartless.

Not this flesh and blood, puzzling and disturbing man who threatened to see all too clearly something she'd never let anyone see in all this time. This desperate disguise she'd adopted might have served her well before, but now it was as if it had just been sheared away like wool from a sheep.

But if she really was hiding behind these clothes she wore, as he'd said, from what—or from whom—was she hiding? From herself—or from him?

Chapter Six

That evening at supper, Rolant sat on Gwennan's left. There were only four of them at the high table, although it could have sat half a dozen. The rest—the entire household apart from the men on watch—filled the tables that flanked the central hearth on three sides.

And as they ate each and every one of them in turn—man, woman, young and old—stared at him. Some were curious, some fearful and some suspicious, but all without exception were hostile.

On Gwennan's right sat the grey-haired old warrior called Meuryn ap Hywel, who watched over the Princess like a guard dog. Rolant had no doubt that, but for his worth as ransom, the man would happily slit his throat from ear to ear and throw his carcass over the walls for the wolves.

'Your man, there.' He gestured with his eating knife. 'Does he never leave your side?'

The Princess turned her head, which had been pointedly turned anywhere but towards him until then. The honey-brown of her eyes was cool this evening, as on previous nights, despite the heat in the hall, for the fire blazed even though it was summertime.

But tonight there was an added wariness in their depths—one that he'd seen kindled there that afternoon on the parapet. As usual she wore a tunic, not a kirtle, and although the material was finely woven and trimmed with thread of gold, she looked no different in her simple attire from any other of her people.

'When I sleep!' she responded, flippantly yet with a wary edge to her tone. 'Of course he leaves my side when his duties take him elsewhere.'

Rolant took up a piece of bread, dipped it in the meat juice that had congealed on his wooden trencher. The food was plain fare—oatcakes, rye bread, roast mutton and fowl—unflavoured by sauces or spice, with no sweet pastries or cakes to please the palate afterwards.

'And who guards you at night?' he asked, mid-chew.

And why was there no husband in her bed at night? She was of marrying age, and even in those clothes and with her unusually short hair, her beauty was enough to draw any man's eyes, Welsh *or* Norman.

But perhaps she was betrothed and the wedding interrupted by war. It would be hard to believe there wasn't a man eagerly waiting somewhere.

'Meuryn sleeps in the room next to mine,' she informed him 'Within earshot should I call.'

Rolant put aside the bread, which was as tough as shoe leather, and wiped his mouth. 'Do you have need of a bodyguard, then, even here in your fortress?'

'Meuryn is my *penteulu*—my captain—and also my uncle, though not in blood.'

'How so?'

'He is my father's foster brother.' There was impatience in her tone now, a barely audible sigh, accompanied by a pointed lift and fall of her shoulders. 'But, yes, to answer your first question. He guards my life as he would his own—since my father is not here to do so.'

Rolant looked across at her uncle to find the man staring back at him without even a blink. Over one eyelid ran a scar, the mark of a blade, that scored from brow to cheekbone, and the eye behind it was glazed and white—blind. A good choice of captain, even with one eye sightless.

'Is one's family so tightly knit here in Wales, then?' he asked, returning his gaze to the Princess.

'Of course.' Her face was incredulous. 'Is it not so in England and France, and all other lands too?'

Rolant shrugged and, lifting his cup to his mouth, took a swallow of mead. 'I cannot say.'

Once he would have answered that with certainty, and from his own experience. But if that experience had taught him anything, it was that the ties of family were only so strong. If pulled too tight, or pulled two ways, those bonds would snap like string.

'But you have, or have had, a family of your own, surely?'

Rolant looked away down the hall, his mind whirling, seeking a suitably subtle evasion. The wooden walls were bare of hangings and the rushes on the floor were thinly spread, though not foul. Above the round hearth in the centre the aperture in the roof was inadequate, and thick grey peat smoke hung about the rafters, stinging his eyes and lining his nostrils.

'Yes,' he replied. A lie would have sufficed, but whatever else he was, he wasn't a liar. 'I had a family.'

'Had?'

At the fireside, a young minstrel sang disjointed verses accompanied by a stringed instrument. He had a pure and high voice, like a monk in a cloister, but the unintelligible lyrics and strange tune grated in Rolant's head.

'Had,' he confirmed, hoping that would be the end of it. But he was wrong.

'Your parents are dead, then?'

He drained his cup and looked back into her eyes, drawn against his will. Why and how had they come to this topic of conversation? He'd started it, hadn't he, by asking about her family? Damn it! He should stick to conversation about defences and strategy and the inevitable retaliation of his overlord, already overdue.

'My parents are alive and well in Normandy, as far as I know.'

A servitor approached and Rolant held out his cup for more ale, although by habit he drank little as a rule. But his throat was parched, and it wasn't just because of the peat smoke that filled it like a thick choking cloud. It was the irresistible questioning of the woman sitting beside him.

'It is *I* who am dead to them, *Arglwyddes.*'

He swallowed deeply of the honeyed mead and then pushed his cup away. No more. He needed a clear head, not a muddled one. The brew—unlike any he'd ever tasted, and far more potent than any honey—had already begun to addle his brains and loosen his tongue.

But how could he speak of his shame, his pain, his guilt over John and the estrangement of his family? Maladies that had no cures in this life or the next? Far better to speak with glib and throwaway words that had no meaning and were soon forgotten.

'But I still retain my lordly tastes.' Rolant turned his eyes to meet hers once more as his sorrow, despite his flippancy, squeezed tight around his heart. 'And while I am here, as hostage, I would welcome a more comfortable room and also some exercise or activity.'

Gwennan had known it was a mistake to seat him next to her, but he was a guest under her roof and it would be expected that he sit at the high table, enemy or not.

'I suppose you would like a feather bed too?' She girded her inner defences, making them strong like the chainmail hauberk she'd divested him of three days ago. 'And to go hawking and hunting outside the walls, no doubt?'

He chuckled, though there was no laughter in his eyes as he took up his chunk of bread again, biting into it with strong white teeth. 'That would be a start, certainly.'

Gwennan stared at his mouth. The full lips, the flex of his jaw—clean-shaven once more—brought a blush into her cheeks. Or perhaps that was just the heat in the hall, which tonight was almost suffocating.

'You have missed my point. None who have known no roof at all but have slept under the stars would scorn the strong room as you do.'

She'd done that for the last year as a fugitive, forever running and hiding from the Normans. Sleeping under the stars, or in caves, in woody hollows and friendly hovels, wherever she and her men had found shelter.

'I'm not averse to sleeping under the stars. In fact, on a summer's night like this it is pleasant and preferable to a hard pallet.'

A vision of him lying under his blanket in that forest clearing swam up unbidden, and her eyes slid to the wound on his cheek. A warrior would be proud to carry such a scar if it had been won in battle. A warrior might boast about how he'd earned it in his cups around the campfire.

But how could a man like this—hostage, yes, but still cloaked with undeniable nobility—admit that a mere woman had hit him with a rock?

'Although even that has its perils.' He touched his forefinger to his cheek, rubbing it lightly, his eyes twinkling now as bright as any star. 'It doesn't pain me much, if that is what you are wondering.'

Gwennan drew a silent breath. It was as if he saw right through her skin into her mind, and into her soul. 'It wasn't,' she said, tartly. 'But the wound is showing signs of infection and needs to be treated.'

'And who will treat it?' He smiled suddenly, brilliantly, his mouth as dazzling as the humour in his eyes. 'You? That would be a fitting recompense, would it not, since you are the one who dealt the blow?'

Was he jesting or accusing? Baffled, and feeling an unwelcome niggle of remorse, Gwennan pointed down the hall at the minstrel. 'Ywain Gerddor was a novice and herbalist at the *clas* of Aberdaron until the Norsemen burned it. He might provide you with a suitable balm if you were to ask him nicely.'

Tomorrow eve, and at all the mealtimes to follow, she would seat him further away. Keep him at a distance and not be lured into searching those eyes and wondering what lay behind them. Less still be tempted to examine the responses his nearness sparked deep inside her...physical and emotional needs she'd long since buried.

At that moment, seeing her attention on him, her *bardd* and her herbalist—also her clerk—glanced up. He moved his stool from the hearth and set it down again in front of the high table.

'A song, mistress?' he said in French—meant no doubt to impress their guest!

Gwennan, no expert in the Norman tongue, inclined her head, since she could hardly refuse.

Ywain began to play a love poem, his eyes not on her but on Nest. And, despite being weak-sighted, they burned with an ardour that put even the torchlight to shame and brought flames into the cheeks of her maidservant.

Some of the men in hall were also staring at Nest, the light of appreciation in their eyes fuelled by ale. Gwennan frowned. She should reprimand her poet for his boldness, for daring to play court to her maid in front of the whole hall, thus slighting his Princess, whom he *should* be praising!

And she should admonish, too, those others who coveted Nest with their eyes. But her maid was beautiful, her face pale, her skin soft, her manner demure. Her hair, long and golden, hung in a thick plait over her shoulder, glowing bright against the homespun russet gown she wore.

Gwennan looked down at her own clothes, also homespun, if made of finer weave. Suddenly they were ugly and uncomfortable. Her hair had hung like that once, soft and thick to her hips, and her hands had been delicate too, instead of the callused sword-scarred paws they were now.

Then, as she raised her eyes again, her cheeks were made as hot as Nest's by the searing gaze of Rolant Guyarde, who was not staring at her maid, like the others, but straight at her.

Quickly, she looked away, but all through the song she felt the green eyes scorch her skin, until she had to fight the urge to press her palms to her cheeks, to try and cool her blush.

But when Rolant spoke, in the space of silence between two verses, his startling question drove every drop of heated blood from her face, leaving her skin as cold as ice.

'Why is it you have no husband? Or is there a betrothed somewhere, biding his time and counting the days?'

Gwennan's vision suddenly went black. She balled her hands in her lap until her knuckles locked and her fingers began to hurt. But the pain was nothing compared with the stab to her heart that his careless words had brought in their wake.

The notes of Ywain's song drove into her skull like nails under a hammer. The *bardd* had sung and played at her wedding too…songs full of hope and promises that had come to nothing. Because the Normans had come first.

'I *had* a husband—and brothers, and a mother and a father too.' Slowly she turned her head to look at Guyarde. 'Until the Earl of Rhuddlan's men came and took them from me.'

The scraping of Ywain's bow on the strings of the *crwth* seemed to urge her onwards.

'Why do you look shocked, Sir Rolant? You—Robert of Rhuddlan's own man!'

His hand stilled in lifting his cup to his mouth and a muscle tensed in his jaw. 'I was not in his service then.'

'Perhaps not, but you have no doubt heard of it? How we resisted for three months of siege? Until we were starving and sick and people began to die of hunger and thirst and disease?'

Gwennan launched the accusations at him like arrows, wanting to hurt him even as it hurt her to voice them, not caring that it was not he but his overlord who should be the target.

'I knew of the siege, yes, and of the taking of this fortress…the imprisonment of your parents.' His eyes narrowed as he drank from his cup, holding hers over its brim. 'But that is all.'

All? The inadequate and insulting excuse came as if from far away, yet was loud enough to be heard over the singing of the poet. His song was a lively one now, with a jollity that clashed agonisingly with the raging sorrow that engulfed her.

And anger…so much anger that Gwennan thought her bones would crack with the shaking of her limbs.

She put her cup down, spilling some of the mead over its brim, staining the sleeve of her tunic. 'No doubt this is the moment where you tell me that such things happen in war? That lives are cheap—especially Welsh lives—and only victory matters, as long as it is a Norman victory?'

His face seemed paler suddenly. 'No, I would not tell you that, Gwennan.'

Gwennan? She stared at him, aware that her mouth had dropped open in mute astonishment, and in outrage that he should address her with such irreverence. Insult her by using her name so familiarly, especially now, at this moment.

But worse was to come. Ywain's song had changed

again and—pitifully oblivious to the carnage that was unfolding in front of him—he'd turned from a love song to a praise poem. One she'd not heard played for a long time, nor allowed to be sung, and so had all but forgotten.

Gwennan Fwyn, geneth firain,
Calon annwyl, glan glwysgain

Gwennan's heart shuddered to a stop. *'Taw, nid y gân honno, y cnâf!'*

The poet bit off mid-note, his lips rounding in horror and his face blanching. He could not know why she'd snapped and called him knave…why she couldn't bear to hear that song because of the bittersweet memories it conjured.

'Canwch gerdd arall!'

As she ordered him to sing a different tune, with different words, she saw her uncle glance across at her, his face troubled. Rolant Guyarde still looked at her too, his eyes dark and speculating, not troubled but puzzled.

And a moment later the question Gwennan had dreaded came—soft, yet penetrating, ripping into wounds already laid open and made raw by the innocent choice of a song.

'Gwennan Fwyn…' His accent made the word ache even more painfully in her ears. 'Gwennan is clear enough, but what does *fwyn* mean?'

Her heart twisted as if he'd reached right inside her and closed his fingers around it. No man now called her by that name—Gentle Gwennan—her childhood endearment and then Rhys's name for her. And only her husband had ever said it the way Guyarde had just done.

Even before the words had faded on his lips, the anguish of a year ago tore through her, sharper than any blade. That last goodbye…the worry while she awaited her husband's return…the shattering grief when he didn't come. And finally the hollow and overwhelming sense of loneliness when she knew he would never come again.

Although he *had* come home eventually, his corpse tied onto the back of a horse, his flesh rotting from his bones, seeming nothing like her husband at all.

'It means nothing,' Gwennan said, her voice quivering and her soul wailing in her breast.

And it must *never* mean anything—not ever again. She didn't think of herself as Gwennan Fwyn now. She didn't even think of her herself as a woman, let alone a gentle one as the endearment claimed.

Even if she had been so, once upon a time, she wasn't Gentle Gwennan any longer.

Not since she'd taken up her sword, put off her gown and hidden her lonely grief behind men's clothing and a cause.

'We sing different songs nowadays,' she went on, looking away from Rolant and down the hall. 'Songs more fitting for times of invasion and conquest and butchery.'

But now, for the first time in a year, Gwennan found herself mourning more than the loss of her husband. Something deeper dragged heavily at her heart. And tonight she felt lonelier than she'd ever felt in her life.

Rolant lifted his cup again and studied Gwennan's stony profile over its rim. Her face had blanched, but the torches lit sparks in the hair that fell like chestnut fire to her shoulders and turned her face from pale to wan.

War was bloody, brutal and greedy, and this invasion of Wales was no different. And he was a part of it. But a faceless, nameless enemy was one thing. Sitting here by the side of a flesh-and-blood enemy, sharing food and drink, was quite another.

'I am sorry,' he said at last, the words insufficient and inadequate. 'About your family...the death of your brothers and husband.'

She turned towards him, her mouth curling with scorn. 'Who are you trying to absolve, Rolant Guyarde, with your false sympathy? Your overlord or yourself?'

'Neither.' That at least was true, though the admission left a sour taste on Rolant's tongue. 'And nor is my sympathy false. Even Normans know loss and grief and sorrow.'

Instinctively he reached out and lightly touched her sleeve, in a gesture of comfort. He felt her flinch, but instead of snatching away, as he'd expected, she lowered her gaze to his hand briefly and then lifted it back up to his face.

'Even you, Rolant Guyarde?'

Rolant nodded. 'Even me.'

There was a long moment of silence. The air between them was poised and taut, distant and disconnected from the noise in the hall. Their eyes held and he saw hers darken even as he knew his own did.

Beneath his fingers, through the linen sleeve, her skin was warm, soft, as beguiling as her gaze. Their words hung in the air while beneath them, unspoken and unheard, a host of feelings hovered.

Her eyes flickered from his to the wound on his

cheek, and then to his mouth. Her lips parted and he heard her breath catch sharply. Then she gave her head a little shake, as if answering a question that hadn't been asked—at least not out loud.

She got to her feet and the whole hall rose too, the legs of the benches scraping. Rolant followed suit, and as one the voices fell to murmurs as the exit of their Princess signalled the end of the evening.

'Ywain Gerddor.' She called the poet forward. 'Our guest, as you see, has been injured. Do you think you can concoct a balm to heal the wound on his cheek?'

The poet hitched his instrument over his shoulder and, leaning across the table, peered into Rolant's face. Then—doubtless aware of the cause of the wound, as was everyone else—he grinned and nodded to the Princess.

'Yes, *Arglwyddes*. I can treat it. Mouse-ear would be best, or mayhap vervain, and tansy for the bruising... Although I think it will leave a scar, even so.'

'Then see to it tonight—before bedtime, if you please.'

The youth retreated, casting a last lingering look from under his lashes at the Princess's maidservant. The two women turned, went to go through the curtain behind. Then Gwennan seemed to change her mind and took a step towards Rolant instead.

'Outer wounds are easily mended, so let us hope Ywain's ointment can heal yours.' Her body was held rigid, but the words on her breath trembled. 'As for the inner wounds...there is no suitable balm for them. No mending them as you would a scratch on your skin. You can only bury them deep inside and let them fester unto death.'

Rolant's heart jerked against his ribs and it was as

if he was on his knees once more, in the courtyard of his former home in Normandy, with the sun and the silence beating down upon him. The hard ground cutting into his knees as he'd stiffened his body to wait for the blow that hadn't come.

And now, as the Princess held his eyes, he saw the vision in his mind reflected back at him, dark and damning. Had she seen his shame, his guilt, that day she'd held the sword up in front of him? Had she known he was ready to die and wondered why?

'Perhaps some things are better left buried,' he replied bluntly, severing the thread of empathy that threatened to connect them.

He was here to conquer, not to ask for comfort—less still to seek salvation. He hadn't sought salvation during the last five years, so why should he want to reach out and grasp it now, when he didn't deserve it? And why, when throughout those long years he'd been ready to pay for his mistakes with his death, did he now feel himself lusting for life again?

'Perhaps they are... I only wondered...'

The Princess stared a moment longer into his eyes, as if to ascertain some truth—or some lie. Her eyes seemed darker, and he saw the centres had grown large even as he felt his own do the same.

Then another connection was severed as she turned abruptly away, shaking her head. 'But I was mistaken. Goodnight, Sir Rolant.'

She passed through the curtain, her maid at her heels, and the heavy linen swung back into place. The hall erupted into noise again—voices rising, tables being stacked, trenchers and platters being gathered up and taken to the kitchens.

His guards, surly and silent, escorted him to the strong room. The bolt was shot on the door, leaving him in darkness.

Rolant sat on his pallet and leaned back against the wall, his arms crossed on his knees. Gradually, as his eyes adjusted, the light grew brighter. Not the sort of light a torch cast into the gloom, but the inner glow of a soul in the wilderness that glimpsed redemption.

He shook his head and dragged his fingers through his hair. Foolish notions. Brewed by honeyed mead, love songs, and the look and scent of a woman. Such things were for youths and poets, idiots and dreamers, not for him.

And yet yesterday, when Gwennan had struggled not to laugh when that plank had come loose and hit him, and tonight, when he'd reached out and touched her and she hadn't flinched away, something had shifted inside him.

The aloneness that was his constant companion in the absence of his family had weighed less heavy. And he had glimpsed something…even if not salvation. Still out of his reach, but there none the less.

A purpose for existence when a week ago he hadn't even known he wanted or needed one. And a latent and treacherous desire—which was a weakness he'd thought he'd conquered and would never have to do battle with again.

Chapter Seven

It was the eve of Lammas, the beginning of harvest, when word came.

Gwennan was in her chamber. The daytime meal had finished long since and everything was quiet. The afternoon was hot and she was restless. But in truth she'd been restless since the day the Vikings had burned Tywyn.

The residue of Rolant's sunlit gaze, his rich laughter, his fingers around her wrist…all had lain under her skin ever since, itching and nibbling and occupying her thoughts day and night.

Worse, his accusation that she was hiding from something had made her feel more unsettled every time they met—as if he'd laid bare a raw nerve and was now able to see right down into her very soul.

A knock came at the door and Nest, sewing under the window, went to open it. Meuryn stood on the threshold, holding a parchment in his hand. Gwennan knew, even before he announced it, from whom it had come.

'A message from the Earl of Rhuddlan,' her uncle said, holding the roll out to her.

When she didn't take it, but stared at it instead as if it was a viper in his palm, he closed the door quietly behind him.

'Shall I read it?'

Gwennan nodded, her heart leaping into her throat as Meuryn broke the seal. He smoothed the parchment out on top of the oaken table in the centre of the room and began to read it out loud.

The missive was written in Welsh, Robert of Rhuddlan clearly having employed a local scribe among his household. But the words, as briefly put as they were, would have been as bitter in any language.

When her uncle had finished relating the Earl's refusal, he looked up at her. 'I had hoped it would be otherwise, Gwennan.'

'So had I.' Gwennan's hopes sank into the rushes beneath her feet. 'But that man has no honour, no compassion, no mercy.'

'Or he fears your father too much to let him loose.'

'And my mother? Surely he can't fear her as well!'

'If your mother were free, her family in Ynys Môn would not keep the peace, as they are forced to do now. They would rise and drive the Normans from the island.' Meuryn looked down at the parchment again, and the hand he rested upon it curled into a fist. 'Your parents' captivity is too good a security for him to relinquish—for now anyway, Gwennan.'

Gwennan paced to the window, where the afternoon sun slanted in, bringing with it not beauty and warmth but cold and bitter fury. 'Curse that man's evil soul!'

The wonder was that he hadn't killed her parents already, as he had killed her brothers and her husband—if not by his own hand, then on his orders.

'The Earl states his own demands in this letter too, Gwennan,' her uncle went on. 'That you surrender yourself to him and relinquish Carn Egryn.'

'Never! If I surrender, who will carry on the fight? There is no one left.' Gwennan turned to face him, her hands twisting helplessly together. 'Gruffudd ap Cynan rots in Chester castle, leaving his forces in Gwynedd without a leader. The Normans are in control of Ceredigion, and Powys is as yet uncertain. We are alone, Meuryn!'

Her uncle nodded, scratched his beard. 'But if Robert of Rhuddlan comes in force, as he did last time, we have little chance of holding here. It might be best, instead of facing another siege, to flee into the mountains again... bide our time until the fates turn more favourable.'

The tidings of doom grazed over Gwennan's skin as her uncle repeated what Rolant Guyarde had said on the parapet—if not in the same words. But to yield her home now she'd got it back! To surrender herself to the same fate as her parents!

She went over to the table and stared down at the parchment, willing its message to be different. Then, on a savage impulse, she snatched it up and tore it into pieces. But she couldn't tear up the meaning of the words themselves, and they left her with an impossible choice. Or rather a number of choices.

Try and hold here, resist the Earl, and risk her parents' lives. Or become a fugitive again and go on fighting. But for what? Until sooner or later, she also perished under a Norman sword or at the end of a Norman rope?

And there was another life in the balance too—that of Rolant Guyarde. What was she to do with her hostage now he was declared not worth the ransom asked? Would she—could she—really order his death?

Gwennan pushed her hair from her brow, the tremble in her hand mirroring the trembling of her heart. 'Leave me now,' she instructed her uncle. Talking wouldn't help her sift through those choices, but only make them more muddled. 'I must think on this.'

As Meuryn went out, leaving the pieces of parchment where they were, Gwennan sank down on a chair next to the window. The late-afternoon breeze fluttered in, stirring the hair at the nape of her neck and rustling the vellum where it lay in shreds on the table.

Nest, on a stool opposite, had been sitting quietly all this while, having taken up her sewing again even though the light was fading. After a moment, she lifted her head and spoke. 'I'm sorry, *Arglwyddes*.'

Surprise broke through her preoccupation with the moment. Since her violation by those soldiers of the Norman garrison Nest had spoken seldom, and kept herself to herself to the point of invisibility. Her ordeal had all but erased the girl she must have been before, and the way she melted like a cat into corners whenever a man passed by spoke plainer than any words.

Gwennan stared at the mending in the girl's lap. The stitching was neat and precise and it was excellent needlework—a skill she herself lacked. Or rather she'd jettisoned the needle for the sword and had almost forgotten how to wield the former.

'You have parents, Nest, in the village?'

'Yes, *Arglwyddes*, and two sisters still at home. My brother Berian fights in your service.'

'Then what would *you* do if you were in my place... your parents in danger, the enemy all around?' she asked. 'You may speak your mind, since I would welcome your thoughts.'

The needle in her maid's hand paused. Soft grey eyes lifted and amid the sadness shone a quick flash of fire. 'I would do whatever I had to, to save those I loved.'

It was as if a sliver of cold steel had cut a path down Gwennan's spine. Nest was right—she would do whatever it took. She'd already done so many things, hard and sometimes terrible, but all necessary. Things she would never have done before...

She sat back and reached for some mending, taking up a short riding cloak that had a hole in it. Her fingers felt rusty and her eyes—keen in scouting distant horizons for signs of the enemy—were unused to close work.

Perhaps if she didn't try and think at all the solution would come. But as she took up a needle it slipped through her grasp and fell down to the floor. A sigh rose and almost became a sob as Nest leaned forward to retrieve it.

Gwennan forced a smile of thanks and, bending her head, began to sew, slowly at first as her fingers recalled what to do, and then with growing assurance. As she worked, not thinking of anything but the homely task in front of her, a sort of peace descended. The world outside the window receded for a moment, leaving an inner stillness of spirit that she hadn't known for a long time.

And as a lovely sunset began to slant into the room, casting dusty shadows across the floor, her needle began to weave in and out of the material almost as fluently as Nest's did.

In the hall, Rolant sat down next to the messenger who had come from his overlord. In a piece of luck, it was Alan Fitz Osbert, one of his own men—or had been when he'd been in command of them. Now he doubted he'd ever be given a command again—by his overlord or any other—after this debacle.

Yet another misjudgement…yet another mistake… yet more dishonour.

Alan, a bachelor knight as he himself was, had come under safe conduct with three men-at-arms. These sat at a table further down the hall, partaking of the refreshment that had been laid before them on Meuryn ap Hywel's orders.

'Did all my men make it safely to Caernarfon, Alan?'

'Ay, Rolant, every one of them.'

'Thank God for that.'

'Though the Earl was incensed by the turn of events.'

'Naturally.'

Rolant smiled wryly as Meuryn disappeared into the rear chamber at the back of the hall, hidden by the heavy curtain behind the dais. It was the inner domain of the Princess Gwennan and a room he'd never been admitted to, or even glimpsed.

They began to talk quickly, in lowered voices, since Alan clearly had a good deal of information to impart— including the news that the King was on his way to Wales.

Rolant whistled through his teeth. 'King William Rufus is at Shrewsbury?'

The knight nodded. 'He has come to deal with some trouble in the Middle March.'

'And the Earl of Rhuddlan?'

'Summoned to the host, as is his cousin Hugh d'Avranches. But Rufus won't tarry long, since further north is his main concern. Malcolm of Scotland is mustering on the border and threatening Northumberland.'

Rolant nodded as an idea sparked in his head. A king facing unrest on several fronts might be a king open to suggestions... 'And what of King Cynddylan and his wife in Rhuddlan?' he asked.

'They say the Welshman suffers from a wasting disease and is not expected to live much longer.' Alan shrugged and lifted his cup to his mouth. 'Of his Queen Angharad I know nothing.'

'Then pray the saints give Robert the sense to show mercy for once and release them.'

'I wouldn't like to place a wager on it.'

Rolant shook his head. 'No, nor would I, Alan. Did the Earl send any message for me explicitly?'

'None.' The knight frowned. 'Rolant...if the Earl refuses to release his Welsh prisoners, what of you? Your life may well be forfeit come sunrise.' He leaned closer. 'If, when we leave, we wait outside the walls, you might make a dash for it and escape with us. Even if my horse has to carry us both it is worth a try.'

Rolant considered. There was no dishonour in a man trying to save his own life, and yet...

He shrugged the temptation away. 'I have given my word. Besides, I have another idea—one that might entail less risk to you and me both.'

At that moment Meuryn reappeared through the curtain behind them, drawing it securely back across as he always did. Coming to the table, he addressed Alan in fairly good English.

'The Princess will need to consider her reply carefully before she sends it to your lord. There is no need for you and your men to remain.'

Rolant bit back a smile. Welsh courtesy only went so far, it seemed. He rose to his feet and grasped Fitz Osbert's forearm in farewell.

'It has been good to see you, Alan, and thank you for your...offer.'

As he said it, the suggestion of making a bid for freedom hovered in front of him once more, like a tempting piece of fruit on a bough just within reach. But to try and squirm away like a cornered rat—to attempt to save his own life when the lives of others hung in the balance—was cowardly. And the plan that was taking shape in his head would have a far more honourable outcome—if it worked.

'God keep you and your men, and speed you all home.'

His former comrade nodded and got to his feet too, signalling to his men that they were leaving. 'God protect you also, Rolant. You might need it!'

Gwennan must have dozed, because the knock at the door made her start and leap to her feet. Nest had gone, though her maid had draped a woollen *brychan* around her and lit some candles. The daylight without had turned to twilight, and a blue hue seeped in through the un-shuttered window to blend with the soft gold light that shone from the sconces.

'*Dewch!*' she called, and the door opened to reveal Meuryn on the threshold once again. But this time behind him stood a second man—Rolant Guyarde.

At once her body stiffened, and a force seemed to shoot through her like a bolt of lightning. Dropping the blanket onto the stool, she smoothed down her tunic where it had rucked up around her thighs. Her hands were trembling and she clenched them tight. But she could do nothing about the heat that began to creep up into her cheeks.

'Rolant Guyarde would like to speak with you, Gwennan,' her uncle said. 'A matter of urgency, or so he claims.'

Gwennan hesitated. This chamber was her sanctuary, the only place where she was able to be alone. Since Rhys had been killed no man—apart from Meuryn and, when it was necessary, her advisors and her clerk—had been allowed to intrude.

And this Norman wasn't going to intrude either—not now, not ever.

'Is it quiet in the hall?' she asked of her uncle. 'If so, I will see him there.'

But even as she spoke the sounds of preparations for the evening meal drifted in from the outer room. The scraping of tables and benches…the clatter of trenchers on boards…the hiss and spit of the fire as more peat turfs were thrown onto it.

It was sorely tempting to order the hall emptied again, to delay the hour of supper. But that would be unreasonable, as well as foolish. The men were hungry and tired and night was drawing in.

There was nowhere else to hear in private whatever it was that Rolant Guyarde had to say. Or to tell him, as she must, what response had come from his overlord.

'No matter.' Gwennan squared her shoulders, but her heart began to gallop in her breast. 'I will speak with him here.'

Meuryn withdrew and the Norman stepped past him over the threshold. Immediately the chamber seemed smaller, everything in it shrinking as if overwhelmed by his large presence. It had felt warm enough before, but now it seemed stifling as she folded her arms and spoke first, bluntly coming straight to the point.

'You should know that Robert of Rhuddlan has declined the exchange of your life for the lives of my parents.'

There was no surprise on his face, she noticed, though a flicker of something moved across his features. If Nest had lit more candles she might have been able to read whatever it was. But the room was only softly lit and dark shadows lurked in the corners.

'It is as I expected,' he said.

Gwennan turned and put a taper to another of the candles, lighting another and then another in an attempt to bring light and clarity of thought into the room. She wouldn't hide, as he'd accused her of doing, not even in the darkness of her own chamber.

When there were no more candles to be lit, she turned back towards him. 'And that leaves me with a problem.'

A smile hovered over his mouth. 'What to do with me?'

Her gaze flickered briefly to the wound on his cheek, almost healed now, though it would leave a slight scar after all. Ywain's balm had done its work; now she had to do hers—though it might prove far less remedial.

'I can hardly let you go free.'

'No.'

His calm voice, the measured nod of his head, unsettled her even more. Moving to the window, Gwennan began to put the shutter across. But that only seemed to trap her even more with the man in the room, so she left it open.

'But there might be a way to resolve the situation, *Arglwyddes*—to the advantage of us both—if you will hear it?'

His words hadn't been a request, despite their polite inflection. Perhaps he was a man who never *asked* for anything—not even his own life. Or mayhap—like all his people—he was simply secure that his arrogance would achieve all!

Gwennan turned to face him, steeling herself not to be swayed by false words, and found her heart beating faster than ever. 'What sort of resolution?'

'The King is currently at Shrewsbury—'

'How do you know this?'

'The messenger who came is—or was—one of my own. He told me that the King has come to deal with some unrest in the Middle March.'

She frowned. How did her enemy, confined as he was, cut off from all his kind, know things *she* should know?

'So what are you suggesting?' she asked. 'That instead of submitting to Rhuddlan I go to Shrewsbury and deliver myself into the hands of your King himself?'

'Not deliver yourself. Go as a potential ally—not as an enemy. Seek peace with him, or at least a truce. A submission need not be a total surrender.'

He moved closer and Gwennan felt a thrill run over her nerves. Despite all the distance she'd maintained between them since that day on the parapet, and that night at the table, she was always aware of his presence. And his very presence now—here in her inner sanctum, her safe place—made her think things she shouldn't think. Feel things she didn't want to feel. Doubt things she'd never doubted before.

'Very well, I am listening,' she said, folding her arms as all those things rose up inside her in spite of her efforts to tamp them down. 'Tell me of your solution.'

Rolant hadn't intended to come quite so close to her. Yet, even as a part of him wanted to step away again, and put a proper distance between them, the other part had to fight a compulsion to move closer still.

It wasn't as if she'd let him come near her again. She even seated him at the other side of Meuryn at mealtimes. Yet somehow—and for reasons he couldn't begin to fathom—her very remoteness, her stubborn strength, her pride, her courage, her impossibly precarious situation, had reached out and found him all the same.

He couldn't stand apart this time and do nothing. He had to try and prevent an ending that would surely be inevitable if she continued to resist his overlord.

'Why not go over the head of the Earl altogether?' he said. 'Appeal instead to the King for your parents' release, and in return offer him fealty and a pledge to keep the peace in these parts.'

'You are suggesting I become a vassal of the English King?' Her eyes widened, and then a little knot formed between her eyebrows. 'What would that avail? Why should *he* grant me what the Earl would not?'

Rolant felt his breath catch at the back of his throat. She was beautiful, standing there in outrage and defiance, framed against the purple-black sky beyond the window. A sliver of moon was rising, and the stars were thickening in the heavens like jewels against velvet. And she was shining the brightest of them all.

He fought the impulse to move closer, to cup her face and find out if her skin really was as soft as it looked. He knew already that it was, and so instead he turned away and crossed to the table. A torn parchment lay there with the seal of his overlord, blood-red and ominously indestructible.

'The King might listen if you went to him personally,' he said, touching a finger to the wax. 'I could accompany you, since I knew him well in Normandy.'

'But my parents are in Rhuddlan's custody—not the King's.'

Rolant took up a piece of the parchment, studied the Welsh words intently for a moment. 'William Rufus is on his way north, to deal with Malcolm of Scotland, so he could do without yet more unrest in Wales too.'

Talking of strategy should be simpler than this, surely? More clear-cut, swift and decisive and then done. Did it seem so complicated now because Gwennan's fate had suddenly become his cause?

'Also, he is newly returned from campaigning in Normandy,' he said, putting the parchment down and turning abruptly to face her. So doing, he caught the naked reactions that flitted across her face—surprise, doubt, suspicion, and something else that he had no hope of deciphering.

'So his resources for war are already thinned,' he added, trying to decipher it anyway, 'which might also work in our favour.'

'*Our* favour? Why should the King favour *us* over Robert of Rhuddlan?'

'William Rufus is…an unusual man. Eccentric, even.' That was putting it mildly, Rolant thought, but the description would suffice. 'The Earl of Rhuddlan is powerful, and a little put-down of a too-ambitious vassal might just appeal to the King.'

He leaned back against the table, curled his fingers around its edge. There was a long silence while they stared at each other. He saw her shiver slightly, though the breeze that came in through the window to play gently over her hair was warm rather than cool.

'I fought alongside the King in the rebellion of the barons,' said Rolant, aware of the note of urgency that had entered his voice as, desperate to convince her, he fought the pull of his eyes to her hair.

What had it been like before she'd cut those chestnut tresses to her shoulders? Had it skimmed her waist—her hips, even—when she'd loosened it here in this very room?

'And so…for all those reasons…he might listen to me if I spoke in your support,' he concluded, as the breeze stirred the curtain across the room that divided the living and sleeping areas.

His gaze strayed to the partition. Had she lain with her husband in that bed beyond? Had he threaded his fingers through those silken strands as he possessed her? Perhaps he had loved her—not just possessed her—and she had loved him.

'No, it would be madness to go to Shrewsbury.'

Her voice broke into his thoughts as curtly and as dismissively as if she'd read them.

'It is a day's ride there at least, and another day to

ride back. And I would be going straight into Norman-held lands.'

Dragging his eyes and his thoughts back under control, Rolant stepped towards her as his persuasion threatened to come to nothing. 'In the March you will be under my protection, and crossing through Welsh lands with luck we shouldn't run into any brigands.'

'I wasn't thinking of danger in *my* lands!'

Her indignity rose up like a flame, and even as her cutting sarcasm made him suppress a smile of admiration his blood sparked hotly. Why did this woman—one who vehemently renounced her womanhood—make his body disobey him and crave things long since denied it? Make his senses rebel and his mind want to believe things he'd long since renounced?

'If you don't go to the King sooner or later you will face far greater danger. Now may be the only opportunity you will get.'

He watched as she absorbed his words, chewing her bottom lip, the revealing impulse drawing his attention once more to her mouth.

'I will consider the option,' she said finally. 'But if we do go we must take an escort for safety.'

'We would be conspicuous that way, and it would be quicker to go without. The King will not waste much time in the March, so we must move swiftly if we want to catch him.'

She looked at him sharply and then gave a short laugh. 'If *we* want to catch him? You almost make me believe you actually care, Sir Rolant!'

What could he tell her? That he *did* care what happened to her, far more than he wanted to? More than he should? She would hardly believe him—and, anyway, his plan benefited himself too. If it succeeded, he would regain his freedom and be gone from here. Gone from *her* and out of reach of the temptation that threatened to undermine all the vows he'd made to himself and thus far kept faith with.

'Why should I not care to preserve my own life?' he asked. Although not so long ago he hadn't cared much whether he lived or died. 'Also, do you not want to be rid of me?'

'I… Yes, of course.' She stood taller, lifted her chin, although there was something more defensive than defiant in the gesture. 'But that still doesn't mean I should go to Shrewsbury with you, or that I should trust you.'

Rolant moved closer, halting a foot or so from where she stood. There he drew a breath and braced himself to say what he had to. To tell her what she needed to know even if it would wound her to the quick.

'I asked Alan about the welfare of your parents. Your father is very ill—perhaps even close to death. You have no choice, Gwennan. If you want to secure their release…save their very lives, perhaps…you *have* to trust me.'

Chapter Eight

Gwennan's stomach heaved. Spinning away, she placed her palm on the window frame and clutched it tight. A splinter pricked her skin, but she felt only the fear that rose into her mouth.

Trust him? How could she? Yet…how could she *not* if she was to save her parents? And, if her father truly *was* ill, how could he—how could *either* of them—survive much longer?

Outside, the moon was higher now, and somewhere in the sky an owl screeched ominously. The terrified shriek of its prey—some mouse or shrew—followed, short and fatal. That was how she felt—trapped as fatally as any prey, with no means of escape but a glimmer at least of hope…if she had the courage to grasp it.

Nest had been right. She would do anything—whatever it took—to secure her parents' safety. Even if it meant riding into England with Rolant Guyarde and bowing down to the Norman King.

Yet still she hesitated, arguing against the inevitable. 'Ten years ago, Gruffudd of Gwynedd rode to parley with the Earl of Chester,' she said. 'Instead he found himself in chains, where he still rots. Why should I not suspect the same treachery?'

'You will not be going to any ambitious Marcher lord but to the King himself. William Rufus is chivalrous, renowned for his fair treatment of enemies and his sense of justice.'

Gwennan laughed, the sound a choke in her throat. 'So *you* say!'

'I have never lied to you, Gwennan.'

Gwennan again! When had she given him leave to use her name? She hadn't—any more than she'd given him leave to invade her country, her home, her chamber, her thoughts.

'Why not? What would stop you?'

Behind her, his voice came quietly, so close she could feel the words on her neck.

'I have many faults, but dishonesty is not among them. And my conscience would not rest easy if I didn't try and help you.'

Her hand on the window frame started to shake. 'That still doesn't induce me to trust you. It only tells me that you might actually possess a conscience!'

'Gwennan...' She heard him take a deep slow breath, exhale even more slowly. 'You *must* trust me—even if only because there is no other course left to you.'

Her heart thudding, Gwennan turned slowly back to face him. As their eyes met she knew, suddenly and startlingly, that he was right. She *had* to trust him. She had no options left, no alternative course, no other choice. All her decisions had been made for her already.

She nodded. 'Then we will leave at first light.'

His shoulders seemed to relax, as if he'd been as tense as she. 'You should prepare an appropriate missive. We will need to submit that to the King's officials and beg an audience, first and foremost.'

Beg? Yes, that was what she would have to do, wasn't it? Get down on her knees and beg the English King to be merciful. Well, so be it. Now the decision was made, there was no point in tarrying over the necessary practicalities.

'Very well.'

Gwennan crossed to the door and called for Ywain. She dictated the letter slowly and carefully in Welsh, which was translated into Latin. The fine, ink-stained hands were painstaking in their transcribing. Ywain's sight was weak, though his letters were elegant none the less.

When the writing was finally done, she looked up at Rolant, aware that as the words had formed on the page it was as if a wheel had turned. No longer was he simple hostage, but now advisor, advocate and protector as well.

'Is anything else necessary?' she asked, feeling the reality of that dependency closing around her heart and squeezing tight. 'Is there any more the King will expect?'

'I should also dictate a message of my own to him.'

Ywain looked up her, a question in his brown eyes. Gwennan inclined her head in agreement. Rolant leaned on his palms on the table and began to dictate in English, briefly and to the point.

As she watched, the scratch of the quill on the parchment seemed to scrape over her skin too. It was as if all her senses were heightened to everything around them. The resonance of his voice—the flicker of light on his face—the hiss of candle tallow—the scent of the night air through the window—the noise from the hall beyond.

All of it sealing her fate in his hands.

The two messages were tied securely and bound with thin strips of leather and Ywain left them. A heavy silence fell, as if now the business was done neither had any wish to speak of anything. Or perhaps now the business was done more personal matters had entered the room. Slipped in through the door unnoticed as the clerk went out, to lurk in the corners with the shadows and render ordinary speech impossible.

Gwennan folded her arms across her body—a defensive attitude that she only seemed to need with him. 'Ywain Gerddor should come with us tomorrow. We may need a scribe at the King's court,' she said, more out of a need to dispel the tension than of necessity. 'He knows Norman French as well as Latin.'

Rolant nodded. 'And your maid too, as would be fitting.'

'Yes, I suppose so.'

She dropped her hands to her sides, unsure what to do with them, aware that her fingers were curling and uncurling, unable to stop them. Rolant still stood at the other side of the table, staring at her intently, imposing, expectant, and looking as ill at ease as she must.

Was he waiting for her leave to go—or for her permission to stay? They'd said everything that needed to be said, so what was it that suddenly began to whisper around the walls of her chamber?

Gwennan cleared her throat, the sound too loud in the silence. 'Is there anything more, Sir Rolant?'

'Your attire…'

'My attire?' She looked down at her clothes. 'What about it?'

'It would be as well if you present yourself to the King dressed as a lady and a princess, not as you are now. If you want him to take your plea seriously you must play by the rules of etiquette. Otherwise you risk him dismissing your plea—and you also—as being of no consequence.'

Gwennan started to shake her head, her body instinctively shrinking deeper into the concealing garments he was advising her to take off. The words he'd spoken on the parapet—when he'd accused her of hiding—echoed again in her ears, like a drum coming ever nearer.

Yet how could she kneel before a king dressed as she was? How could she ride into his court and risk being a laughing stock to all?

Lifting a hand, she touched her hair—a self-conscious and betraying gesture she regretted immediately. A flush warmed her cheeks and she became keenly aware of her sex. As any other woman would be in the presence of a virile man. And, worse, she was unable either to hide or deny her reactions.

His eyes were resting on her hair, dark and assessing. Then they came to rest on her face, and all at once her mouth felt softer, fuller, her skin smoother, paler. It was as if her whole body was naked and glowing hotly beneath his gaze.

'I will pack a gown for the occasion, but will ride as I am.' Even her voice seemed lighter, more breathy, goading her into a cutting and defensive sarcasm. 'Mayhap I can pretend to be your page, Sir Rolant! That would be most fitting now, would it not? An apt disguise indeed, if an ironic one!'

His eyes narrowed, concealing whatever thoughts might lie within them. 'It might be safer that way.'

Safer for *her*, certainly.

Gwennan knew she hadn't moved a muscle, had hardly drawn in or let out a breath. Yet her whole being seemed to be sending out betraying signals that even in the dim light must be as blindingly clear to him as they were mortifying to her.

She inclined her head. 'Until the morrow, then...'

He gave a nod in return, and with one last searing look turned and crossed to the door. There he paused, his hand on the latch, his head half turned, as if she might bid him stay. And for a brief instant Gwennan felt an overpowering longing to do just that.

But she didn't, and the next moment he was gone.

Raising her hands to her face, she found her cheeks aflame, her palms moist, her fingers a-tremble. And, low down inside her an agonising and long-forgotten ache began to tug, like a rope twisting around her entrails.

Forwyn Fair!

But calling on the Blessed Virgin for help was almost blasphemy. Because even though she was still fully clothed, it was as if every strip of material had been peeled away from her body, leaving her nothing to hide behind.

Gwennan knew it was wrong to cross the room and draw back the partition curtain that concealed the sleeping section. Wrong to light a candle and go to the coffer on the floor at the foot of her bed. To kneel down and open it...

Wrong to look inside and touch the colourful garments within and remember how it had felt to wear them in days long since, when she had not been as she was now and life had been so much simpler. The kirtles and shifts, the veils and coifs, the stockings and soft leather shoes and slippers, the belts, the jewels…

She pushed her hand deeper, right down into the bottom of the chest, to the lowest layer of all. To the gown of dark red she'd worn on her wedding day, which Rhys had peeled from her body with gentle and patient hands as they'd lain together for the first time.

A sob caught in her throat and she snatched her hand out of the coffer and slammed the lid down. Oh, why had she kept these things? Hidden them safely from the invaders? Restored them to the foot of her bed when all they did was torture her? Why!

'Oh, Rhys!'

Resting her forehead against the hard oak, Gwennan squeezed her eyes tightly shut. All the tears in the world wouldn't bring back the man who'd been her husband. The man she'd known for as long as she could remember and had loved since the day she'd first seen him… the day she'd discovered what love really was.

The man she'd thought she'd spend all her days with, no matter what dangers came, because they'd face them together.

The man she would have died for if she'd had to.

But he had died, not her.

Rhys was gone, and gone too was the woman he'd loved in return. All that was left was his sword and her memories—and these hidden garments that she'd almost forgotten about. Garments that now brought it all back—the memory, the pain, the loss of not just her husband but herself too.

And now she had to put these garments on again, and she knew they would feel not like clothes but like the remnants of a life of promise, of joy and hope and desire, of love that had died too soon. Of things that had been once upon a time and could never be again.

Rolant Guyarde was right. She *had* been hiding all this time—firstly from herself and lately from him! And now, by uncovering her self-concealment, he had also unleashed all these things she'd never allowed herself to mourn and had thought never to know again. Things she'd never *wanted* to know again until *he'd* come.

Shrewsbury was the biggest town Gwennan had ever seen. Looped on three sides by the River Severn, it was dominated to the south by the Benedictine abbey and to the north by the castle of the Earl of Montgomery.

A symbol of invasion, the motte and bailey of stone and timber had been built nearly a score years ago, when the Norman noblemen had been given free rein to plunder and conquer as much of Wales as they could.

Noblemen like Rolant Guyarde.

Even after three weeks as her hostage, with none of the luxuries he was no doubt used to, he was riding up ahead, talking and laughing with Ywain as if he'd known the man all his life. His helmet gleamed in the sunshine and he looked as fresh as if he'd risen that morning from a feather bed, not a mean pallet on the floor of her strong room.

As they rode over the wooden bridge and into Shrewsbury, Rolant's stature seemed to grow ever larger. His height, his strong-featured face—stern below his Norman helmet—and his noble bearing set him far apart. And while many glanced at him, some with envy, some with admiration, Gwennan drew no attention at all. More than likely everyone really did take her for his page!

Rolant suddenly drew rein to let her catch him up. His knee bumped hers as he leaned in to make himself heard above the noise in the street. 'The King will be lodged in the castle, if he is still here. We will try to find beds at the abbey hostel.'

Gwennan nodded and then, as a passing merchant bowed to Rolant and ignored her completely, indignation flared up inside her.

'Yes, my lord knight,' she said with a bow, low down over Tarian's neck. She glared pointedly at him as she straightened up again. 'Doubtless the Lord Abbot will find *you* a nice comfortable bed and *me* a place beside the pigs in their sty!'

His brows shot up and then he burst into a laugh, his teeth strong and white in his face, deeply bronzed now from the sun.

'I don't think it will come to that! If it does, then I shall take the pigsty and you the feather bed...*Gerallt.*'

Gwennan scowled, the sound of the name as much as the twinkling eyes and easy humour bringing yet more indignation. Muttering an oath under her breath, she moved Tarian away a little, so that there was a gap between them again.

The town was suffocating her...as if its streets were wrapping around her throat and squeezing so tightly she could hardly breathe. But most suffocating of all were the things that came in the wake of that laugh: those sunlit dancing eyes, that presence that she couldn't ignore, no matter how hard she tried.

Had he sensed that beat of taut silence last night in her chamber? When they'd seemed to be the only two people in existence? When her legs had turned to water and her belly had filled with longing? When her heart had thundered so loud in her breast that she had been sure he must hear it?

Pray God he hadn't seen or heard anything at all. Even if she couldn't hide from herself any longer, she had to keep hiding from him. Had to conceal this inner turmoil, try and subdue it, and then—once he was gone from Carn Egryn—forget it all as if it had never been.

As they ascended an incline to where three streets converged, the noise around them grew louder. A mass of people were gathered there, but it was only when they drew nearer that it became clear what it was.

A public hanging.

Gwennan's stomach lurched and she tried to turn Tarian away. But the crowd had closed in around them, everyone eager to watch the gruesome entertainment, and they were swept along with it.

It was like a market day, with vendors selling their wares, pie men their pies. On a chain, a bear danced cruelly. All was a spectacle worthy of a nightmare, but for the moment they could go neither forward nor back. They could only watch.

The man at the end of the rope was already half dead, his thin and unkempt body jerking feebly. Even above the sound of the watchers—some gasping in awe, some wailing in pity, some laughing in callous derision—his terrible, struggling breaths rent the air with an agonising clarity.

'Public hangings are not a pleasant sight.'

Rolant, without her knowing it, had come to her side once more, his horse between hers and the gallows. His face had darkened, all humour gone, and his mouth twisted with disgust.

'And yet folk enjoy them like any other holy day! We may be stuck here for a while, so best avert your eyes.'

But Gwennan couldn't look away, no matter how much she tried. As if mesmerised by the horror, she watched life leave the man's body, his suffering over in a final rattle of death, one last twitch of his limbs. Her eyes were dry, but inside she wept a thousand tears.

The crowd began to jostle and disperse in disarray. Rolant's horse cannoned into hers, the gelding rearing in alarm, and she heard him curse.

'If I'd known this was happening I would have avoided the Cross altogether and taken another route.'

Gwennan was deafened by the clamour of tongues, speaking every language on God's earth, it seemed, even Welsh. The stench of the town, the houses that flanked the streets and hemmed them in, the awful delight of these people in the suffering of a fellow creature—all of it brought a rush of vomit up into her mouth.

She couldn't bear it any longer. Sliding from the saddle, she landed on her knees, felt the crowd parting, someone's boot accidentally stamping on her hand. She staggered up again and, blinded by panic, pushed her way through the mass of bodies. From somewhere behind her she heard Rolant call her name, but his voice was swamped by the other voices, howling like a pack of wolves all around her.

Gwennan began to run, although she couldn't see where she was going. At least it was away from that hideous sight. Away from the unbearable pain and haunting loss it had evoked.

She ran through twisting streets, passed faceless people who stopped and stared at her. She ran until she all but hit a wicket fence that blocked off the end of a narrow alleyway. And there she sank to ground and began to retch.

'Gwennan!'

Through the fog in her head, her name came dimly. She felt someone kneel at her side, felt their arms go around her, their hands scoop her hair back from her mouth. She remembered this had happened before, some time, somewhere, someone...

She retched and shook, until her soul felt empty and her heart so lonely that she thought it would break. And in her vision it wasn't that pitiful felon but Rhys who swung back and forth, back and forth, the rope creaking, the watchers gloating, as he died all over again.

Gwennan covered her face with her hands, but the vision still speared through her fingers. Then she felt that soft touch on her hair again, heard a voice that spoke softer still. And all at once she remembered that same voice, that same touch, that same man in the forest.

'What is it, Gwennan?' Rolant's question came close to her ear, gentle as a caress. 'Did that scene upset you so much?'

She nodded, the tears she wouldn't cry blocking her throat, pain building up behind them like a dam. *'Y crogi...yn union â Rhys...'*

'I don't understand.' Even more gently, his breath touching her cheek, he probed, 'Tell me.'

She tried to swallow the words as they rose, but it was impossible to stem the outpouring of grief that— stifled for too long—suddenly knew no restraint.

'The hanging...it was...how Rhys died.'

'Rhys?'

'My husband.'

'My God.' His body stiffened. His breath halted, then came again on an oath of disgust. 'And you witnessed it?'

Gwennan shook her head and stared at the ground in front of her, at the rent in the knee of her stocking, the bruise on her hand. 'He was captured in battle with Robert of Rhuddlan's forces…where Caradog and Cadell, my brothers, were killed.'

She squeezed her eyes shut. 'They didn't grant him the quick death that he, a prince, should have had. They hung him from a tree and watched him suffer. Then they left his body to rot, swinging from the rope, food for the carrion.'

Rolant's arms were still around her, and she leaned her head into the hollow of his shoulder.

'Oh, it was a cruel end, a shameful way to die, Rolant! They should have cut him to pieces with their swords. At least that would have been a noble death…a warrior's death…worthy of the man he was!'

A church bell rang out the hour of Nones somewhere in the town, drowning her words, but she went on, needing to finish, to say it all now she'd begun.

'Days later, some of our men brought him home on Tarian's back, his bloodied and mangled body covered with sackcloth.'

The bell stopped and her voice rang out suddenly loud.

'I took off the cloth and made myself look at him, so that I would never forget. But his face… *O Grist annwyl*, Rolant, it wasn't the one I'd known…'

'Stop, Gwennan.' He tipped her chin up and turned

her face to his. 'Don't think of him thus. Remember him as he was in life, and then as a man who died bravely, if despicably, and be at peace with that knowledge.'

Gwennan stared into his eyes, saw them crease at the corners, deep with concern. Too deep, too caring. His arms were close around her and she wanted to bury herself deeper inside them. Draw on his strength, lean on him, trust him.

Instead, she wrenched herself free and pushed herself up from the ground, steadying herself on legs that felt out of joint. And she girded her heart again the way she would gird her body before battle.

'How can I be at peace when the war still goes on?'

He rose too, towering over her as he always did, his face dark. 'If all goes favourably with the King, there may yet be peace.'

Gwennan bent to dust off her clothes, but her head was dizzy, her nose full of the stench of nausea, and she swayed slightly. When Rolant put out a hand to steady her she ignored it, and hated herself for being so ungrateful.

'Then we'd best make haste and go and ask for that favour, hadn't we? I apologise for delaying us,' she said, her voice hard, so as to keep herself upright and not fall back down and weep her heart out all over the street. All over *him*! 'After all, we mustn't keep your King waiting!'

As she brushed the dirt off her hose Rolant noticed the tear in them, and the cut on her hand a vivid slash against her pale skin. Her face was even whiter and her eyes red, even though she'd shed no tears.

'I had thought your husband killed in battle,' he said. 'I'm truly sorry for the way he died.'

Her eyes flashed into his, glittering and yet somehow desolate too, as if what she'd just revealed had left her empty inside. Perhaps it had.

'I don't want your apologies or your compassion, Rolant Guyarde. I just want this day over.'

Pushing past him, she walked away, back up the alley to where Nest and Ywain waited with the horses. Her steps were like those of a sleepwalker, unsteady and without direction.

Rolant walked in her wake and cursed under his breath. For Rhuddlan to have hanged her husband like a felon for committing no crime but defending his land was an act unworthy of any man. And, not for the first time since he'd entered the Earl's service, a taste of personal dislike soured his mouth.

It was a taste that persisted and grew more and more rancid as they threaded their way through the streets towards the abbey hostel. Near the Foregate, he nodded to someone he knew slightly—a knight in the service of the Earl of Montgomery—but the man didn't recognise him.

And as they dismounted at the gates Rolant hardly recognised himself any more. He felt like a stranger, an alien, for all his Norman trappings. An impostor, wearing garments that fitted his body but didn't clothe his soul. A soldier who forgot his duty, sickened instead by violence and war.

At the pilgrims' hostel he issued instructions to the monk who greeted them with more haste than was polite.

'Ywain and I will seek a bed elsewhere,' he said, after securing private lodgings for the women.

He was lucky to do so. Ironic that it was Rhuddlan's

own silver, part of the supplies meant for the ousted Norman garrison, that was paying for the luxury.

'The hostel is full now.'

Gwennan was handing her horse to a groom, stroking the stallion's nose lovingly, as if loath to let it out of her sight. She hadn't met his eyes since they'd left the alleyway, nor spoken a word, shunning his conversation as she had his compassion.

'Do you require anything, Gwennan, before we take our leave?' he added, when she still didn't look at him.

'No.' She turned at last. 'Just to know at what hour I should be ready for the King.'

There was the barest tremor in her voice and his gut clenched. Exposing her to that hanging had been bad enough, accidental though it had been, and an accident he'd give anything not to have caused. But had he done the right thing, bringing her to the King at all? What if he'd misremembered or counted too much on Rufus's chivalry? What if the King upheld Rhuddlan after all and Gwennan was taken to join her parents in his dungeon or face an even worse fate?

'As early as we can,' Rolant replied, keeping all those fears from his voice. To air them would serve for nothing, not now. He had to keep faith that this time he *had* done the right thing. 'I'll take our letters to the castle tonight, to try and hasten proceedings.'

'Then goodnight…and thank you.'

He gave a short nod. It was too early for thanks—even grudgingly given, as hers had been. And come tomorrow she might have little to thank him for anyway, if things turned out ill.

'Goodnight, Gwennan. Until the morrow.' Rolant remounted his bay and gathered the reins, needing to be gone, yet reluctant to leave. 'Be ready by the hour of Terce.'

Her chin tilted up. 'I shall be ready for dawn, if need be!'

Rolant stared down at her. Shadows lurked under her eyes and her hands were clasped tightly together in front of her. All at once his compassion and his desire became one and began to leak out of his heart, drop by drop, like his life's blood.

He turned his gelding swiftly for the castle and drove his heels into its flanks until its hoofbeats muffled his nagging doubts. There was no room for weakness or for doubt, and he could do nothing—as yet—about desire. He'd taken his stand, chosen his side, pledged to help her.

But if he should fail...

No! There could be no failure. There mustn't be. Not this time. He'd let everyone he loved down once, by not standing on one side or the other, being too weak, too deluded to see clearly. Now that he'd chosen Gwennan's side—because his conscience couldn't let her stand alone, a plaintiff without an advocate, before the King and all his court—he would help her win this victory. Or else fall with her in her defeat.

Chapter Nine

'Will you wear the coif or the veil, *Arglwyddes*?'

In the simple but thankfully private room she and Nest had been given at the abbey hostel, Gwennan stood still as her maid dressed her. She was shivering, but not because the room lacked a hearth for a fire or a window to let the sun in. She shivered because as every garment went on she felt a layer of skin come off.

'The veil would be more fitting, I think.' At least the tremor in her voice might be mistaken for the chattering of her teeth. 'And the circlet.'

A clean shift was placed over her naked body, then a grey kirtle and a pale green over-gown. Around her waist was looped a fine leather girdle, with a soft pouch hanging from it in place of a dagger.

Like an obedient child, she sat on the bed for her maid to wrap woollen *socasau* on her legs and then put on her boots. Finally, Nest fixed a white veil of fine linen on her head and secured it with a delicate circlet of bronze.

These clothes were soft, like silk, compared to the rough weave of her tunic. They covered her body just as they should. But putting them on was like taking a step back onto a path she'd left long ago. Now it was unfamiliar, frightening, and she didn't know where it would lead her—backwards or forwards—or if she could ever step off it again.

And something was absent from this attire—and sorely missed. Cleddyf Gobaith, left behind at Carn Egryn, for she could hardly take it with her to meet the King.

In less than one day she had taken off the disguise adopted out of necessity, which had kept her safe from her enemies, and disarmed herself of the sword that had sustained her for the last year of flight and fight.

Crossing to the table, she poured some wine and forced it down her dry throat. There was no stepping off the path again now...no more disguise. No going back either—only forward to whatever today would bring.

'Will you put on your cloak now, *Arglwyddes*? The bell has already rung Terce and Sir Rolant said we must be ready for this hour.'

Nest's words were tremulous and, turning, Gwennan saw the shadow of fear behind her eyes. Her maid would be going into the lion's den too...if not into the presence of the King himself.

And, before that, what if they had to pass again that hideous spectacle on the gallows at the Cross?

'Yes, bring my cloak if you please,' she said, as calmly as she could, setting an example even though her fear was no less than Nest's. 'God forbid we keep Sir Rolant waiting!' '

Nest had seen the hanging yesterday too, yet *she* hadn't run away like a frightened deer. And neither should Gwennan have run, nor emptied her stomach into the street. And, worst of all, she should never have leaned into Rolant's embrace, opened her heart and poured out all her sorrow.

Because when his hand had brushed the hair from her face, touched her cheek so gently, she could so easily have stayed there in his arms for ever. Closed her eyes, gone to sleep, forgotten everything and just given herself up to his strength, to his care.

Just as she was now entrusting him with her hopes, her future, and perhaps her very life. She would be in his debt for whatever this day brought, be it good or bad.

Her maid fastened a mantle of russet-brown at her throat with a golden brooch, and then stood back to inspect her mistress's appearance. 'You look fit enough to meet the Holy Pope himself, not just the King of England.' Then her maid hesitated and her colour deepened. 'May I speak to you of something, *Arglwyddes*, while we wait for Sir Rolant?'

'Of course, Nest. What is it?'

'Ywain Gerddor wishes to wed me.'

'Does he?' Gwennan adjusted her headdress, marvelling at how soft the veil was…how she'd forgotten. 'And what are *your* wishes, Nest?'

'My parents would like to see me wed, and Ywain is kind and good. He says he doesn't care that…that I am not a virgin.'

'Through no fault of your own,' Gwennan reminded her gently. 'Do you *want* to be wife to Ywain?'

'I don't want to be alone all my life.' The girl chewed her lip. 'And if I don't accept Ywain it might be that no other man will ever ask me again.'

'Then, if you do accept him, you have my permission and my blessing.'

It seemed Ywain's eyes, as poor-sighted as they were, still saw clearly, and more compassionately than those of other men.

'I will give you a dowry and a gown for your wedding day.'

Nest stepped forward and straightened a crease in the russet cloak, her face both relieved and worried at the same time. 'Thank you, *Arglwyddes*...but may I remain your handmaiden even after I am wed?'

'I would like that.' Gwennan smiled. Perhaps, over the years, she and her maid might even close the gap of diffidence between them, cement the companionship they'd found the evening they'd sat and sewed at the window. 'Although if you get with child at once we may have to make some alternative arrangements while you are confined.'

'I don't think I can bear children.' Her maid's eyes clouded. 'There was no babe before, and I...I had to lie with those soldiers not once but many times.'

Gwennan reached out, touched the other woman's cheek. 'God spared you from a babe to be born out of such abomination, Nest. It will be different when you and Ywain are wed. A child—many children, perhaps—will be born into a blessed marriage.'

'Perhaps. I hope so. Every woman wants to be a wife and a mother, after all, do they not?'

The innocent words scraped over Gwennan's heart like a blade. Once, she had wanted that too. To be a wife and mother, to provide her husband with heirs that would continue the line, raise daughters to the kindness and beauty of life, not war and death. But now she was the last of the line.

She left Nest's question unanswered—pretended it

wasn't a question at all, but a commonplace remark that didn't apply to her. 'Then if that is what you want, it is settled. The banns will be read once we get home.'

A knock came at the door, making them both jump. And before Gwennan could call 'enter' it opened and Rolant Guyarde stepped over the threshold.

Rolant stopped in his tracks. Gwennan was standing in the middle of the room with her maid, but he hardly saw the other woman. Even when Nest curtseyed and melted into the shadows, as she always did when he appeared, his eyes saw only Gwennan.

A Gwennan he'd never seen before. And he couldn't have torn his gaze away even if his life had depended on it.

She was the same, yet different. Her gown flowed over her body like a caress, outlining small breasts and slender waist, curving over the slope of her hips. Her white veil hid the fire of her hair, yet framed her face as tenderly as a man's hands might.

And even though the bronze circlet around her brow and the clasp of gold at her throat were the only jewellery she wore, both caught the honey of her eyes and turned them to stars as bright as any in the heavens.

Rolant swallowed and bowed his head, feeling desire flame into his loins. 'Good morn, Gwennan, I hope you slept well?' He paused, lifted his eyes again, and asked what had to be asked. 'And I trust you suffered no more ill effects after yesterday's occurrence?'

'I am well enough, thank you.' Her chin lifted. 'You need have no fear I'll vomit before the King! But I think today, of all days, addressing me by my title would be more appropriate.'

'In the presence of the King it would, but we are not there yet,' Rolant replied, behind a silent sigh of relief. At least if she were indignant she might forget about that hanging rather than dwell on it. 'Besides which, I called you Gwennan yesterday without a reprimand.'

Her eyes flickered away for an instant before coming back to his. 'That was yesterday.'

Yesterday—when she'd run through the crowd and out of sight...when he'd caught her and clasped her to him, held her close. He could so easily cross the floor and take her in his arms again today, forget going to the King's court altogether.

'So it was,' he agreed, trying to keep the desire out of his voice. 'But we are not at Carn Egryn now, and I am not a hostage with you my host. Today we are just Gwennan and Rolant.'

Her gasp filled the room. Then her shoulders squared and she drew herself taller, looking even more magnificent in her new clothes. '*Sir* Rolant will do for me, thank you!'

Rolant grinned. 'We have advanced quite a long way, have we not? There was a time when you called me a Norman dog, and worse.'

'How do you know I don't call you that still, in my heart?'

His smile faded as quickly as it had come. How could he know what was in her heart when he couldn't even tell what was in his? Even if she was a dream of desire, standing there in front of him, nothing had really altered with her change of clothing.

'You can call me whatever you wish, Gwennan, in your heart or out loud. But now it is high time we left.'

She hesitated, and a little frown creased her brow.

'Before we go…is my appearance…fitting? Suitable to meet the King, I mean? Nest says so, but you might know that best.'

The words—proud yet quietly imploring—hit Rolant like a punch. Fitting? In the almost bare room, with its pious paucity and lack of colour, Gwennan shimmered like a rare and precious gem.

'You are perfectly attired to meet the King,' he said, and only his ears were aware of the tone of awe that might betray his thoughts. 'You need have no fear of that.'

He was the one who should be afraid. Of his longing to peel that gown from her body—even though it had been he who'd advised her to put it on. Of wanting to dismiss her maid, bar the door and remain within these four walls. All the things he shouldn't want to do.

'And now we must make haste.' He gestured to the door. 'Every moment we tarry, we risk missing the King altogether.'

Once they were mounted and riding towards the castle—Gwennan at his side now, not behind him—Rolant kept his eyes fixed dead ahead. He had no business being dazzled by a gem in female form, less still feeling this craving to touch, to taste, to possess.

He'd forbidden himself such things long since, because they'd swayed him once—with tragic consequences. And if he was to avoid the same outcome now, he had to keep all those treacherous needs well out of it.

Walking into the great hall of Shrewsbury Castle was indeed like entering the lion's den. Although it was hardly larger than her own hall, Gwennan found it bursting to the walls with people standing in tightly pressed ranks, all eager to see the King, and all of them her enemies. Even the Welsh who were present were those who had capitulated, either from fear or for gain, and sided with the Normans against their own countrymen.

At the back, she and Rolant waited as the hours dragged by—one, two, and then a third. And through every moment of those slowly passing hours Gwennan felt the presence of the man at her side like an encroaching and irresistible flood, coming nearer and nearer.

He didn't speak, he didn't touch her, he didn't even look at her…but every inch of her skin, every pulse of blood through her veins, every beat of her heart felt him.

And she knew that he felt her too. How could he not when between them the air was taut with feelings so powerful that they screamed louder than the deafening noise that surrounded them?

Then, suddenly, she heard her name being called and she jumped out of her skin. It was then that their eyes met at last. And it was as if a jagged fork of lightning had come right through the roof and pierced a path into her womb.

'Are you ready, Gwennan?'

His voice was jagged too, and the sharp blades of his cheekbones had turned a fiery red. His gaze was more a glare, and darker than Gwennan had ever seen it.

She nodded and swallowed down the sudden dryness in her mouth. 'Yes.'

Her reply was a whisper, and when he held out his arm and she took it the lightning lanced again. She saw in his eyes the same expression that had been there when he'd entered her room at the abbey earlier, and looked at her as if he'd never seen her before.

If she'd had a mirror, perhaps she wouldn't have recognised herself either. But she recognised the responses that sparked deep down inside her as his eyes devoured her, as consuming as any fire.

Her name was called a second time. One of the King's harassed officials strode up and with glowering impatience beckoned them forward. Somehow she moved her feet—which seemed to have become stuck to the floor—and walked forward on Rolant's arm.

But even though the air still crackled as that unknown storm moved down the hall with them, her mind took control of her body at last. And the fire inside her was a cold one now as she stared, mesmerised, at the sumptuously dressed figure seated on the throne.

With his thatch of flaxen hair and ruddy cheeks, William Rufus looked more like a labourer of the fields than a king. However, as she drew nearer the shrewd glint in his eye and the firm set of his mouth told her he was nobody's fool.

It went against the grain to relinquish Rolant's arm, to lift the hem of her gown and curtsey low, but she did it. At her side, Rolant went down on one knee and, taking the hand the King extended, kissed the largest of his copious rings.

'Welcome, Rolant Guyarde.' The King's voice was gruff, impatient, a little weary but not dismissive. 'It has been a long time.'

'It has, my liege.'

As he rose to stand again Gwennan did the same. She had no idea of the etiquette at the Norman court—how could she? But it seemed that women—even the few Norman ones present—were as invisible here as they were everywhere. Because at once the King switched to French and began to converse with Rolant as if she wasn't even present.

And she knew then that she'd not only crossed a border between two lands but also entered another world altogether. A world in which she had to make herself heard and hold her head high if she wanted to gain what she'd come here for.

As soon as there was pause in their speech, Gwennan stepped forward and, her heart thumping, addressed William Rufus directly and in English. 'My Lord King, I am the daughter of Cynddylan Fawr, ruler of Dysynni, and I am here on an important matter.'

'I know who you are, Princess, and why you are here.'

The bright blue, slightly bulging eyes flickered to hers. The full mouth twitched, and for a moment she wasn't sure if he was going to smile or scowl. It was even more unnerving when he did neither.

'I have read your plea already and I have been discussing with Rolant the reasons why I should grant it— or why I should not.'

Gwennan's heart missed a beat, but she steeled her nerves. 'Then I would ask that you discuss that with *me*, not with Sir Rolant, and in a language I can understand.'

'Would you, indeed?'

His eyes narrowed in his fleshy face and she braced herself for the wrath that would surely burst forth. But instead the King broke into a laugh that echoed around the hall.

'Then tell me—in plain English—why I should grant your request. One which I understand my Earl of Rhuddlan has already deemed it wise to refuse.'

Gwennan moistened her lips as perspiration ran down between her breasts. The gown she wore sud-

denly seemed to crush the breath from her body and the
circlet around her brow squeezed like a vice.

'Lord King…' she began. 'My parents…my home…'

Her voice faltered and her mind emptied. After all,
why should he grant her anything when he couldn't even
address her with respect but only laugh at her? How
could she hope for his mercy even if she flung herself
down at his feet and wept over those fine leather shoes
of his?

Then, so gradually that he seemed not to have moved
at all, Rolant brushed her arm with his sleeve. He didn't
speak, or turn his head, but the warmth of him seeped
through her like a welcome fire on a dark night. And
all at once, from nowhere, in the midst of her enemies,
Gwennan felt an ally at her side.

'My Lord King…' She cleared her throat and began
again, her voice steady now. 'I have come to beg for the
release of my parents and the restitution of my home.
The Earls of the March pledge you fealty for the lands
they hold. Why should I not do the same for mine, and
hold them in agreement with you as they do?'

The King stared at her, his gaze unreadable, his
mouth pursed. Rolant still said nothing, although she
could almost hear his thoughts…feel his silent strength
passing from him to her as if by magic.

'I am only one of many dispossessed Welsh rulers,
who might come to friendly terms with Your Grace if
you would only give us the opportunity to do so.' Gwennan lifted a hand imploringly, feeling her argument flow
now like the river outside the walls. 'We might then
co-exist in peace, instead of conflict that benefits neither side.'

William Rufus's face turned very red, very slowly. Presumably nobody—man or woman—should tell a king what he should or should not do...not even a princess of royal blood. But what had she to lose? Only her freedom, and perhaps her life. And if she didn't succeed here today, those would be forfeit anyway.

The silence stretched out, and as the speculative murmuring around them hushed into expectation even the rafters of the roof seemed to tremble. And then softly, yet so strongly, Rolant's fingers linked with hers.

She looked from the man on the throne to the man at her side, and so did William Rufus. Rolant's profile was stern, his gaze fixed on his monarch, his eyes unwavering. And as the two men stared at each other the knight seemed more regal, more powerful, than the King.

And it was the King who broke the eye contact first. Leaning back, he let his gaze flicker over them, from one to the other and then back again.

'So...you support the Lady Gwennan wholeheartedly in this, Rolant?'

'I do, sire.' Rolant spoke at last. 'I think it a just and wise proposition. And all it will cost you—or rather cost the Earl of Rhuddlan—is the release of his prisoners, one of whom is a woman and the other ill and aged. Where is the benefit in their continued captivity if you can obtain their loyalty instead?'

'Loyalty for now, perhaps, and possibly peace for a while—but for how long?'

The King rubbed a hand over his chin, his rings gleaming in the torchlight, and Gwennan knew instinctively that his decision was still far from made. And she was right, as his next words insulted her people, her status and herself all in one blow.

'I have heard it said by many here in the March that the word of a Welshman counts for naught—on either side of the border.'

At his side, Rolant heard Gwennan gasp. He'd said the same thing to her weeks ago, as they'd ridden through her lands, she his captive and he her captor. Then he'd half believed it, but now he knew better. And for reasons that were personal, as well as political, he would challenge anyone who dared utter it—even his King.

'I cannot speak for all of her people, my liege, but that same slur is often pointed unfairly at the enemy in times of conflict.' He stepped forward, driving his words home. 'And I can assure you—from my own knowledge—that the word of the Princess Gwennan is true and trustworthy.'

His sovereign smiled, but not with mirth. 'Still the misguided champion where women are concerned, Rolant? I thought you would have learned better, but it seems not.'

The distant abbey bell tolling Sext rang loud in Rolant's ears, muffling the whispers coming from behind him. Probably half the assembly knew what had happened in Normandy—of his disgrace and how his father had disowned him, or rather how he had disinherited himself. But, being distant kin to Adeliza, the King knew why.

'I don't expect you have seen your parents, under the circumstances, but perhaps you have heard that the Lady Adeliza has recently wed the Count of Briouze?'

Rolant shook his head, his mind numb and his face

frozen into a mask while the King's torturing arrows buried their tips into his flesh. Deeper than his flesh—right into a heart that he'd thought better defended after all these years.

Out of the corner of his eye he saw Gwennan's brow crease, her lips part in confusion and wonderment, and the King went on, deliberately and for some reason mercilessly.

'So you can speak eloquently enough in support of the Welsh, but are struck completely dumb when it comes to your own concerns?'

Rolant gritted his teeth and held his tongue before Rufus's taunting. To loosen it here—to try and defend and justify his past mistake—would not only deflect form Gwennan's cause but would be futile to boot. There *was* no defence or justification he could utter to his sovereign—to anyone.

The King sat back in his throne, his fingers drumming on the velvet-covered arm for a long moment. 'So...a silent but united front...'

Then he shrugged, as if suddenly bored with the whole interview. A gloved hand lifted and beckoned his clerk forward.

'Very well, Rolant. For the sake of friendship I will grant this boon for your lady. Robert is tardy in answering my call to arms, and since he is not here to dispute it I will waste no more time on this matter.'

The King barely paused for the clerk to put quill to parchment.

'I hereby grant the release of the two prisoners at Rhuddlan forthwith, and place the Princess Gwennan under my royal protection.'

Rolant waited for the rest. He knew William Rufus

as well as any, and while Gwennan's face had lit up and a sound of relief had escaped her lips, he knew there were bound to be conditions.

'But I will not be as trustworthy nor as foolhardy as *some* might be...' Rufus eyed him keenly. 'The lordship of Carn Egryn will be held in fiefdom of the Crown. Fealty will be due to me, and sworn in person once a year, together with a payment of coin, cattle and produce to the amount of ten pounds per annum.'

'Ten pounds!'

This time Gwennan's gasp was one of shock and outrage. Rolant felt her begin to tremble at his side, but before she could say more he spoke first.

'Sire, coin is not common in Dysynni. Commerce is by way of produce. The land is not fertile, and the demesne was ravaged by the late siege and occupation—'

But Rufus held up a hand—a warning that his patience was nearing its end. 'Then the tribute will be in cattle and other livestock, together with a portion of whatever grain *does* grow there, with a year's lieu before payment begins. Does that satisfy you, Rolant?'

Rolant inclined his head. What else could he do? The King didn't even bother to ask if Gwennan was satisfied, and he wouldn't have received an answer if he had. Because her face was blanched to white, her expression one of horrified disbelief, and her whole body rigid with shock.

The clerk scribbled furiously to keep up with the torrent that had tumbled out of his master's mouth. But when the quill finally paused, its point hovering nervously over the parchment, even Rolant didn't expect the King's next pronouncement.

'I elevate you, Rolant Guyarde, to the title of lord of

those lands. I remove you from Robert Earl of Rhuddlan's household forthwith, and make you my vassal.'

The words echoed around the room and the murmurs suddenly became a roaring river of astonishment. The flagstone floor below him seemed to open up like a trap he hadn't seen, let alone had imagined might be set for him—or for Gwennan—and together they fell straight into it.

'And, finally, as surety for the keeping of my peace in the lands of Dysynni, and to ensure continued fealty of its rulers and their heirs, the Lord Rolant and the Princess Gwennan will marry, the wedding to take place as expediently as is possible.'

Chapter Ten

'I mislike this as much as you do, Gwennan.'

Gwennan made no reply. Out of the corner of her
eye she saw Rolant drink his wine and immediately
call for more. That was unlike him. At table in Carn
Egryn he drank but moderately. Perhaps here, among
his own kind, as a landed lord now instead of a land-
less knight, he was showing his true colours and toast-
ing his success!

She looked about her, misery filling her stomach instead of the rich food dished up for the King's presence
at supper. The great hall of Shrewsbury Castle was full
to the brim, and Gwennan was seated not on the high
table, like at home, but halfway down one of the two
long tables that ran the length of the room.

On her left sat a nobleman who'd introduced himself as Lord Peverel and then not spoken another word
to her. On her right sat Rolant Guyarde—her husband-
to-be by the order of the King! Just like Rufus's invi-
tation to them to dine here tonight, instead of leaving
Shrewsbury at once, had really been a command.

She looked at William, son of the Conqueror, dominating the table on the dais. Flanking him were his brother, Robert Curthose, his chaplain and justiciar Ranulf Flambard, and the Earl of Montgomery and his wife. All of them were resplendent in the most elegant clothes Gwennan had ever seen.

'Are you not hungry?'

At her side, Rolant's voice came again. And again Gwennan didn't answer. She hadn't had any words for him, or anyone else, since they'd bowed and backed their way out of the King's presence earlier that afternoon.

'Then will you at least take some wine?'

A note of weary impatience had entered his voice. She curled her hands in her lap and stared down at her untouched plate, at her eating knife still unused in its pouch.

'Gwennan…'

'What?' Jerking her head up, she met his gaze at last. 'What do you want me to say, Rolant?'

His eyes narrowed, their greenness muted in the smoky light of a hundred candles. 'Anything, as long as it is conversation!'

'We have nothing to say to each other.'

'Nothing?' He drew in a long breath, let it out slowly, as if controlling his temper. 'Then ours will be a very tiresome union indeed.'

'There will be no union—tiresome or otherwise!' Gwennan shook her head, words coming fast and flowing as freely as the wine now. 'This will not be a *real* marriage. It is…ludicrous…impossible.'

'Make no mistake, Gwennan, it *will* be real and it is very possible. The King has decreed it.'

'This is all *your* doing!' The accusation was as bitter

as poison on her lips, but she couldn't help herself. 'If you hadn't agreed so readily to his terms, none of this would have happened.'

'And your parents would remain where they are,' he countered, retaliating with what she knew to be the truth. 'And the Earl of Rhuddlan would have a freer hand than ever in Dysynni.'

Gwennan shook her head, misery churning like bile in her stomach as the reality of this day's work hit her fully at last.

'I cannot pay ten pounds a year—in produce or anything else. My people barely eke a living from the land as it is! How can I ask them to hand over their grain and meat to fill the bellies at the King's court, which are full enough as it is?'

'Count yourself fortunate, Gwennan.' His voice was sombre. 'For North Wales, Rhuddlan pays forty pounds a year into the royal coffers.'

'Paying for land that doesn't even belong to him?'

The impudence of that made her ball her hands until her knuckles hurt. Such payment would fall hard on her tenant farmers and their families, not just on her, even if they could meet it—which was unlikely. Not that either Rhuddlan or Rufus would care if they all starved to death this coming winter.

'Then he's a fool as well as a monster, and your King is even worse.'

She glanced up to the high table again. A jester was amusing the company with some lewd song that she was glad she could neither hear nor understand. It was a far cry from the sweet music and learned poetry of her own *llys*, and it made her feel even sicker.

As she looked, the King's eyes shifted to stare pensively straight back at her. Even from that distance she saw a gleam of something—amusement, mischief, malice, perhaps—in the shrewd eyes.

Whatever it was, Gwennan itched to slap it from his face. Because in taking her lands under his protection and granting the freedom of her parents, he'd not only bound her to a marriage, but chained her to an impossible agreement in every respect.

'What the King decrees has no authority or validity in Wales,' she said, through a scowl. 'When my father is home again he will have something to say about this *union* of ours—and this unjust payment for our own lands. He will not see our people suffer to make the King richer still and neither will I.'

'There cannot be two lords in one household, Gwennan.'

'So you have already taken my father's place? Seated yourself in his chair at table?' She glared into Rolant's green eyes, their calmness kindling her frustration even as their beauty tugged at a place deep down inside her, despite everything. 'You are presumptuous indeed to think to usurp either his title or his person.'

'And you are too innocent if you think the oath you promised the King today means nothing.'

'An oath under duress *is* nothing—least of all honourable or binding.' Gwennan pushed her untouched trencher away and started to rise. 'And neither is this decreed marriage honourable, less still binding. I wish to return to the hostel now.'

'You cannot leave until the King does.' His tone was firm as his hand on her sleeve detained her. 'No one can. We are not at Carn Egryn now, Gwennan.'

Slowly she sank back down onto the bench, her heart

sinking too. No, they weren't at Carn Egryn—and more was the pity she'd ever left it!

'If you are wise, you will stay here in Shrewsbury and let me return to Wales alone.' Gwennan shook his hand off as she spoke, but her voice began to quiver with entreaty. 'You can tell the King whatever you like— make any excuse. Say that I fled rather than wed you.'

Rolant's gaze darkened. 'And undo all we've achieved here today?' He shook his head. 'You have gained nothing in real terms yet—only the King's favour and a promise. If you are not careful, you might forfeit even that.'

Gwennan groped for her cup as the blood chilled in her veins and her heart shuddered to a stop. She tried to drink but her throat had closed with fear. He was right. Her parents weren't free yet.

'Do...do you think the King will keep his word?' She put her cup down again, her hand trembling too much to lift it to her mouth. 'Will he truly order my parents' release?'

'I trust the King, yes.' Rolant gave a slow nod, but there was a discernible lack of conviction in it. 'But whether Robert of Rhuddlan will comply remains to be seen.'

Gwennan shook her head as dread filled her stomach and spilled over into her voice. 'But he *must* comply! He would not disobey his king, surely? He *can't*!'

Rolant looked towards the high table, his face suddenly like stone and an odd grimace on his lips. Gwennan followed his stare, and her blood ran even colder as Rufus raised his cup in a salute.

Swamped by her preoccupation over the day, gripped by her worries, she'd almost forgotten where she was.

Slowly she looked around her at strangers who sat and ate and drank and laughed. Each and every one was her enemy, not a friend among them—not even the Welsh, who sat and drank and laughed with their Norman neighbours.

An icy realisation settled over her heart. She'd undoubtedly made a mortal enemy of the Earl of Rhuddlan today, even more so than before. It wasn't only she who'd gained, though, was it? Rolant had gained too. With one word from his King he'd achieved the very thing he'd come to Wales to take—lordship of her lands.

Time swooped backwards, to the day she'd made him kneel and kiss the sword. Had she been blinded by false victory? Had he set a trap for *her* instead? One she'd not seen, even though it had been right before her eyes?

Duw Trugarog! When he'd held her yesterday in the alleyway, and today when he'd taken her hand as her knees had threatened to buckle before the King, she'd almost begun to believe that he might actually care. But now...

Now her whole world was tipped upside down and the freedom of her parents, the safety of her lands, the survival of her people seemed as far away as it had been before she'd ridden over that bridge yesterday.

'And what will you forfeit, Rolant, if we do not wed?' She turned slowly to meet his gaze, her question bitter and to the point but her voice quivering like a reed in a sudden blast of wind. 'Since today the King gave you exactly what you wanted all along—Carn Egryn and Dysynni.'

The green eyes held hers without a blink. 'That is true, but I didn't expect to get a wife into the bargain.'

His response was as blunt as her question had been. 'So you didn't plan this all along?'

'No, I brought you here in good faith.' He frowned, and something moved deep within his gaze, mysterious and impossible to interpret. 'But, as I just said, I have no more wish to marry than you do.'

A sort of hollow opened up in Gwennan's stomach, but it wasn't due to the absence of the food she'd disdained that night. His words cleaved into her heart like an axe.

'Then it seems we have both been duped by your King!'

He shrugged. 'It would have been naive for you to think the King would grant your request without conditions that would benefit him.' Then, to her surprise, his hand covered hers where she'd clenched it on the tabletop. 'There was always going to be a price to pay, Gwennan, and it could have been much higher.'

Once again, Gwennan felt the strength of him seep through her skin and into her bones. And despite everything—despite this travesty of a marriage neither of them wanted, despite the rocking of her faith since nothing was really certain yet—her hand warmed under his and her pulse began to beat hard.

'It is a price payable by others, not just me. By my people and perhaps by my parents, if the Earl will not release them. But he must...'

Her voice failed her and the noise in the hall seemed to grow dim until it almost faded away. The jester somersaulted down the hall, but Gwennan's heart turned over higher and faster. She stared down at their hands. Rolant's with the scar on the back—the first thing she'd noticed about him in the forest. Then it had been the hand of her captor. Now it seemed it was the hand of her possessor, her fate, her future.

'By us both, if we can become allies instead of enemies.'

Easing her hand from under his, Gwennan wanted to believe him—she really did. But what if…? She drank deeply from her cup, even though she wasn't thirsty, but his next comment made her choke on the richly spiced wine.

'And mayhap one day we might even become friends too.'

The jester tumbled his way back up the hall, a flashing of green and crimson, a tinkle of tiny bells. Rolant's comment was made even more absurd by the frivolity of the fool, and Gwennan felt an awful urge to laugh, and then in the next instant to weep.

'Are you in earnest?' she asked.

His quiet, measured reply seemed to ring louder than all the voices around them. 'I am always in earnest, my lady.'

His lady? Yet there'd been mention that day of another lady—a name that had dropped lightly and yet so pointedly from Rufus's lips. And now the name formed on her own lips before she could stop it.

'Who is Adeliza?'

The colour left Rolant's face, as it had done when the King had spoken the name, but his answer came without hesitation.

'She was my betrothed, once.'

Gwennan stared at him, her thoughts flying in all directions and then coming back again, like bees into a hive. 'Yet you did not wed?'

'No.' This time there *was* a hesitation as Rolant toyed

with his eating knife, burying the point of it deep into his trencher. 'She spurned me.'

'Why?'

'Because of something I did…and did not do.' His gaze met hers again, frank and yet as bottomless and as far away as the sea. 'But either way the consequences were the same.'

Gwennan searched the shadows of desolation that both filled and emptied his eyes. The same shadows she'd seen that day he'd knelt before her and kissed the sword. But she'd seen so many expressions in those eyes over the last weeks that she wasn't sure any more.

'What happened? And what were those consequences?' she asked, her heart beating wildly with the urge to know and yet the fear of knowing, of being sure one way or the other.

'Death, sorrow, shame. My disinheritance and estrangement from the family I loved…still love.'

There was the sound of sudden activity at the high table. The jester's bells ceased as the scraping of chairs and the rustle of rich clothing announced that the King was retiring. Rufus tossed the fool a ring from his finger, and then the royal party proceeded down the hall.

Everyone else got to their feet too, and bowed low as the King passed by. When he'd exited, Rolant turned to her. There was nothing at all in his eyes now, as if the departure of the King had ended what had only just begun between them, leaving all the questions, the doubts, hanging in the smoky air.

'You may return to the hostel now.' The hand he held out shook slightly and his mouth was grim. She couldn't read the expression on his face. 'There will be a strict curfew tonight, because of the royal presence.'

The outstretched hand was the one with the scar on it—a jagged white line running from the knuckle to disappear beneath the cuff of his tunic. Hiding. Disguised. Dissembling. As he himself did?

And, unbidden, into Gwennan's mind flashed a question she'd never thought to want the answer to. Was Adeliza the reason Rolant had no wish for this wedding? Was it Adeliza he desired and wished to marry, not her?

She pushed herself up from the table, ignoring his courteous helping hand. And then perversely—since she should be relieved that he wanted neither her nor their marriage but somehow was left only confused—she launched an attack.

'So you accuse me of hiding, Rolant Guyarde—but are you not hiding too?'

His lashes flickered and a muscle moved in his lean cheek. Then his head tilted and his shoulders lifted in a shrug. She didn't know what any of those gestures meant, nor could she hope to guess, but every one of them proved the truth of her accusation.

Without another word, Gwennan walked away down the hall, beckoning to Nest and Ywain to follow. Behind her, she heard his footsteps. Rolant—her hostage turned ally, husband and lord. A man she'd thought she was beginning to know, had almost begun to trust, but now seemed hardly to recognise.

The following morning Gwennan rose early—not that she'd slept much. The abbey bells ensured that no one lay abed long anyway, as they greeted the dawn with glorious Lauds. And as she sat in the fireless room and sipped some sour ale, every toll, every peal, seemed to shatter her head, leaving it filled with a dull ache.

'Will you wear your gown, *Arglwyddes*?'

She stared at the kirtle Nest held out, then shook her head. 'No, there is no need now. I will ride home in my usual clothes.'

'Oh, I thought...' Her maid flushed but left the comment unsaid and began to fold the garment for packing.

Gwennan felt a prickle of irritation. 'What, Nest? Do you disapprove too?' She stood up and banged her cup down. 'Speak freely, do! I should hate to be a laughing stock and not know it!'

Nest's hand flew to her mouth and her cheeks turned from pink to white. 'N-no! I... I merely thought you looked so beautiful yesterday it would be a shame not to dress like that again today.'

Gwennan's shoulders slumped and shame fell down upon her like dust from the rafters, as heavy as her worries. 'I'm sorry, Nest, I didn't mean to be sharp. All the same, I cannot ride in skirts today, so please pack them.'

Cannot? Or would not? Nest would be riding in skirts, with no hindrance or excuse or fear. But then Nest's fear was not like hers. Nest was braver. She was facing her fears by marrying Ywain, willing to lay the pain of her past aside and embrace the joys of the future.

Could she do the same? Lay aside her pain and sorrow, mistrust and fear? Open herself to belief instead, even hope for joy, some day, when she married Rolant? The reading of the banns didn't necessarily mean the wedding would ever take place. But if it didn't what of her parents, her people, her lands, her home? All of them still hanging precariously on the whim of the English King?

Gwennan didn't wait for her maid to dress her but did it herself. Sitting on the bed to pull on her boots, she tried not to look as her kirtle and veil were placed in sacking, ready for the horses to carry them home.

She hadn't felt beautiful at all yesterday—just uncomfortable, and vulnerable, and afraid before the King. But she had felt different, and somehow stronger, without her disguise. As if by throwing it off she'd broken past a barrier that, while keeping her safe, was also holding her back from something.

A knock on the door broke into her thoughts. Nest went to open it, just a crack, and Rolant's voice came from without.

Hastily, Gwennan pulled her cloak around her shoulders. 'We are almost ready!' she called, nodding to her maid to admit him, wishing she could tell Nest to bolt the door instead. And at the same time tamping down a strange sort of longing to see him…one that set her heart racing for reasons she didn't want to examine.

But when he stepped into the room and bowed there was no welcome in his eyes, despite the greeting that fell stiffly from his lips. The vivid green gaze was guarded and his whole being seemed impenetrable beneath his chainmail.

His voice, too, was without expression. 'We will ride to the bridge along the river, not through the town.'

Gwennan nodded and, feeling a blush steal into her face, hid it behind the act of adjusting her belt. They'd ridden to the castle yesterday by the same route, and she hadn't had to ask the reason why they'd avoided the streets—so they didn't have to pass the hanged man, doubtless still on his gibbet, his flesh being feasted on by crows.

When she looked up again, she caught his eyes flickering over her appearance, lingering for a heartbeat on the tear in the knee of her stocking. She clasped her hands in front of her, lifted her chin and waited for the inevitable question. But it didn't come.

Instead his eyes flared wide as they held hers, and a blaze of colour shot along his cheekbones. Gwennan held her breath as between them the air seemed to vibrate with feelings unvoiced but so powerful she could almost hear them.

Then, with a nod, he bowed and departed, the curt words he threw over his shoulder cutting clean through the tension that still hovered. 'The horses are ready whenever you are, my lady.'

Gwennan's hands fell to her sides, her arms hanging loose, even though she wanted to wrap them around herself, as his arms had done in the alleyway. Wanted to recapture something she hadn't even known she'd needed…a closeness she hadn't known she lacked until he'd offered it.

And now it seemed their enforced union had driven a wedge between them and that offering—like that crack in the door just now. Not shutting it completely but jamming it where it was, half open and half shut.

Was his manner such this morning because she'd asked about Adeliza? Or had his mind—now cleared of the drowsy comfort of wine—realised the enormity of the yoke the King had tied around their necks?

Gwennan helped Nest gather up their bags and they went out into the courtyard, where Ywain aided them to mount. Rolant was already astride his bay gelding, his head turned to the river path, his back towards her.

He looked at her once, but said nothing as they moved off. The turbulence in those green eyes today was as far away as a distant forest. But she felt his presence still so near that she could have reached out and touched it.

Just like in the great hall yesterday, when they'd waited in that invisible yet potent storm to see the King.

It was the heralds that Rolant saw first as they approached the bridge that led out of Shrewsbury towards Wales. Their banners blazed in the sunlight, the flashing bold colours of one, the lupus argent on azure of the other, both unmistakable. And an instant later the gasp from behind him told him that Gwennan had seen them too—and recognised them.

'Rhuddlan!'

The name on her lips sounded like both a curse and a prayer. Her hand went to where her sword should have been, had she been carrying it. Her gaze dropped to the place, her face showing a brief frown of puzzlement. Then her eyes lifted to his again, bright with fire and bloodlust.

'Give me your weapon!'

Rolant shook his head. 'We will not need weapons, Gwennan, God willing.'

Swiftly, he assessed the approaching column of men. Less than forty—an entourage, not an army. And at its head the Earls of Rhuddlan and Chester. Close-knit cousins and the most powerful nobles in the March. Behind them rode another of Rufus's favourites, Robert of Limsey, Bishop of Chester.

'Let me do the talking,' he muttered quickly, before they came into earshot. 'They are between us and the bridge, so we cannot avoid them.'

A horn blew and the entourage slowed. Dust from more than a hundred hooves filled the air. Then the two

Earls, dressed from head to foot for war, rode abreast to where their little group waited.

'So…' Robert of Rhuddlan folded his hands on the pommel of his saddle. His keen eyes swept over each of them in turn, resting longer on the grey stallion, puzzlement glinting. And then his thin mouth set in a line of suspicion. 'What have we here, Guyarde? A welcome party?'

Rolant inclined his head. 'Greetings, my lord Robert…my lord Hugh.'

Gwennan was sitting as still as a statue, mute and as white as death, all fire and bloodlust gone. Dressed as she was, she would pass for a boy, but the pity was that she hadn't ridden in her gown. This wasn't a moment for disguise but for open proclamation.

'I did not expect to meet you here in Shrewsbury,' Robert went on. 'The last I heard you were held hostage in Wales.'

'We had some business with the King, my lord, and now that business is concluded we are bound for home.'

'Home?' The Earl's gaze flickered again to Gwennan's horse, then upwards to the rigid figure in the saddle, and then back to Rolant. 'I have spied that fine steed somewhere before, I think.'

Robert wouldn't have recognised the Princess dressed as she was, even if he'd ever seen her in person. But the stallion was memorable, and as his former overlord finally located it in his memory Rolant confirmed the fact.

'The horse belongs to the Princess Gwennan of Dysynni.'

The Earl's expression didn't alter, but something

about his stance was suddenly menacing. 'I see you have been busy, Guyarde, while you have been in Wales.'

Rolant felt a tingle creep along his nerves. 'We have, my lord, and you may as well read the fruits of our labour for yourself, here and now.' Turning, he beckoned Ywain forward. 'Please read to the Earl the King's decree.'

The clear voice of the clerk-cum-minstrel rang out over the hillsides, sweeter even than his *crwth*. And with every word Robert of Rhuddlan's face grew redder and redder, until it seemed the very blood vessels below his skin would burst wide open.

A long silence followed the reading, and then the Earl smiled a serpent's smile. 'Neatly done, Rolant.' He threw his cloak over his left shoulder, revealing the hilt of the sword that hung from his belt. 'I applaud you on a *coup* that even *I* could not have achieved.'

Rolant tensed, but kept his hands steady where they rested on his horse's withers. His gaze flickered briefly to Hugh d'Avranches. The Earl of Chester had been sitting silently all this time, at the side of his cousin, but his eyes were keen and his ears missed nothing.

'I planned no *coup*,' he said, bringing his gaze back to Rhuddlan, 'but merely adapted my tactics to the lie of the land.'

'Lands that are now lost to me and gained by the Crown! Lands that are now given to be held by you via a cunning and very hasty marriage agreement.' Robert's voice dripped with malice. 'Politic indeed. Or perhaps you have bedded the woman already and secured yourself an heir into the bargain, Guyarde!'

Rolant felt his face flame. The slur was deserving of instant challenge, yet he dared not fling his gauntlet in Robert's face. To do so might unleash violence that would end in his death—an 'accidental incident' that the Earl would be pleased greatly to embellish and justify to the King.

'And where is the lady, may I know? Confined in childbed already?' Rhuddlan laughed, his lizard-like eyes darting over their party and finding Nest. 'That meek mouse is not Cynddylan's famous daughter, surely?'

Ywain's muttered Welsh curse was audible though unintelligible as he moved his horse nearer to Nest's. Rolant lifted his hand and gestured to Gwennan, but she'd already sent her stallion forward. Its nose almost met that of the Earl's destrier and her voice rang out even louder, even sweeter, than Ywain's had done.

'I am Gwennan *ferch* Cynddylan, Princess of Dysynni.'

Chapter Eleven

Gwennan gripped her reins hard as the face of the Earl of Rhuddlan swam in and out of focus, the rat-like features blurring, then sharpening, then blurring again. She was shaking so much she could hardly breathe, let alone speak, but somehow she did both.

'I am the Princess of Carn Egryn and I would know how my parents fare and when I can expect their return?'

Something shifted in the Earl's eyes and for a moment his face paled. Then he laughed and addressed the large man at his side, who hadn't spoken a word thus far.

'God's blood, it's a woman after all, Hugh! A wench in braies!' He turned back to Rolant, his expression ugly with mock pity. 'You were ever a dark horse, Guyarde, but now you have surpassed yourself. What kind of bed sport you prefer is your own affair, but that the King should demand *this* match is an abomination.'

Gwennan felt the scorch on her cheeks, saw colour flood into Rolant's face too. For a moment nobody spoke, but the look that held between the two men was as lethal as any blade.

Then a cold rage filled her veins and she stopped shaking. Her decreed marriage was an abomination to her too. Not in the way the Earl had implied, but the fact that he dared to do so made her hate him even more.

'My Lord of Rhuddlan,' she said, her voice like ice as somehow she channelled that hate into contempt—the only weapon she had to hand. 'Do not mistake my attire for anything other than a convenient manner in which to travel. You yourself have made sufficient inroads into my lands to know that a lady can hardly be carried through them in a litter or ride in a fine gown without tearing and soiling a costly garment.'

The man's jaw dropped, but she went on, driving her words into him like daggers.

'As for the King's demand for this marriage, that is not a topic for jest—by you or anyone else.'

Her disdain was loud enough for all to hear, but below it, and only audible to herself, there was desperation.

'I asked you a question a moment ago and have yet to hear your answer. How fare my parents?'

Robert shrugged and shifted in his saddle. 'How do you expect me to know? Do you imagine that I go down to my dungeons each morning and enquire after my prisoners' health as I serve them breakfast?'

Gwennan felt the reins grow slippery in her sweat-bathed palms. Tarian tossed his head and began to champ at the bit, as if he too sensed they were face to face with the persecutor and murderer of her family. She leaned forward and stroked his glossy neck, calming both him and herself.

This wasn't the moment to give vent to vengeance, or to pull that jewelled dagger from Rhuddlan's belt and slit his throat from ear to ear. If she did, she'd never get an answer at all.

'I don't imagine that at all, my lord—quite the opposite,' she said, levelling her eyes on his again. 'But at least you must know if they are alive...or dead?'

There was a pause. The Earl was clearly unable—or unwilling—to answer. Then Rolant was at her side. The clink of iron as their stirrups clashed rang out like a bell in the thunderous air as he addressed the other man.

'Since King Cynddylan is to be my father-in-law, I would also ask this question of you.'

Rhuddlan's eyes shifted from side to side, like those of a dog caught stealing a goose from the kitchen. He shrugged his shoulders once more, but it was an evasive motion that belied his words. 'They fare well enough, I believe.'

The answer reeked of guilt, and Gwennan's fury turned to a sickening sense of foreboding. He was lying.

Rolant spoke again. 'Then I would advise you to heed the agreement we have made with the King and release them at once.'

There was no plea in his tone, as there had been in hers, only unrelenting command.

'And I would advise you also to leave the Princess Gwennan's lands alone. I give you the same advice, Lord Hugh. She is now under the Crown's protection, and under mine too.'

Gwennan's heart drummed heavily in her breast. What had the King said? A united front? It seemed so as her ally—one she was glad of at that moment—went on, not just protecting her, but defending her honour too.

'And as for your remark about bed sport, that is an insinuation that we will forget we ever heard, since it is an insult not fitting to be uttered anywhere but in the kennels.'

The Earl's thin mouth began to work, as if he was chewing gristle. Gwennan had heard that his temper was notorious, his nature unstable, and she braced herself for whatever outburst was coming.

'You do well to speak of kennels, Guyarde! You, a treacherous dog who bites the hand that feeds it! Did you not bite even your own sire's hand?' Rhuddlan's fingers curled around his sword hilt. 'And now you bite mine and double your dishonour!'

'Brawling like a common cutthroat is not my manner, even if it is yours, my lord.' Rolant's tone was enough to chill the summer's day. 'But if you wish to answer for that insult in front of the King himself, in man-to-man combat, please say so.'

The Earl spat a scornful response. 'Under other circumstances it would be my pleasure, Guyarde, to rid the realm of a coward and a traitor. But we are summoned to join the King's army for Scotland.'

Rolant smiled, and when he spoke his voice was like iron coated in velvet. 'Then I suggest you make speed…for only yesterday he noted your absence and was not at all pleased.' Then the velvet fell away and the cold steel rang out loud. 'And since no honourable man should insult a lady in public hearing, or anywhere else, before you depart you will apologise for what you said to Princess Gwennan.'

The Earl spat again. 'Go to hell, Guyarde.'

Rolant moved so quickly that Tarian reared and Gwennan had to cling to his mane. When he settled again, Rolant's bay courser was in the middle of the road, before the Earls' horses, barring them passage.

'I told you to apologise, my lord. Or perhaps you need to be told twice?'

The challenge was left hanging as the two men sat and glared at each other like lions. Rhuddlan's face was working and sweating, but Rolant's looked as calm as a sheet of still water. She knew that beneath it tumultuous currents swirled, ready to break the surface. And perhaps that tumult would have broken, too, had not the large man whom Gwennan hadn't looked at clearly before moved forward. As he placed his hand on Rhuddlan's wrist the white wolf's head insignia of Hugh d'Avranches blazed into her vision.

'Stand back, Lord Rolant. My cousin will not apologise, as you well know, but I will do so on his behalf.'

He turned his head and his eyes locked on hers. There was no threat in his manner, but even so a shiver crawled down her spine. Because this was Hugh Flaidd—the Wolf—and he was every bit as cruel and merciless as his cousin.

'Princess Gwennan, my Lord Rhuddlan begs your pardon for any unintentional insult given here today, as do I.'

A vicious curse burst out of Robert's mouth, but Chester's hand was like iron on his sword arm, preventing him from drawing. 'You will appreciate that your clothing misled us, and you were unwise to attire yourself so. Therefore the confusion was on both parts—do you not agree, my lady?'

Gwennan swallowed and gave a nod. What else could she do? She saw Rolant glance at her quickly, and as his brow lifted she sent him a look of pleading. This had to end now, otherwise there was only one way it could finish: in spilled blood.

Not just hers and Rolant's, but the blood of Nest and Ywain too, as well as those innocent souls who on coming and going from Shrewsbury, had gathered to watch. She hadn't noticed before, but a crowd of people surrounded them, all of whom would surely get caught up in the flailing of swords and iron-clad hooves.

He read her look accurately, and with a barely-there nod returned his gaze to Robert of Rhuddlan. 'Then, since we are all agreed that the Earl is indeed sorry, even if he has difficulty in forming the words himself, we will leave it at that.'

With a bow of his head, more in warning than deference, he moved his horse aside for the Earls and their retinue to pass.

Rhuddlan gathered up his reins and dug his spurs into his destrier's flanks, holding it cruelly on the bit as he did so. 'You are riding high now, Guyarde, but you have gone too far this time. In choosing the wrong side you have made an enemy of me here today.' His piercing eyes flashed to her. 'And so has the woman who is to be your *wife*!'

Then he kicked his horse forward without a backward glance. Hugh d'Avranches paused and cast them a speculative look before he, too, turned his mount towards the town.

On his heels, a bishop rode, dressed for war under his rich cloak. He drew rein briefly, and drove condemnation straight into Gwennan's heart. 'Daughter, you are breaking God's laws, and the laws of the Church, by wearing such clothes. I advise you, for your soul's sake as much as your future husband's shame, to discard them and dress as a noble lady should.'

Then, making the sign of the cross, he rode on.

The entourage filed past and gradually the colours and the sound of hooves and boots faded into the distance, swallowed up by the dust and dirt of Shrewsbury.

Gwennan turned Tarian in the opposite direction— away from the churchman's damning words. On the bridge she gave him his head, and his hooves hammered over the wooden planks, the sound pounding in her ears and shaking her whole body.

To the west, the mountains hovered like an island in the mist, calling her home. Among them, behind them, veiled in that mist, she would hide again, be safe once more.

But as they galloped like the wind for Wales, behind her the hooves of Rolant's horse pounded too. And as the wind whipped her face and brushed unwept tears onto her cheeks, Gwennan knew there could be no more hiding now.

Not from the Church, nor from the King, and nor from her lord, ally and husband.

It was many hours later, and then only at Rolant's insistence, that they broke their journey at the little religious house of Llangadfan. Gwennan had forced a breakneck pace until, convinced she meant to gallop the whole way back to Carn Egryn, he'd persuaded her to slow.

They sat and took some food under the trees outside the small wooden church, their horses drinking thirstily of the stream nearby. The branches overhead covered them like a nave and the breeze was cool. No one spoke much, and even Nest and Ywain talked only in whispers.

Rolant sat with his back against the wicker fence that

enclosed the church, the sweat of his body making his chainmail chafe his skin through his shirt. And as he ate the bread and cheese, drank ale warmed by the sun, he returned Gwennan's fixed and unfathomable stare.

She was sitting opposite, her back against an apple tree, as far away from him as she could be. She ate but little, and her fingers frequently went to her knee, worrying at the hole in her stocking. Her features looked bruised, as if the last two days had inflicted physical blows on her skin.

Invisible blows that he'd helped deal—albeit unintentionally.

If only he'd known when they'd set out to seek the King's favour how it would result. If only he hadn't taken her by way of the Cross and that hanging... If only he hadn't encountered the Earls at the bridge... If only...

But he *had* done all that, and now the consequences were laid down as indelible as ink upon vellum. And perhaps the most resented consequence of all, at least on her part, was this union that the King had bound them to. How could it be otherwise, when she hated him almost as much as she hated Robert of Rhuddlan? And she loved her dead husband still and ever would.

And even if she *hadn't* hated him, even if Rhys had never been, how could he—a man who'd hurt the people he loved, broken apart his home—ever forge such ties again? Build a life, take a wife and be part of a family, when he'd forfeited all that long ago?

Yet how could he not, if he were to protect her?

She got up suddenly and came over to him. Rolant stiffened as her shadow fell upon him, but he didn't get up. He might as well be slain for a sheep as a lamb!

But to his surprise, after a moment's pause, she sat

down beside him and leaned back against the wicker fence.

'I'm sorry.'

He put his bread and cheese aside and turned to look at her. 'For what?'

'For what I said at supper last night…when I blamed you for everything.' She didn't meet his eyes, but a pulse beat visibly in her throat. 'None of this is your fault. You tried to help and couldn't have foreseen the result any more than I could.'

Rolant took up the skin of ale and drank deep before he answered. 'No, neither of us could have envisaged marriage.'

He passed the ale to her but she shook her head. Drawing her knees up, she wrapped her arms about them. Beneath the hole in her stocking, the graze on her knee was bleeding again.

'No, we couldn't have envisaged that. But what if it has all been for nothing, Rolant? What if my parents are already dead?'

'Don't dwell on that. Not until we know one way or the other.'

We? Yes, that was correct now, wasn't it? Rolant leaned his head back against the wood and closed his eyes, feeling the sun warm his face even as a startling realisation stirred the ale in his belly. It wasn't he and she any longer, but *we…us…*whether she hated him or not!

Robert of Rhuddlan had called him a traitor. Well, no doubt he was—in one respect. But the Earl had been right when he'd said he'd chosen his side. Or perhaps it had been chosen for him. Not by the King, but by his own actions.

Either way, there was no going back now. The border was far behind them and he'd never cross over it, or any other, as the man he'd once been.

'Yes, that is best.' Gwennan's voice broke into his thoughts. 'We mustn't think the worst...not unless... until it happens.'

He half opened his eyes and glanced across at her. She was staring over to where Nest and Ywain sat, near the stream, their heads close together, their hands entwined.

And suddenly a yawning ache filled his heart. It was hard to look at love and know it could never be his. Harder still to have the promise of it sitting so close he could touch it, yet to know he could never do so.

Some insect, spotted red and black, alighted on Gwennan's shoulder, and carefully Rolant reached out and picked it off. She turned, startled, and then a smile transformed her mouth as she looked down to where it sat in the palm of his hand.

'Buwch goch gota.'

Her eyes lifted to his and for a moment he smiled too, feeling his heart turn over.

'Ladybird...or Our Lady's Beetle, I think the Saxons call it.'

'And in French it is *coccinelle*,' he said, hearing his heartache tremble in his voice.

Her eyes sobered again and she looked away once more. He blew the insect gently from his palm and they both watched it flutter away, to land in a nettle bush growing nearby.

She watched it long after his eyes had turned away. 'I want to thank you, Rolant,' she said.

'What is it you would thank me for?' he asked.

For a moment just then they'd almost seemed to exist in the same time and place. But that must have been an illusion, since she could feel nothing of his heartache, only her own. And her heart ached for another, not for him.

'For standing up for my honour when Rhuddlan called me a wench in braies.' Her lashes flickered and her mouth set in defiance, yet there was a sort of anguish there too. 'When he condemned our marriage as an abomination, and that priest said…what he did.'

She leaned her chin on her knees, her profile pale and frowning. It was all Rolant could do not to reach out and smooth the worry from her brow, caress her mouth and banish its downward droop.

And then more. Tilt her face back towards him and take her lips with his…lay her back in the grass and let the sun warm them both as he peeled away her clothes.

'No knight worth his salt would stand apart and let a lady suffer such an insult, Gwennan,' he said, cursing his lustful thoughts and the weakness of his flesh. 'As for the Church…it is often too ready to condemn where God himself would not.'

As if in echo, the sound of plainsong came from within the church. The voices might have been in accord with the words he'd spoken, or in discord with his desires here in this peaceful place. But it amounted to the same thing in the end.

Because lust was only part of it.

He hadn't just been ready to fight the Earl over Gwennan's honour—he'd been ready to die for her.

'What was said by the Earl and by the Bishop means nothing,' he went on, his voice almost inaudible below the chanting that now swirled eerily yet beautifully in the treetops. 'Put it out of your head, Gwennan. Don't let it hurt you.'

She turned and looked at him, colour surging into her cheeks. 'But…what about when he said I shamed you by dressing thus?'

'You would never shame any man, no matter how you were dressed.'

Rolant felt his own face burn too, with a fire that reached up from his loins and consumed him as the truth of his words outdid the pure plainsong around them.

There was a silence as their eyes held and their thoughts flowed, in quiet harmony with the singing from the church. Perhaps it was the plainsong, or the stillness, or the nearness of her, but at last he said what had been waiting on his tongue for too long.

'Tell me about Rhys.'

Immediately Rolant sensed her withdraw, turning her eyes away and folding invisible wings around herself, like that little *coccinelle* might do. He half expected her to leap to her feet and walk away from him in anger that he should dare ask. But a long moment later, she spoke, her gaze far away, her voice even more distant.

'In Wales, the sons of ruling families, when they are young, are placed into the houses of other great rulers to forge ties, strengthen loyalty… Rhys came to Carn Egryn because he was the son of Meirion Goch, our ally to the north. He was ten years old, the same age as me, and…'

Rolant saw the arms around her knees tighten, as if she needed to hold herself together, and then she went on, her voice almost a whisper.

'We were the best of friends…always together, never

apart, the whole time we were growing up. I knew from the beginning that I would love him for ever, and he me.'

'And so you became betrothed?'

She started, as if she'd forgotten he was even there, sitting at her side, and then nodded. 'We married when we were eighteen. I thought life would stay the same and that our love, our happiness, would never end. But then Robert of Rhuddlan came.'

Her eyes closed and her mouth trembled. Rolant hardly dared to move or breathe. Then she shook her head and leapt to her feet and the moment of intimacy and confidence was over.

'The rest you know about. And now we should be on our way, before darkness falls.'

He stared up at her. Her face was white, drawn, as if saying all that had drained her of her life's blood.

Gathering up the remnants of his meal, he took up his helmet and got to his feet too. 'Thank you,' he said.

She looked at him, a frown in her eyes. 'For telling you?'

'For trusting me.'

Her gaze became dark with emotions that he tried to read but failed. It wasn't as if a shutter had come down, but rather as if a door had been flung wide open to reveal too much for the eye to take in all at once.

Then she gave a short nod and walked away from him. Nest and Ywain had risen too and were walking hand in hand towards where the horses waited.

They left Llangadfan with its haunting plainsong behind and made their way wearily homewards, towards the setting sun. And as twilight darkened the sky behind them Rolant felt himself to be riding into unknown realms, even though he'd travelled this route once before, when he'd come to conquer.

Now he was the one who'd been vanquished, and not by the sword—though the impact was just as fatal. When the Bishop of Chester had chastised and damned Gwennan for her clothes, he'd have offered up not just his life but his soul instead of hers, and willingly cast himself into damnation in her place.

The irony of that was bittersweet, like the scented night that enfolded around them as they sighted Carn Egryn. Now he knew the extent of her love for Rhys he knew it would be impossible for her ever to love *him*. And so he was halfway to hell already.

In the room that had been her parents', Gwennan dug her fingers into the bed coverings while Nest, sitting at her side, brushed her hair, ready for bed. That day they'd sat long at the high table—she, Meuryn and Rolant—and speculated, debated and argued until there had been nothing left to say.

As dusk had fallen like a seal on all their talk even Meuryn had seen the sense in it, the benefit to them all, and the necessity of the King's protection against the Marcher lords who had their sights set on Dysynni.

During all the debating she'd not once looked into Rolant's face. They hadn't exchanged more than a few necessary words since Llangadfan, and when possible she'd addressed all her words to Meuryn, speaking through her uncle. Still trying to hide and more afraid now of discovery than she'd ever been in her life.

She moved her head out of reach of the comb. 'That's enough, Nest.'

Her parents' chamber seemed cold, lifeless, since it had been unoccupied this last year. Although the Norman garrison had made use of it, of course—or rather *misused* it. The first thing she'd done on retaking Carn Egryn was erase every trace of them and their filth.

Rolant had offered to take this room and leave her own to her. Given his elevation, the strong room wouldn't do now, naturally! But she'd have died before seeing him in her parents' chamber, so she had moved instead. And even though he was just the other side of that wall…she missed his presence.

'Bring my shift, if you please, Nest.'

Gwennan stood for her maid to slip her linen night shift over her head. One step at a time… Soft linen tonight and then tomorrow the flowing folds of kirtle and veil. And soon the heavy wedding gown that waited in the bottom of her coffer.

'Will you take some ale, *Arglwyddes*?'

She shook her head. Ale wouldn't numb her senses in the way she wished it would, or dull her quivering awareness of the occasional sound from the room next door.

'You may go and take supper in the hall now, Nest. I don't want anything, so please inform my…my uncle that I will not be joining him.'

Gwennan bit her lip. She'd almost said *my betrothed*! A flash of heat and then a cold chill ran over her skin and, moving to the bed, she took up the homespun *brychan* that served as a coverlet.

'I suppose you will be supping with Ywain?'

'Yes, *Arglwyddes*.'

Nest seemed suddenly younger, and yet somehow

older too, shy and worldly at the same time. And the glow in her cheeks gave Gwennan her answer even before she asked the question. 'You have accepted him then?'

'Yes, I gave him my answer when we stopped at Llangadfan. I think I will be happy with him. He is not as handsome as your lord, of course, but—'

Gwennan waved a hand, shooing her maid towards the door. They might both have gained a future husband in Shrewsbury, but that was where any similarity ended. 'You'd best hurry or supper will be over before you get there and Ywain will think you have changed your mind and jilted him!'

As she might soon jilt *her* husband-to-be!

After Nest had gone, she sat down at the hearth. There was no fire, since the night was warm, but even so she pulled the *brychan* tightly around her. Across the room her discarded tunic hung on a peg, a remnant of her old life. And there, at the foot of the bed, stood the coffer that held the trappings of her new life, all the fine gowns and veils, soft and feminine and fitting.

Gwennan laid her head against the wall and closed her eyes. She must think only of the good that would come out of this, and of the release and safe return of her parents—if they still lived. And even if they were dead the protection and prosperity of her lands, freedom from the threat of conquest, would be some comfort at least.

And all made possible by Rolant. The man who'd stood with her in front of his King. The man who'd defended her before his own kind. The man who'd begun to creep into her heart—not just because of that, but because of the way he'd listened as they'd sat beneath the shady branches at Llangadfan and she'd told him about Rhys.

Gwennan opened her eyes with a start and her heart turned over. Cleddyf Gobaith! Where was it? She leapt to her feet, scanned the room, searching every corner. It wasn't there. And if it wasn't here, there was only one place it could be. Next door—in the chamber that now belonged to Rolant.

She chewed her lip. He would still be at table at this hour. She only had to slip into his chamber, retrieve the sword and slip out again. It would take no longer than a moment to achieve. She wouldn't even waste time in dressing, since nobody would see her.

Pulling the *brychan* tightly around her, Gwennan opened the door and stepped out. The noise from the hall filled the passageway and sped her footsteps as she crept to the adjacent door, not a yard from her own. Then, after lifting the latch softly, she inched around the doorjamb and stepped inside.

And her heart stopped dead in her breast. Because Rolant wasn't at supper at all, but lying on the bed, his eyes closed. The light of a single torch lit the room, but dimly, casting light and shadow over his face and body.

He wore only his braies. His calves and his upper body were uncovered. One arm was flung up behind his head, the other lay loosely at his side, but the fingers of both hands were tightly clenched into fists.

Gwennan took a hasty step backwards, feeling silently behind her with her toes. But her care not to rouse him was all for nothing. She stepped on the bottom of the *brychan*, lost her balance, and went toppling into the door.

She bit her tongue over a curse as the impact of her body slammed the door shut with a bang. And by the time she'd righted herself Rolant had leapt off the bed and to his feet.

Chapter Twelve

There was a moment of stunned silence as their eyes locked across the room, his dark with surprise and question. Hers, Gwennan knew, had flown wide with panic—and not just at being caught like a thief in the night. She felt for the edges of her blanket, pulling them tightly together, trying to stop her gaze dropping from his face to his body.

Because he was magnificent, standing there before her. His black hair was tousled and the muscled expanse of his chest, lightly dusted with hair as dark as that on his head, filled her vision and flooded her blood.

He was the first to break the crackle of quiet tension. 'Did you want something, Gwennan?'

Want? Gwennan searched her mind, found nothing except the sort of want, the kind of need, she had no right to find. 'I… I forgot Cleddyf Gobaith.'

'Your sword?'

He took a step forward and she knew then he hadn't been sleeping at all, because the vital green eyes were more than awake—they were alive. He must have heard her slip into the room, for all the stealth she'd maintained. Why had he pretended otherwise?

'I had noticed and meant to return it to you tomorrow.'

Gwennan stared transfixed at the bare broad shoulders, the expanse of chest, the taut muscles of his stomach beneath skin that glowed as rich as bronze. His body bore scars, like the bodies of most men who lived by the sword.

The one she knew about on his forearm stretched from knuckles to elbow. There was another across his right ribcage, and yet another at his collarbone—a long thin sliver of a scar, old and faded to white now against the golden tones of his flesh.

'But you may take it now...since you are here.'

He crossed to where the sword lay flat on a table, his strides lithe and easy. There was another scar on one shoulder blade, the star shape of a dagger point, but when he turned back she saw nothing of his scars at all.

Gwennan saw only the unmistakable hardness of his loins, and she felt the wave of heat that engulfed her in response. As he held Cleddyf Gobaith out to her in his upturned palms the burnished metal seemed to accuse her. Not just for forgetting all about it, but because it saw her weakness, her shame and, clearest of all, her desire.

Stretching out her hands for the sword, she didn't feel the *brychan* fall from her shoulders to the floor.

His eyes dropped from hers and moved over her like a caress. As his breath hitched and a flush rose up into his cheekbones a heavy ache settled low in her belly.

Gwennan clutched the sword with desperate hands as he bent to pick up the blanket. She quivered as he replaced the *brychan* over her shoulders, covering her once more. It was the inner trembling she had to conceal now, so deep inside her that it would never be visible again.

A smile touched his mouth, although his gaze didn't match it. Rather the green eyes were serious, turbulent. 'You never cease to surprise me, Gwennan.'

Gwennan pressed her back hard against the door, drawing on its solid surface to hold her upright. 'What do you mean?'

'You've been clinging to your tunic and hose all this time, as if removing them might be fatal to your health. And yet here you are, in my room, wearing hardly anything at all, and it's not even our nuptials night.'

The mocking words—because surely that was what they were—flayed her flesh and brought her wits hurtling back. 'You forget that this was *my* room! And I doubt there will *be* a nuptials night after my father returns.' She wound her hands tighter around the sword hilt, clutching the steel for strength of will. 'You yourself said there cannot be *two* lords of Carn Egryn.'

He shrugged, and the broad shoulders drew her gaze, making her want to reach out and touch.

'Then we must deal with that when we have to.'

'You underestimate him.' Gwennan dragged her eyes back to his. 'Do you really believe that Cynddylan Fawr will relinquish his status and his title? That he, a Welsh king, will bow down before your English King like any common vassal?'

'He may have no choice, Gwennan.'

Gwennan shook her head, but suddenly the supporting door behind her seemed to crumble away, leaving her suspended. And as she forced words out through trembling lips her heart trembled even more at the reality of them.

'And neither will he see his daughter wed to a Norman enemy. Because when my father returns he will kill you on sight.'

For the briefest of moments Rolant heard similar words—his own—urging his father to kill him. Unanswered pleas that echoed down the years, never silent, always begging to be heard and granted.

But then they were gone, fading far into the past, leaving only a distant and barely heard note. He dragged in a deep breath and the note vanished completely, and there was only the aroma of heather and rosemary.

'That might solve our immediate problem,' Rolant said, his nostrils and throat thick with the scent of Gwennan's hair and skin, while her honey-coloured eyes drew him deep down into them, until he saw and heard nothing but her. 'Though I suspect he will not be so rash.'

Even before she'd entered—clearly thinking him asleep and unaware—he'd been surrounded by her essence, the presence she'd left behind along with her sword when he'd taken this chamber from her.

So instead of going to sup in the hall he'd lain on his bed—*her* bed—and let himself drown in that essence.

'But if that is what you want, Gwennan—to be rid of me—why don't you do the task for him and save him the trouble?'

Her gaze flew wide and her mouth dropped open, but no words came out. She stared up at him, the glow from the torchlight touching her cheekbones, casting her eyes into dark pools.

'It would be easy to do,' he went on, trying to ignore the heaving of her breasts beneath the blanket, the way her breath came fast and shallow on his throat. 'You have your sword in your hand. All you need do is thrust and your problem will be solved. It wouldn't even take much of an effort, since I wear no armour.'

Rolant took a pace forward until there was less than the space of a handspan between them. 'You vowed once to kill me—do you remember? When you came back for your sword in the forest.' His fingers itched to lift to her face, to cup her cheek, feel the softness of her skin and thread into that fiery hair. 'And here you are, come for it again. Why do you want it so badly, if not to use it on your enemy?'

'It…it is Rhys's sword.'

Rolant gritted his teeth and hissed in a breath. Here he was, her living husband-to-be, the would-be protector she didn't want. And there was she, clinging to the sword of her dead husband as if it was a talisman to ward off the devil himself.

'Rhys…' he echoed, the sound of it nearly choking him.

She flinched, as if the revered name on his tongue, coated with his accent, was an insult. Irritation vied with desire and some demon settled on his shoulder, poured poison into his ear. The bitter irony of wedding but never really possessing this woman induced him to listen to it.

'Your dead husband that the Normans hanged, like that felon in Shrewsbury?'

She nodded, then blinked, then shook her head, saying nothing. Her lips quivered, but it was her eyes that spoke, wide and raw and bright with anguish. Yet still he needed to hear the words—if not from her mouth,

then from his own. The man might be dead, but he was
far from buried.

'That's why you hate us, isn't it, Gwennan? For taking your husband as well as your lands? Why you hate
me? Would killing me make you feel better, even though
you know it won't bring him back to life?'

As he spoke, the words came back at him, loud as
a bell in his ears. And he realised that his own death
wouldn't have brought John back to life five years ago
either. Vengeance was an empty and futile thing—
meaningless, harmful, bringing only more sorrow in
its wake.

Even if his father *had* executed him, the hurt, the
loss and the betrayal would have lived on in his parents'
hearts. It *did* live on, and whether he lived or died now,
nothing would alter that.

But the present could be altered, and it was in his
power to do so. He could help Gwennan even if she
resented that help. He could save her despite herself,
despite her pride, her hate, her stubborn passion for resistance.

Rolant reached out and placed his hands over hers,
where they clutched the hilt of the sword. Slowly he
drew her towards him until only the sharp steel of the
blade lay between them, shockingly cold on his naked
belly.

'But you're not going to use that sword, are you?
Just as you didn't use the knife that night in the forest.'

He felt the tremble of her body through the metal, felt
it move into his limbs like a raging fever passing from
her blood and infecting his. Lust flared in his loins and
there was nothing he could do to douse it.

'Because you know, deep in your heart, that I'm not your enemy now, even if I was once... Gwennan Fwyn.'

Her head snapped back. 'D-don't call me that!'

'Why not?' Rolant ignored the stab of quick remorse as his demon drove him on as fast and relentlessly as his lust did. 'Because Rhys called you Gwennan Fwyn? Was it *his* name for you and only *he* was allowed to say it, none other?'

Her face blanched and he hated himself. But he couldn't stop hurting her, nor torturing himself either. Any more than he could stop himself from imagining what would happen if he gave in to his desire, here and now.

Would she return it? Repel it? Deny that she could ever feel the same burning need as he did?

'But do I not have the right to use that name? As your husband?'

'You are not my husband yet!'

She tried to pull free and the blanket parted, slipped lower on her shoulders. Her breasts beneath the linen shift she wore pressed against his bare chest. Her head turned one way and then the other, like a cornered animal seeking escape. And then, as her eyes met his again, they began to swim, filling with tears he'd never witnessed before.

Rolant cursed himself. God and all the saints in heaven! What was he doing? He should comfort her, not torment her. Beg her forgiveness for causing her pain. But his blood was aflame, his heart was thundering, and his whole being centred at one point—on her, and nothing else.

He lowered his head and let his mouth hover just over hers, tasted the breath that clashed so violently with his.

His lips burned to kiss her but he refused to let them. Not until he was invited, allowed to do so.

'I know you'll never forget Rhys, Gwennan, and nor should you. He was your husband and your love.' Rolant steeled his voice into softness, despite the raging hardness of his loins. 'But there is all of life left for you yet and you must live it—as must I. Deny it all you like, but I will be your husband too.'

She froze in his arms for an instant, her eyes full of anguish. Then she pulled her hands out from under his, the force of it sending her flying backwards into the door.

'How dare you say such things?'

The sword clattered to the floor, breaking the dangerous moment, shattering his fantasy. Her fingers found the edges of the blanket and she clutched it tightly around her.

'I cannot...*will* not think of you as I thought of him—ever!'

Rolant fought for breath, the frustration of his body rendering his mind hardly his own any more. Sweet heaven! Would she never let go, just a little? Just enough to begin to live again! Would she never remember that she was a woman, alive and beautiful, and not a corpse as good as in the grave herself?

And would he ever be allowed to remind her of that?

'You can't cling for ever to a dead man as you do his weapon, Gwennan, for your own sake.' At least his voice was clear, even if his head was anything but. 'If you go on living in the past there will be no future for you, or for us, whatever the nature of our marriage turns out to be.'

She looked down at her hands, as if suddenly realising the sword was no longer there, and his gut twisted.

Not with carnal need now—though that still ravaged him mercilessly—but with contrition.

'And your father will not object to our union, because to do so would forfeit everything you have gained for him—his lands, this fortress, your life and the lives of your family. I will not let that happen.'

She shook her head, as if she tried to block out his words, even though she must know the truth of them. All at once she looked so lost and so utterly defence-less in a way he'd never seen her before. And his demon fled in shame.

'Now, I think you had better return to your chamber—before I forget that we are not yet married, that I am not yet your husband, and that our nuptial bed is not yet blessed and ready for us.'

Rolant stooped to retrieve the sword, but even before he'd straightened up again she was gone, the wind at her heels. He heard her chamber door slam shut with a sound that shook the wooden walls and then there was utter silence.

Closing his own door, he crossed the room and placed the sword back down on the table. Running his finger over its carved and ancient hilt, he cursed its dead owner once more, for the power the man wielded even from the grave. The power to hold a woman's love. Even though the blessed, saintly, courageous, in-furiating Rhys was a rotting, rancid cadaver, fit only for the worms.

Rolant dropped down on the edge of the bed and, leaning his elbows on his knees, rubbed his hands over his face. Just because she'd come into this room half naked, it didn't mean he had to turn into a rutting stag, butting heads with a man who didn't even exist any more except in her heart. Less still punish her with hurt-ful words for causing this torture to his body.

That was what came of five years of celibacy! He should have given in to his needs long since—slaked his lust with camp followers and light-skirted women, like his comrades did, instead of clinging to his mor-als and his vows.

A wry smile pulled at his mouth. What had his men called him? Virgin and monk! Well, if they could see him now they'd swallow those words back, whole.

He was a man like any other. And, like any other, prey to lust and needs. But his despicable behaviour this night had been much more than a base carnal urge. He'd needed to kiss Gwennan as he needed to breathe. He'd needed to feel her body against his more than his blood needed to flow through his veins. He'd come vio-lently to life just at the thought of bedding her, and his heart had lurched into a frantic wish to beat again, to live again, to love again.

But since *her* heart beat and would always beat for another man, he must learn to accept that and be con-tent. And she must never know nor guess how much he envied her dead husband. How much he yearned to taste, feel, enjoy the things he had when he had lived, breathed, loved.

Gwennan slammed her door shut and leaned back against it, her eyes stinging, her breath sobbing in her throat. Slowly, she let her body slide down to the floor and sat there, hugging her knees to her chest.

A groan rose into her mouth and she stifled it with the palm of her hand, even though it choked her to sup-press it. Why had she been so foolish? Why had she gone into that chamber? Why hadn't she sent Ywain or Nest or someone else for the sword?

Now she'd lost it for ever. Worse, she'd thrown it away. It might just as well be lying at the bottom of Talyllyn Lake, rusting beneath the turbulent green waters, discarded, forgotten, betrayed.

Because when Rolant had placed his hands over hers and drawn her close...when his eyes—deeper than any lake and far more turbulent—had stared into hers...she had forgotten Rhys, forgotten everything.

When Rolant had breathed desire into her face and his mouth had hovered over hers...when his body had hardened and his manhood had pressed urgently against her belly...only he had existed.

Gwennan closed her eyes. Rolant was to be her husband now, just as he'd said, and he was alive, real, vital—not a fading memory. So very alive that her body clamoured for him whenever he came near her, looked for him when he wasn't there, craved him night and day. She'd tried not to notice, to suppress, to disbelieve, to deny, but it was all in vain.

Instead, her soul had been awakened as if from a long sleep and her spirit had started to sing. And her heart sang loudest of all.

Ignore, suppress and deny all she might, it was no use. She didn't just desire Rolant—she loved him. She'd loved him when he'd run after her through the streets of Shrewsbury. When his fingers had locked with hers before the King. When he'd taken her side at the bridge, before the Earls and the Bishop.

When he'd listened, without speaking, in the warm grass at Llangadfan and a sort of peace had calmed her inner turbulent world.

And now—he *was* her world.

But when her father came back... Surely it could only be death for Rolant? His life would be forfeit, payable for all the wrongs done to them. Or at the very least he would be banished from Carn Egryn. And for her the loss would be as great as the loss she'd known a year ago.

But Gwennan's father would never come back. At least not living.

A fortnight later, on an overcast summer's day, Rolant stood in the gateway with Meuryn ap Hywel and watched as the body of Cynddylan Fawr was carried up the hill on the shoulders of six of the men from the village.

Both he and Meuryn, without the necessity of words spoken between them, had stayed at the gates, giving Gwennan and her mother the private moment they needed. Now the Welshman muttered under his breath as mother and daughter stood clasped in a long embrace, each seeming to hold the other upright.

'God curse you Normans for this day!'

Rolant didn't say it aloud, but he too cursed Robert of Rhuddlan for this deed. For the grief of the two women that weighed down upon him and upon the whole household. They had gathered behind him, and their eyes pierced his skin like spikes, their hatred sharper even than on the first day he'd come here.

Only a few short weeks ago he wouldn't have cared if they'd rushed at him and torn him to pieces. He hadn't desired or deserved to live then, and death would have been just and welcome. Now... Now he needed to live for Gwennan's sake.

Even so, a blackness even darker than the clouds over-head settled over Rolant's soul—because he watched not one but two such tragic homecomings.

His brother John had also been brought back like this—a shrouded corpse, his body ravaged by the points of swords and arrows. Death wounds that had been in-flicted on the wrong man for the wrong reasons.

Then, like now, he'd stood at the gates, his presence a curse and not a comfort to his parents. He'd wished it was *his* corpse on the bier instead of John's, as it should have been if he'd acted otherwise.

But he hadn't done otherwise.

He'd lived and John had died.

Although he'd died too, in a way. In his heart, as well as in the hearts of his family.

The slow cortege finally reached the gates and Meuryn ap Hywel rushed forward to help Gwennan's mother, Queen Angharad, down from her horse. Rolant stepped forward too, and as she looked at him it might have been his mother's accusing eyes in that grey and lined face.

'You are Rolant Guyarde?' She didn't wait for an an-swer. She didn't even seem to want one, apparently find-ing him already condemned. 'Then it is you I have to thank for my release.'

Rolant bowed and went to take and kiss her hand, but she curled it away into the folds of her skirt. 'No, it is not I,' he said. 'It is your daughter you have to thank, *Arglwyddes*.'

'Yes, I know all about the agreement made at Shrews-bury.' Her thin shoulders lifted in a little sigh, though it seemed even that might shatter them, so brittle the bones looked beneath her stained cloak. 'And I know also that you are to become my son-in-law by the order of the King of England.'

The sagging skin of her jaw tightened and her mouth set firm. Her eyes—Gwennan's eyes—flashed, briefly, but brilliantly, and Rolant saw that she must have been beautiful once.

'It is almost a comfort to me that my husband died before he had to know any of this shame.'

Then, without another word, she moved past him and into the stunned silence of the compound. Her people parted to let her pass, their faces shocked and angry in equal part. Even the dogs were silent, their tails between their legs. Meuryn walked close at her side, supporting her stumbling progress, his face the angriest of all.

Then Gwennan came on foot at the head of the bier, and Rolant's breath hitched. Because it seemed that a light had been extinguished within her soul, leaving it in pitch-darkness.

Grief was etched on the wan face as if a knife had carved it into the bone, indelible and irreparable. Deeper even than it had been on her mother's, since Angharad had had more time to absorb it.

He put out a hand and touched her sleeve, and she stopped and turned slowly to face him, as if she'd only just realised his presence. There were no signs of weeping in her eyes—not even now.

His mother had wept even as she'd struck his face with the palm of her hand. His father had wept and yet still drawn his sword at her bidding, held it to his bared neck, ready to slay him.

Adeliza too had cried—easily and often. Copious tears that in the light of hindsight had been nothing but false gems—worthless for all their glitter, meant to dazzle, deceive and coerce.

It was Gwennan's lack of tears now that told him the truth of that. And it was her grief, her naked sorrow, that made him feel humble, and yet somehow strangely alive, even in this moment of death and despair. Rolant almost wished she *would* cry, purge that desolation and so allow it to pass and heal.

'I am sorry, Gwennan. Even I didn't think the Earl would stoop so low.'

'Sorry? But you should be *glad*, Rolant!' The dulled eyes flashed briefly bright. 'There is no one to stand in your way now. My father is dead, my mother is ill… her spirit broken…' Her voice cracked and something in her face seemed to shatter too. 'All is yours now, to take as you please, to rule as you will.'

Rolant felt the sweat cool on his brow and pool in the hollow of his throat. The hush all around them filled his ears until they threatened to burst. The men carrying Cynddylan's corpse still hovered, half in and half out of the gateway. The villagers behind waited to pass through; the household within wondered at the delay.

This was a moment of testing—for him as much as for her. This moment, as grief-filled as it was, was when he had to mark out his place here, establish his position, make these people his people. Win them over or else dominate them.

Because with Cynddylan's death he was—as Gwennan had said—their lord and ruler. And he was *her* lord and protector, even though she didn't want him.

Dragging in a silent breath, he offered her his arm. 'Come, Gwennan. I will escort you into hall.'

His words hung in the air, vibrating until the wooden

palisade itself seemed to shake with them. But it wasn't really the walls that shook. It was he. Though none saw—not even she, standing so close.

If she refused him, it wouldn't change anything. He would still be her lord. He would still be her husband. And once they were wed he would have the right to her hand on his arm, the right to possess her entire body whether she wanted him or not.

But if she accepted his arm now something *would* change…however small. He couldn't erase the past, but if Gwennan allowed him to help her now perhaps he could make some sort of repair, even if only in the sight of God.

But reject him she did, passing him by and walking with her head high towards the hall.

Rolant followed in her wake, looking neither right nor left at the people who stood with eyes wide and mouths open.

At the doorway, she halted, turned, and nailed him with a bitter glare. 'You may be my betrothed and the lord of Carn Egryn, but only by command of your King. He is not *our* King. But I will do whatever it takes to ensure my mother's safety.'

Her chin lifted higher and her tone became ever more bitter.

'I will even wear fine gowns, as befits the lady of a lord, but do not expect to find a willing wife below them—because you will not.'

And then she went through the doors and into the shadows.

Rolant stood on the threshold and stared after her. It was a long moment later that he became aware of the silence behind him. Turning, he saw the household still waiting. None could enter the hall before him, of course. He was lord now.

He looked slowly from face to face, high to low, soldier to peasant, man to woman. None of them held any warmth or affection, although each and every one wore a mask of respect. It would be no easy task, winning the trust of these people, and impossible perhaps ever to win their affection.

But trust and affection might prove even more unattainable from Gwennan herself. She'd spoken for both of them when she'd said she would obey the King's command, as would he, since neither had any other option. But she was wrong in one thing.

He would never expect to find a willing wife beneath her gowns because he would never allow himself to look for one. The night she'd come for her sword had proved that all his restraint of the last five years held for nothing.

He desired her—wanted her so desperately that he would forget all his vows and bed her in a heartbeat should she only say the word. But she never would—not now, with this latest wrong.

How could her hate ever fade when surely it was enflamed even more?

And how could he presume or hope that this union would be anything other than what she'd called it in the great hall of Shrewsbury?

Impossible—in every way.

Chapter Thirteen

It rained the day they buried her father. Just a fine, light rain at first, a shower of sighs from the soft grey sky. But by the time the prayers were over the rain had turned to needles that stung Gwennan's face and pierced her heart as she stood at the graveside with her mother and uncle.

The grave was filled in and a slab placed over the earth—one more addition to the line that held the bodies of her husband, her brothers, her grandparents. And now her father.

Or what was left of him. Nothing but ravaged cheeks and sunken eye sockets and rotting flesh. Nothing left of Cynddylan Fawr—Cynddylan the Great—called so for his valour as well as his strength. The father she'd worshipped, adored, emulated.

'Come inside now, Gwennan.'

The rain became heavier, but Gwennan shook her head. 'You go,' she replied. 'I want to remain for a little longer.'

Her mother looked up at her, her gaze bewildered. Before, it had been Gwennan who'd looked up, since Angharad had been the taller. But her year in prison had shrunk her stature, crushed her bones and rounded her shoulders. Turned her into an old woman even though she had passed no more than forty summers.

'Then don't stay out here too long, *'ngeneth i*, lest you take a chill.'

Her mother's hand touched her cheek briefly, the veins blue beneath the parchment-like skin. Then she turned away and, with Meuryn supporting her, began a slow, shuffling progress back to the comfort and warmth of the hall.

Gwennan preferred the cold and the rain, needing solitude not company. And at long last she *was* alone, the only mourner remaining. Or so she'd thought.

It was a feeling, nothing more tangible, that made her lift her head a moment later and look behind her.

And there stood Rolant Guyarde in the lee of the church wall. He was rain-soaked, like she was, and apparently just as heedless of the fact. How long had he been there? All the time or was he newly come?

'Why are you here?' she asked, looking swiftly away again.

Boots squelched through the mud as he moved up to stand beside her, his presence unbidden and unwelcome. He didn't speak for a moment, but crossed himself and bowed his head in reverence.

Then his eyes lifted, and through the rain they touched her face. 'I am here because it is my duty.'

Cold drips of rainwater oozed down the back of Gwennan's neck. 'As the new lord of Carn Egryn?'

'As your betrothed.'

She drew her cloak tighter around her, the wool sodden now, dragging at her heart as much as it did her shoulders. 'Is that why you kept vigil with me in the chapel too—out of *duty*?'

'No, I did that out of respect and honour for your father.'

Rolant had been at her side on each of the last three nights. She hadn't spoken a word to him, nor he to her. They'd knelt in silence beside her father's shrouded corpse in long, silent hours of vigil that had stretched to eternity and beyond.

But, oh, how she'd longed to lean into him, to feel his comforting arms around her, the touch of his lips to her hair—even if just in sympathy and nothing else. Nothing like the desire she'd felt in him, in herself, the night she'd gone for the sword.

'Rolant...' She turned to look at him at last, her voice shivering with cold. But *was* it cold? Because the rain was summer rain, warm and pitiless. 'You neither knew nor loved my father, so do not pretend you have any respect for him or for my family.'

His eyes, like hers, bore the shadows of lack of sleep. Yet the dark circles below didn't dim their vivid colour, and nor did the lines of fatigue on his face drain it of its vitality and strength.

'I am not pretending anything, Gwennan. I didn't need to know your father to respect his memory.'

Gwennan's shoulders sagged lower, his words muddying her thoughts as the rain turned the earth to mud. Oh, why wouldn't he go away? Why did he stand there, confusing her, making her limbs tremble and her breath suddenly hard to draw?

But he was lord here now, and she couldn't make him do anything at all—not even leave her alone. And, powerless before that knowledge, she clutched at her sorrow for strength, as she'd once gripped her sword to attack her enemies.

'Do you know when he died, Rolant? On the same day we stood before the King. Wasn't that a cruel trick for fate to play? To put us together even as my father breathed his last breath?'

He said nothing, but his tall figure suddenly seemed to stoop a little, as if her invisible blade had actually wounded him.

'And when we encountered the Earls at the bridge,' she went on, hurting herself far more than she did him, 'Robert of Rhuddlan probably knew then that my father was dead, or very close to it.'

He nodded slowly. The hood of his cloak was down and his hair clung to his brow. The rivulets of water that ran down his face and throat might have been tears, though she knew they were not.

'I noticed an evasion in his manner then, and I wondered…'

Gwennan shut her eyes for a moment. 'My mother told me my father suffered terribly at the end. The disease wasted him to skin and bone…took his life piece by piece.'

There was a beat of taut silence and then she felt his touch on her arm, light and yet heavier than the rain.

'Gwennan… I…'

But the sad note of sympathy in his voice was too much to hear today, even if she needed it. Because more than that she needed to hurt him as she was hurting, even if she hated herself for doing so.

'Please don't tell me you're sorry, Rolant. Not again! It is such an easy word to say, but it won't make amends for the tally of deaths that have won you Carn Egryn!'

His face froze, and in the pallor of his skin the scar on his cheek stood out. It was only a small blemish, healed and almost invisible now unless you knew where to look for it—as she did.

'Nothing is ever won by death, Gwennan, only lost.'

'Don't you think I know that only too well?' she said.

His gaze delved into hers, too keen, too perceptive.

'Yes, I do. And I understand how you are feeling because I have also felt like that. I too have lost family. So…if you ever need me, Gwennan, I am here.'

Gwennan willed her eyes not to weep, as her heart had cried throughout those long nights of vigil, when they'd knelt so close and yet so far apart. If she *had* been able to weep then, perhaps it would have helped quicken her healing. But she hadn't been able to, even though those unshed tears had formed an ocean in her heart.

'A sorrow shared and a burden halved?' Gwennan shook her head. 'I don't blame you for this deed, Rolant, since it is not yours directly. But I cannot forgive you for taking my father's place.'

It was a cruel thing to say, and at once she wished it unsaid. But he'd never spoken so deeply to her before, and at this moment of all times, when her grief threatened to crush her, she didn't know if she could stand to hear it.

'Until now I have never found forgiveness for my sins, Gwennan, no matter how much I may need it.'

Gwennan tried not to listen, but the effort was as futile as trying to close her heart. If he would only go away…

'If you are quick, you may yet detain the priest before he departs for Tywyn!' she said flippantly. 'He will doubtless forgive you, if you ask, since saving souls is his business.'

There was a long silence, and then his voice fell like quiet thunder. 'I would sooner ask it of you.'

Gwennan pressed her lips tightly together to stop herself responding. But how could she not when they were standing so close that she felt his need to speak as keenly as she felt the rain on her face?

And if he truly did need forgiveness, how could she deny him?

'Then which sin is it, pray, that you need forgiveness for, but cannot ask a priest?'

Rolant hadn't intended to make his confession to her—not here, not today of all days. And he'd never spoken to a priest because he'd never deserved absolution.

But when they'd brought Cynddylan's body back, when he'd seen the ravaged face of his widow, seen Gwennan crumble before his eyes—inwardly at least—the past and the present had become one.

Now it was almost easy to speak, expecting nothing but release from a burden that he'd carried far too long. Easy to reveal the cause of his own pain and to hope not only for forgiveness, but also for absolution.

'For my part in the death of my brother.'

She turned to look at him. 'The death you spoke of in Shrewsbury?'

'Yes.'

Instead of meeting her eyes, Rolant stared down at the grave. He didn't want to risk drowning in those sorrow-filled honeyed depths when he needed to stay afloat.

With a deep breath, he made himself go backwards in time to a place he'd shunned for too long.

'John was only sixteen, untried in war, too young for battle…'

His brother's eager vitality rose up before him as if from the very ground he stood on.

'My father had a long-standing quarrel with Adeliza's family over some land that lay between our two estates. Land that wasn't worth arguing over, let alone fighting over.'

'Is that why your troth to wed was broken?'

His mouth twisted in a bitter smile. 'Marrying Adeliza would have been a disaster—I know that now. But at the time she was my sun and my moon.'

'And you were hers?'

Rolant pulled his hood up as the rain grew heavier still, concealing his face even as his words revealed him down to the bone.

'No, nor ever was. I saw that very clearly when she called me a coward and a traitor…told me how she hated me for failing her.'

'But how did you fail her?'

He turned to look at Gwennan, expecting scorn, derision, at best a lack of interest. Raindrops sparkled on her thick black lashes and behind them he saw none of those things, only compassion.

'When the quarrel became a conflict, she begged me not to take up arms against her family,' he went on. 'Naturally, my father expected me to fight at his side. It was an impossible choice, so in the end I did neither. John went in my place and he died in my place.'

Rolant's confession faded on his lips and he waited for her response, knowing he'd hammered another nail into the casket of their doomed marriage even as a weight had lifted off his soul.

'So in the end I failed everyone, Gwennan.'

Her eyes searched his, as if she thought there was more yet to say.

'But...if you had gone into battle it might have been *you* who died, not your brother.'

'There have been many times since when I've wished it *had* been me.'

'Adeliza was wrong to accuse you as she did.'

'It was her grief talking.' Rolant shrugged, felt the rainwater soak deeper into his shoulders through his clothes. 'Her father was killed too, in the battle.'

He could hear the blood rushing in his ears, feel his heart knocking against his ribs. There was nothing else to say. Gwennan knew all now—except for one last thing. Something it had taken him five long years to learn, but that suddenly and inexplicably he'd understood today, here in the rain.

'Don't linger with the dead, Gwennan. It is not a place to take up abode. I have discovered that all too well.'

He'd given her advice once before, and although she'd resented it, rejected it, her fortress had been repaired, reinforced, until now it was strong and defensible. Would she heed him about this, which was even more crucial?

'As a soldier, my career is fighting. My purpose, abhorrent though it be, is to kill or else be killed,' Rolant went on. 'When I came here a month ago I was ready to die in battle. And I fully expected to die when you made me kneel in the dirt and waved a sword over my head. But I was given my life instead, and now...now

I find myself whole again, instead of in pieces. I can't explain it...'

No, that wasn't true. He *could* explain, or at least try to, but he wouldn't. Now wasn't the time or the place. They needed a different arena, and different minds and hearts, before he could reveal the rest.

'Now I choose to live, Gwennan, where once I didn't care if I lived or died. And I've rediscovered a meaning to my life that I didn't really know was lost to me.'

The rain glistened on her hair and Rolant remembered that long-ago day when he'd removed her dented helmet and discovered the shorn chestnut locks. And despite the darkness of this day, he couldn't prevent the smile that rose unbidden to his lips as his heart grew suddenly lighter.

'Or perhaps it happened even before—when I found you knocked senseless and clinging stubbornly to the broken reins of that great stallion of yours.'

She stared at him, her eyes wide, her face ashen. Her mouth trembled but no words came out, and then her whole face seemed to crumple, as if the bones beneath the skin had broken into little pieces.

For once, Rolant forgot the rules and stepped across his own boundary line. He gathered her to him, wrapped his arms around her, and drew her into an embrace. Not a carnal embrace, but one of comfort and understanding.

'So while you live, while I live, and while we are husband and wife, I will not fail you, Gwennan, as I failed others. Not now...not ever.'

A sort of choke issued from her and her forehead pressed heavily into his chest. Her fingers clutched and clung to his tunic, and he folded his cloak, wet though it was, around them both.

And Rolant knew that now, for him at least, there was no more hiding. Now she knew him for exactly what he was. Good and bad, no worse than any other, and hopefully a better man than he'd once been.

All at once the rain stopped and the sun showed palely through the thinning clouds. And then, as the strengthening rays made their wet clothes start to steam, he touched his lips to her hair.

'Now come inside with the living, Gwennan, before we both catch our death of cold.'

She lifted her head, her eyes wide, uncertain. Slowly she withdrew from his arms, but she didn't move away from him. Hardly daring to breathe, Rolant held out his hand.

She stared down at it for a long moment and his heart filled his throat as he waited. Then, without meeting his eyes, she placed her hand in his palm. And they walked, hand in hand, back towards the hall.

It wasn't a victory for him nor a capitulation for her. But in that little gain there was hope…even perhaps the beginnings of trust. For now, that was enough.

'I would wed your mother, Gwennan, after the appropriate mourning time has elapsed and if it would be agreeable to her, and to you?'

Meuryn's words were not a surprise. He was constantly at Angharad's side since her return, always within earshot of her door should she call, and Gwennan was glad he wanted to wed her.

What other course was left to a widow, after all, but to take the veil? Or take up the sword as she herself had done a year ago. At the time there had seemed no alternative, but now, with her wedding looming, everything seemed to have come full circle.

'You have always cared very much for her,' she said as they left the church, where she'd lit another candle to light her father's way to heaven.

At her side, her uncle grinned, then touched the scar that split his face—the one that had been there always, though he'd never told her what had caused it.

Now he did.

'I fought your father for her hand when we were all much younger. I got this and he got Angharad! But fortunately we remained friends, all three of us.'

Gwennan stopped in her tracks. 'But…he blinded you!'

Meuryn shrugged. 'He won, I lost, and the fight was a fair one. Your father and I would have fought many times over if we hadn't accepted the wisdom of that. He won her then, but now she needs me to care for her. And even if I can never take his place I'll never fail her.'

She resumed her walking, her uncle's words resounding in every step. Had Rolant meant it, that day at the graveside, when he said he'd never fail *her*? Would he fight over her as her father and uncle had done over her mother? Fight *for* her, as he'd been ready to do that day at the bridge in Shrewsbury? Or would they go on fighting against each other even after they were wed?

A shudder went through her. The ceremony was only three days away, so she would soon find out.

'Then, if my mother agrees, I would like nothing better than to see you wed, Meuryn,' she said. 'She is still sick from her ordeal and we must both care for her now.'

Meuryn and Angharad. Ywain and Nest. Rolant and

Gwennan. Three weddings. But only two of them out of choice and through the heart's desire.

And yet when Rolant had held her at the graveside, as the rain had fallen down upon them, something had broken through her. Broken *in* her. And she had been left empty, yet at the same time full to bursting.

Because her hate had gone that day, leaving her bereft of something—she knew not what—to take its place.

As if her thoughts had sought him out, Rolant came into sight, crossing from the stables towards the hall. Against her will, her heart leapt and began to race in her breast. She'd seen little of him during the last week, except when they sat together at table at mealtimes, and even then they'd spoken hardly at all.

So much had been said already, yet so much remained unsaid. And how could either of them say it when he didn't seem any more eager to do so than she did?

And, anyway, Rolant was too busy going about the business of completing the reinforcements of the *llys*. Even now he didn't see her, but disappeared with long swift strides into the hall.

Meuryn's eyes followed him, as did hers, and then her uncle spoke again, his voice pensive. 'We could have done a lot worse than the Lord Rolant, Gwennan. We have been lucky.'

Gwennan stopped again in her tracks, a gasp filling her throat. 'But… I thought you hated him?'

'I did at first. Now, *myn esgyrn i*, I can't help but like him.'

And, with those astounding words—uttered by *him* of all men!—he took his leave of her.

Gwennan stared after him for a moment, then turned

and carried on her way, his statement still ringing in the air.

At the stables, she noticed Dyfrig ap Iestyn the blacksmith, Nest's father, replacing one of Tarian's shoes—a shoe she hadn't even noticed was missing. Going up to him and placing a guilty hand on her horse's nose, she addressed the smith.

'Who sent for you, Dyfrig?'

'The Lord Rolant did, *Arglwyddes*,' the man replied. 'And he instructed me to check the shoes of all other horses of the *llys* while I'm here.'

'Oh.'

It was all she could say. Less than a fortnight after he'd taken his place as lord of Carn Egryn, Rolant's commands were being obeyed without question, his authority and his presence gradually, albeit grudgingly, accepted.

After their initial shock, then anger, and then resentment, the villagers had been won over. And even more quickly by his elevating of Berian, Nest's brother, to the position of his body servant.

Everyone was carrying out Rolant's wishes as dutifully as they'd done hers formerly, and before that her father's. But what had happened to *her* in these last weeks?

Even as she asked herself that silent and damning question, even as indignant anger lit her blood, Gwennan knew the answer. Rolant hadn't usurped her position at all. She'd relinquished it!

Well, they would see about that forthwith!

She stared down at the smith, but he'd already turned back to his task, as if she wasn't even standing there—

which only proved the fact. 'And where is *the Lord Rolant* now?' she snapped.

Dyfrig glanced up again, his cheeks reddening at her sharp tone and admonishing eyes. 'He...he said he had some business in the hall with Ywain Gerddor, *Arglwyddes.*'

Spinning on her heel, Gwennan marched across the bailey, her blood pounding. The hall was almost empty but Rolant was indeed there, sitting with Ywain at the top table, head bent over some documents.

She halted in the doorway and clenched her fists, gathering her breath and her temper. Documents? What documents? And why hadn't she been informed of any need for documents at all?

Inhaling deeply, she marched up the centre of the hall to the table on the dais. Both men looked up, clearly having not heard or seen her until then. Was she really so invisible now? A wraith that moved among her people unnoticed and unheeded?

'What are you two about here so secretly that I had to learn of it from the blacksmith?' Her whole body was quivering like a bow that had been stretched too tight. 'What matter do those parchments contain that nobody has thought to inform me of it?'

Her words came out in incoherent blocks and she reddened until her ears burned. But her blood was roaring in her veins in a way it hadn't for a long time—too long. And she felt herself rejoice in that feeling.

The two men rose and bowed, and then Rolant placed his palm on the document nearest him, whether in indication or to hide it, she couldn't tell.

'I am writing to the Earl of Rhuddlan, Gwennan, with a copy for the King, requesting—or rather demanding—

monetary compensation for your father's death while in his custody. It will come in very useful when our payment to the King falls due next year.'

Gwennan tilted her chin higher. 'Compensation?' She spat the word out with relish. 'Under Welsh law, he'd pay with his *life*—not with money!'

His dark head inclined in agreement, although his reply contradicted her completely. 'The laws of the March and of England are different. But that doesn't mean we cannot use them to seek justice all the same.'

She leaned her palms on the table and drove her glare like a lance into those cool green eyes. 'Do you think either I or my mother care about compensation?'

Rolant answered her as if he was placating an ignorant child…soft, yet firm. 'I have already spoken at length about this with your mother, and with Meuryn, and they are in agreement that Earl Robert should pay.'

Gwennan went on staring, and slowly she seemed to see him anew. The raven-black hair wasn't so short any more, but reached below his collar, the slight curling at the ends hinting at unruliness. The sun-bronzed skin of his face over strong bones was a glorious proclamation of health and vitality.

His lordly clothes sat upon his magnificent body as regally as if he were any prince or king, while the air of possession and power that emanated from him was total and undeniable.

But it wasn't his clothes, or his countenance, or his authority that showed him to her in a new light. Her other senses saw him too, just as they had that day in the rain, though now they saw even more clearly.

The touch of his lips on her hair…the strong yet tender embrace. The scent of him that she'd breathed and almost drowned in. The warmth of his body as it had poured its life and its strength into hers.

And it was her senses that frightened her now, because she didn't know how to quiet them, control them, deny them. Or hide them as she'd hidden beneath her men's clothing until he'd come with kindness, not cruelty, with the will to understand, not conquer, and stripped her disguise away from her.

'Then why did you not speak with me about it too?' she got out at last, her lips trembling with the knowledge that, beneath her rage, she was utterly naked, wholly defenceless. All she had left was attack. 'Does neither my standing nor my feelings matter here in my own home now?'

Chapter Fourteen

Rolant gathered up the parchments and gestured to the clerk to leave them. 'Take these with you, Ywain. These matters can wait a while longer.'

When the man had gone, he turned back to Gwennan. She was like a flaming statue of cold fire in front of him. Yet her weight was leaning on her hands, as if she lacked the strength to stay upright otherwise.

It had been a sennight since they'd laid her father in the earth—since she'd laid her head on his chest and let him hold her. But since then, instead of passing, her grief seemed to grow heavier. Instead of coming closer, they had seemed to grow further apart.

And every time he looked at her Rolant had no doubt that his presence as the new lord was only adding to that burden and driving the distance between them wider still.

'Sit down, Gwennan.'

She shook her head. The chestnut locks were longer now than when he'd first laid eyes on her—how many weeks ago? He'd lost count. But at the same time every day, every moment, was scored into his memory, never to be erased.

'I don't want to sit! I want to know why I am ex-
cluded from matters that should concern *me* most of
all? Matters that should be dealt with by *me*—as they
were before.'

Rolant drew a deep breath. Her cheeks were thinner
than they'd been, her eyes still dry, but looking more
raw than if she'd wept rivers of tears. Perhaps she did,
in private, but somehow he didn't think so.

'I meant to spare you the tedious task of dictating
this document, but of course would have sought your
approval and amendment of the finished version—as
on everything else.'

She continued to glare at him, mute, but that stark
glare spoke loudly. Rolant went on, choosing his words
with tact. 'But I am aware that you are still grieving,
that you need time, and so—'

'Time? Time for what?'

Her eyes flashed, and despite their sudden fury, despite the sorrow behind them that she couldn't hide, they
were as beautiful as ever. Her body, encased in gown
and kirtle, was beautiful too—so much so that Rolant
longed to reach across the table and touch her.

But he couldn't intrude on her grief any more than
he could expect to enjoy her body—not even after they
were wed.

'Time to heal,' he said.

'It is not true…what they say. Time doesn't heal. It
only stretches out too long, too hard.' She moved away
and, with a sigh, sank down at the end of the bench at
one of the long tables. 'There were two documents, I noticed. What was the other?'

Rolant was unprepared, so his answer came out immediately and without thought. Unlike the document

itself, which had proved far more difficult to compose than the one to the Earl.

'A letter to my father.'

She met his eyes and frowned. 'To inform him of your change in fortune?'

'In part. But also to ask for reconciliation between us.' His heart began to beat fast, though whether that was because of what he was saying or who he was saying it to, he wasn't quite certain. 'It is time now that I try and heal that rift, even if it won't change the past.'

'Do you think he will answer?'

Rolant shrugged, his shoulders not feeling the lightness the movement was meant to convey. 'We shall see. I hope so.'

He walked around the table, took a few paces down the hall. He felt her eyes follow him, pierce through his clothing into his skin. And as he turned his body tightened and fire flared in his loins.

She was so lovely that it hurt his eyes to look at her. Her face was pale in the dim light, her hair falling softly to her shoulders, unhidden by coif or veil. Her blue gown pooled around her feet like a lake, and dust motes sparkled in the air like stars over her head.

Was it because she would shortly be his wife that she seemed to grow in beauty day by day? Beautiful yet untouchable. For how could he ever hope to claim her body, less still win her heart, when he knew both belonged to someone else?

Rolant paced again. Could she really be so unaware of the turmoil within him? Had she not seen his desire, not felt it, that evening in her chamber when she'd come for the sword? Or had she sensed it and found it easy to ignore because she didn't share it?

If so, he would ensure she would remain unaware of it, no matter what it cost him. It would be a high price to pay, but one that he had to pay or lose her completely.

'We are not often alone like this,' he said, coming to a halt. 'And, since we are alone now, there is something I want to say to you.'

In truth, they sat together at every mealtime, and on each and every occasion he had to constantly remind himself that their union was abhorrent to her. That while he might lust for her, whether she was in sight or not, right next to him or further away, she merely tolerated him.

'What is it?' she asked, looking down at her hands, where they lay folded in her lap.

Rolant cleared his throat. 'The King was in error when he decreed that we should wed, Gwennan. But, nevertheless, his reasons for doing so were sound.'

A convincing start, at least.

He drew a breath and ploughed on. 'And if we accept that fact, we can ensure the safety and future prosperity of these lands together...in a way that you couldn't have done alone.'

'Together?'

'How else? I am lord here and you are my lady. We are not enemies any longer.'

She looked up at him at last, her eyes wide, lovely, dark in the paleness of her face. 'Then what *are* we, Rolant? Allies...or *friends*, as you said in Shrewsbury?'

Rolant could have given her an answer to that, but he doubted it would be one she would welcome! 'Enemies have become allies before, working together to achieve a common good.'

'And you think we can do the same?'

He nodded, unlocked the knuckles that had clenched without his knowing. 'And in time perhaps we can be… friends, too, yes.' There—the damning word was out. Now he just had to remember it and adhere to it. 'So, to help ease that process, I will assure you that is as far as our marriage will go.'

She said nothing for a moment, as the meaning of his words dawned slowly over her face. 'Do you mean you will not expect…?'

Rolant spared her the embarrassment of having to finish. 'I will not impose myself upon you in any other way. Though for the sake of propriety you must move into our…your former chamber.'

'You will not insist on claiming your husband's dues?'

The hope in her question struck at his pride as much as his manhood, but he himself had invited the blow.

'No.'

At least his voice was steady enough, but she deserved a reason, and he needed one too—if only to ensure he remembered those words in the nights to come.

'I finally understood something that night you came for the sword, although I have known it long since. You already have a husband—albeit a dead one—and you wish for no other.'

Her face went even paler, and then a surge of colour rushed into her cheeks. She didn't say anything, and as the moment of silence dragged out Rolant felt heat burn in his cheeks too. He'd told her on more than one occasion that he'd never lied to her. And yet now he was about to do exactly that. Moreover he had to make himself believe the lie as well as she, as he told it.

'Fortunately, since I do not wish for a wife either—in *that* sense—it will be a simple task for me to respect your wishes, Gwennan.'

Gwennan waited for relief but nothing came. It was like a tide that lay stagnant, far out at sea, instead of rippling into shore. Or a gift that she'd hoped for for so long but now it had come it turned out not to be the one she'd wanted after all.

She stared at him. The eyes that reminded her of Talyllyn were dark now, in the dim lights of the hall, their vivid surface calm and the depths below hidden from sight.

'Marriage should not be a *task* at all,' she said at last, her voice quivering with feelings she didn't understand. 'It wasn't so with Rhys. But then, I loved him, and he loved me.'

Something moved in his face, a slight flinching of the flesh, and then it was gone.

He came to sit on the bench opposite her, leaning forward, his elbows on his knees. 'Then you were blessed, Gwennan. Not all marriages are so happy.'

If she'd reached out, Gwennan could have touched the black forelock, swept it back from his brow, searched his shuttered eyes for whatever lay concealed there. But she didn't.

'My father and mother loved each other deeply and to the death,' she went on, trying to explain something to herself as much as to him. 'When my father surrendered to the Normans she didn't have to go with him into his dungeon, but she chose to do so rather than live without him.'

Her words settled like specks of dust in the still air, formed yet unfinished, and it was Rolant who completed them.

'And you wish you had gone to the gallows with Rhys?'

Gwennan's heart shuddered to a stop as he read her mind and misinterpreted it. But how could she expect him to understand things she didn't understand herself any longer? She couldn't tell him the truth when she didn't know it. Yet how could she lie, when she didn't know if it *was* a lie? A lie born not of love eternal for a dead husband but of cowardice that she might be able to love a *living* husband. That she might *want* to love him and begin to live again. That she could do neither because she was a coward.

Life could end between one breath and the next, with the stroke of a blade, the thrust of a knife, the kiss of pestilence. Rolant lived now, but he could die too, one day. And when that happened how would she bear yet another loss? Another ending of love? Another fatal blow to her heart?

Gwennan got to her feet, her heart already reeling in fear. 'No, I don't wish that. I don't… I never wished for that. There has been enough death in this house already.'

He rose and looked down at her, his gaze more impenetrable than ever. 'Then we will strive together to ensure there are no more deaths.'

Death, life, friend, enemy, love, hate—too many words to hear, let alone try and find the meaning of.

She nodded and turned away, walking out of the hall and into her new and terrible existence. A world of love and a world of the fear of love. And now she felt she could go neither forward nor back, but would remain in a sort of non-existence for ever. In a state of being but not of truly living, and never, ever loving.

Not unless Rolant took her hand and pulled her— one way or the other.

On the eve of their wedding the horn of the Norsemen was heard again. Rolant ordered the parapet manned at once and was up there himself when Gwennan appeared a moment or two later.

She was far from happy.

'*Nefoedd fawr!* It takes an age to get into this accursed gown! I would have been here in half the time in my…other clothes.'

Despite the Viking threat, despite even the chagrin on her face, Rolant smiled. Then, carefully, he touched upon a subject he sensed still bothered her. 'And defy the Bishop of Chester?'

She glared up at him in the act of smoothing down her skirts. 'Who?'

'The churchman in the Earls' entourage at the bridge in Shrewsbury.'

'Oh…' She looked away, out into the night, her cheeks paler suddenly. 'Is that who he was? His teeth are even sharper than Hugh Flaidd's!'

This time Rolant laughed out loud. He'd picked up a little Welsh by now, and was well aware that the people here, as well as the Saxons over the border, called the great Earl of Chester 'Hugh the Wolf', and not just because of his coat of arms.

'I cannot disagree with you on that point,' he said.

If she could jest about the matter, perhaps the Bishop's barb hadn't gone as deep as he'd feared—or if it had, it had been soon healed.

The sound of the horn came again, a good distance away, carrying on the still air as it had done that night when he'd lain in the strong room.

'How far away are they, would you say?' he asked, feeling his way carefully.

Since their conversation in the hall a sort of truce had settled between them, albeit fragile, and he had no wish to break that tenuous understanding.

Gwennan's teeth worried at her bottom lip as she considered. 'Further south than Tywyn, I think. Mayhap they have their sights set on Aberdyfi.'

She met his eyes, and as the moon came out from behind a cloud her gaze glistened like dark gold. Rolant felt his body tighten, his blood stir. It always did now, whenever she was near—truce or no—and as their wedding day approached he found himself reining himself in even more. Inch by agonising inch...like a belt pulled too tight.

'Then, God willing, they will not come as far as here.'

She nodded, and the moonbeams caught the rich red strands of her hair. 'We should remain alert, all the same.'

Rolant nodded too, his fingers itching to reach out and capture those moonbeams, lift the silken locks to his lips, taste the moon in her hair. 'I will stay guard up here—'

But she spoke at the same time. 'I will stay here on guard—'

He hid a smile, then sobered as he remembered her indignity, her hurt, over his document for Earl Rob-

ert. When he'd made the error of thinking to spare her
the task and ended up causing her pain and incurring
her wrath.

That had been remedied and the missive sent, bearing both his and her seals, blood-red and newly made.
And now she appeared to have accepted his suggestion
that they work together, as allies—if not quite friends—
but never as anything more.

'Then we will both keep watch in turn, shall we?' he
asked, not commanded. He'd given his word that they
would rule Carn Egryn together, and he would never
give her cause to doubt it.

'Agreed.' She turned away, placed her hands on the
parapet wall, looked out to the west again. 'I will not
sleep tonight anyway.'

Rolant leaned on the wall too. Sweat bathed the back
of his neck and seeped down between his shoulder
blades. It was the end of summer, but the dawning autumn was still too warm for either sleeping or thinking.

'Because of the Norsemen or because it is our wedding day eve?'

There was a pause before she replied, 'Both.'

He looked over the dark landscape. It was as familiar to him now as the palm of his hand, even covered
in the blanket of night as it was now.

'Do you remember the last time we stood here, when
the Norsemen burned Tywyn?'

She nodded. 'Of course.'

'I accused you then of hiding behind your men's
clothing. I am sorry I said that, Gwennan. I had no
right.'

Another pause—one so full of tension that he thought
she wouldn't answer, that the insult still stung. And then

finally she spoke. 'You were right. I *was* hiding. But I didn't know it—or refused to know it.'

Rolant studied her profile, lily-pale in the moonlight. 'And now you do?'

'Yes, I know it…now.' She turned to meet his eyes. 'I've always wondered… Why didn't you expose me when you captured me? You knew I wasn't what I pretended to be right from the first, didn't you?'

The moment rushed back to him and he smiled. 'It wasn't that hard to tell once I'd touched your… Once I'd felt for your heartbeat.'

If it hadn't been dark, her blush would have reached out and singed his face. 'Then why keep my secret from your men?'

A breeze lifted, danced in her hair, drew his gaze. 'To protect you—why else?'

'But *why* did you feel the need to protect me? What did it serve you to do so?'

Rolant dragged in a breath. The scent of the hillsides around was as heady as incense, her goading like a sweet torture to his soul. 'It served me nothing, but I could not do otherwise.'

'But what were your *reasons*?'

'God's teeth, Gwennan!' He ran his fingers through his hair, felt them shake. Was she determined to put him through hell, day and night? 'Do you think I would have exposed you to my men? Soldiers who'd been in the field for weeks, without a woman to ease their needs?'

'Or to ease yours?'

A grim smile tore at his mouth as his loins turned to fire and began to consume him. 'Do you think *me* capable, then, of misusing a woman as they might have done?'

She moved a step nearer, and the scent of her was even more heady than the night. Then she shook her head. 'No, I don't think that. But with every answer you give me I understand you less. Nothing you do makes sense to me.'

'Such as?'

Lifting a hand, she gestured around her. 'Reinforcing this *llys*, going to the King, standing up and defending me before the Earls...and even now being here, protecting my home should danger come.'

'It is *my* home too, remember?'

She nodded. 'Yes, but it wasn't when you did all those other things.'

Rolant looked away again, folding his arms over his chest to contain his surging lust. Perhaps it was time to tell her, not merely give her evasive answers. Perhaps, since they were to be wed, she deserved to be told.

'You accused me, the last time we stood up here, of trying to salve my conscience. Do you remember? When I told you your defences weren't enough to save you? You were right. My conscience did come into it, though it wasn't a deliberate intent.'

'How so?'

'Because five years ago I failed to protect John, and he died. I wavered then, torn between two sides, not knowing where to stand or why. I've since learned there can be no wavering—not even in trying to do the right thing by everyone. A side must be taken and adhered to.'

'My side?'

Rolant turned to look at her and his heart turned over. Then all the reasons, all the answers came, like a tumbling, crystal-clear fall of water. And the world—

his world—righted itself at last and everything fell into its proper place.

'Your side, Gwennan, come what may, until I die.'

Gwennan bit back a gasp at his declaration. It was like the words a champion would speak before a battle, the words a husband would say before pledging his life for his lady. Words of commitment, of duty, even of devotion—yet not of love.

She turned and leaned on the parapet wall, her heart filling her throat. 'If the Norsemen come, that might be sooner than you realise!'

'They won't come. Not tonight.'

'How do you know they won't?'

'I won't permit it.'

Gwennan glanced at him and away again. Was he jesting? Making light of his earlier and so earnest words that he'd never fail her? And what of his other words? The ones that had told her he would demand nothing of her once they were wed?

'You mean the horn is far enough away to tell you they are heading in a different direction?'

He smiled. 'That too.' Then his eyes become intense, serious. 'But I am at your side, whether they come or not, whenever you need me—and even when you don't.'

She turned to face him again, some force she couldn't resist pulling her towards him even though her feet didn't move. 'And if I *should* need you...you will come?'

He nodded slowly, deliberately. 'You only have to call me.'

Her body was calling him right at that instant if he could only hear it. Her heart was calling him too, so loudly that its clamouring filled her ears until it was a miracle that he didn't hear it. Unless perhaps he didn't *want* to hear…unless he had spoken truly that day in the hall.

Gwennan felt her breasts rise and fall too quickly, felt her cheeks flush with her need of him right then and there. A need to feel his touch, his mouth on hers, his skin against her skin, with no barrier of clothing or anything else between them.

The night was too quiet, the air too warm, too thick with the scents of a summer that lingered too long as autumn changed the colours of the trees. Even the Norsemen's horn had stopped sounding, removing that barrier too—the safe barrier of outward danger to ward off inner perils.

He took a step nearer and lifted a hand to her face, his knuckles gently brushing her cheek. His gaze locked on her mouth and he stared so intently that her lips parted and her breath stalled in her throat. His fingers moved to her temple and stroked softly over her hair and she began to quiver.

Then he traced a path along her collarbone to her throat, his touch so light it might have been a petal or the wing of a butterfly. Or the Ladybird he'd lifted off her shoulder as they'd sat beneath the trees at Llangadfan, closer than they'd ever been, yet still so far apart.

'I will never come unbidden, Gwennan, I have promised you that.' His gaze became dark, sombre, and a sort of torment seemed to swirl within it. 'And I will never break that promise—unless you ask me to.'

Gwennan's heart faltered in her breast. She swallowed, licked her lips, fought for words, but none came. And with the ghost of a smile he took her lack of an answer to mean what it didn't.

Stepping away, he lifted her hand and kissed the back of it—as courteous and reverent a kiss as she'd ever known. When his lips left her skin again the smile was gone, but the serious intent, the shadow of turmoil, remained in his eyes.

'The Norsemen seem to have gone, so there is no need for us both to remain up here. Go and rest, Gwennan. I will take the first half of the night and then send a man to wake you—if you wish to take over?'

Gwennan nodded, and as he relinquished her hand she reeled away, her mind a blur, her limbs a-tremble. She descended the ladder without feeling any of the rungs beneath her feet. She crossed the bailey without seeing her direction. She entered her mother's chamber and closed the door softly, so as not to wake her, or Nest, who slept on a pallet on the floor.

But she did it all without any sense of doing it. Because all her senses seemed to have remained with Rolant, up on the ramparts, watching the night for danger, when the greatest peril was already inside these walls.

The peril of loving when love brought with it fear instead of joy.

Because she *did* love him—deeply, eternally, and so cruelly. Since it could never be revealed or shared or enjoyed. Because it would hurt too much if it—if *he*—were taken from her.

Gwennan didn't get into bed but sank, fully clothed, into a chair by the unlit hearth. Despite her attempt at silence, a heavy sigh broke from her, startlingly loud in the silent room.

Her mother woke and her voice came out of the darkness. 'What ails you, *fechan*?'

'*Llychlynwyr*—but far to the south, not here. Go back to sleep, Mam.'

A moment later the curtain dividing the room parted and then her mother was beside her, a hand on her shoulder. 'I asked what ails you, Gwennan. Is it thinking of your wedding tomorrow that keeps you from sleep?'

Gwennan nodded. 'I'm...afraid.'

'Of Rolant?'

She didn't answer, and her mother began to stroke her hair, as she'd done when she was a child and hadn't understood war and death. When the only love she'd known was the love of her family, not a man.

If only it were as simple as that again!

'Husbands can die, *'ngeneth i*, as we both know.'

Gwennan leaned into her mother's comforting hand, but the words had chilled her to the bone. Perceptive... a premonition that must never come to pass.

'But life goes on. You deserve happiness, Gwennan, and I pray that you will find it with Rolant. That you will come to see him as I have—as a good and honourable man.'

She glanced up and searched her mother's face, not quite so deeply scored with grief as it had been a week ago. 'Do you really see him like that, after all that has happened?'

'Nothing that *he* has caused. He has instead tried to put things right. I see the proof of his goodness with my own eyes daily, and so do others—Meuryn too. And if Lord Rolant can win over your uncle as he has done, that tells me a great deal about him.'

Gwennan closed her eyes. Meuryn, her mother, Ywain, Nest, Berian, Dyfrig the blacksmith... The list of converts rolled on. 'But not a few weeks ago everyone hated him—and so did I.'

'Then we must cease our hating…stop judging him by what others of his kind have done to us in the past. And accept and respect him for what he is doing for us now.'

Her mother smiled through her voice, as she did more frequently now, since Meuryn had made his intentions and his love clear.

'We must bend with the prevailing wind—for now,' she said. 'Rolant is different from the other Marcher lords, for all his Norman blood.'

Gwennan opened her eyes again. Different? Yes, she'd known that right from the start. And even if she'd disbelieved and denied it then, he'd proved her wrong many times over.

Her mother bent and kissed the top of her head. 'Now, come to bed, *fechan*, and sleep. All things turn out well, sooner or later, even when we think they won't.'

Gwennan rose and followed her mother back to bed, on tiptoes so as not to wake Nest—who was also to be wed on the morrow.

Tomorrow things *would* be different. Everything was different already. But would things be well too? Could they *ever* be well when she would have to live her married life in constant self-deception?

Because how could she continue to hide her love from him as she'd hidden herself from him inside her men's clothes? How, when that love was already bursting at the seams of her heart and tearing her apart?

Chapter Fifteen

Rolant and Ywain stood before the door of the church almost exactly one month to the day since the King's decree at Shrewsbury.

It had seemed expedient to have a double wedding ceremony, since they'd had to send to Tywyn for a priest, there being none in the *llys*. The family priest had disappeared during the Norman siege a year ago. Something else that would need to be rectified.

So, there would be two joinings this fifth day of September—his to Gwennan and Ywain's to Nest. Efficient, economical and totally devoid of emotion—at least on the part of himself and Gwennan. Except for the hidden ones she must never know about.

There was a stirring behind them and Rolant turned his head at the same time Ywain did, to see their brides approaching. Nest was on the arm of her father, Dyfrig the blacksmith, her face radiant in a way he'd never seen it before. Gwennan clung to Meuryn's arm, her face downcast, her mouth set, looking as if she was going not to her wedding but to the gallows.

Perhaps she really was wishing that she'd gone to the gallows a year ago with her beloved Rhys...

Rolant turned away with a grimace. That dead and envied man had no place here, today of all days.

As Gwennan came to stand at his left hand he turned to look at her. She wore a rich wine-coloured gown that only seemed to make her face paler still…as white as the tiny wildflowers that were threaded into her hair. But she was no virgin in either body or heart, because both had already been given to that other man.

At least the ill-robed and rustic priest spoke passable Latin, though with a thick Welsh burr, and knew the ceremony well enough. This marriage would need all the validity possible, since he himself had all but declared it invalid when he'd promised Gwennan he would not insist on consummating it.

An easy thing to say at the time. Now, with his bride looking more beautiful and more desirable than he'd ever seen her, despite her wan face, her lips repeating the Latin almost in a whisper, Rolant knew just how hard it would be to keep to that promise.

After the exchange of rings, the vows and the blessing, when he had to stoop and kiss her mouth, he was beginning to wish he'd never made it…

The wedding feast was merry and loud, and before it was halfway through Gwennan's head began to ache. She tried to blame it on the silver circlet that squeezed tight on her brow, but since the ache was in her heart, too, it couldn't be that.

She and Rolant sat at the centre of the high table, with Ywain and Nest to their left, her mother and Meuryn to their right. Her maid and her scribe whispered and giggled, and her mother and her uncle spoke quietly together—about what Gwennan knew not, due to the noise in the hall. But Angharad's eyes sparkled too, and her smile shone as warm as the torches that burned on the walls.

Perhaps it was because this was their first celebration for over a year, but everyone seemed possessed of a sort of joyful freedom that overleapt the bounds of deference and decorum. And, of course, the free-flowing mead and wine loosened tongues and manners with equal ease.

She and Rolant hadn't exchanged gifts, since there were none, the swift wedding preparations not having allowed time to have any made. She didn't dance, and he didn't ask her to. Nest and Ywain danced enough for all four of them anyway, when the tables were empty of food and only the sweets were left.

They were still dancing, late into the night, when Rolant turned to her and cleared his throat. 'Would you like to retire now, Gwennan?'

There were two answers to that. Yes, she longed to leave these festivities in which she had no part. No, she dreaded retiring to her—*their*—chamber and being alone with Rolant and the love he neither knew existed nor wanted from her.

She got to her feet with a short nod. Her mother rose too, drawing her into a long embrace, and whispering in her ear. 'Remember what I said, *'nghariad ferch*. Put away your hate and let love into your heart again. None of us knows how long we have in this world, so we must not waste a moment of life.'

Gwennan drew her head back and stared into her mother's eyes, saw that she meant what she'd said, and how her new love for Meuryn had made her strong again, instead of the broken woman who had escaped her prison only a short time ago.

And in their reflection she saw her own self, small and white, weak and afraid, as she kissed her mother goodnight.

There was yet another exposing ordeal she had to face. Their leaving of the hall which, as tradition expected, would be both irreverent and lewd.

All she could do was shut her ears to the cheers and banging of cups, the gleeful jests and bawdy comments that accompanied their departure through the curtain behind the dais.

Then Rolant was holding the door open and inviting her to cross the threshold, and thankfully shutting it fast again, before any of the revellers could follow them inside.

Her heart thumping, Gwennan folded her arms around her midriff and stared at the curtain that separated living from sleeping quarters, already drawn back and the bed waiting.

'Will you take some wine, Gwennan?'

'No…thank you.' She wasn't used to spiced wine and her head ached enough as it was.

Behind her, she listened to Rolant crossing to the table and pouring himself a goblet. He'd drunk little that night, nor had he eaten much, and she hadn't either.

'Do you wish to go straight to bed?'

Gwennan stared down at her gown, and her heart froze even as her cheeks burned scarlet. How was she supposed to get out of it?

Of course if this had been any other wedding night, any other man and woman, her husband would have helped her. As Rhys had done on her first wedding night. Yet now she struggled to remember, so far away did that night seem—as if it had never happened, or had been only a dream, from another life, not this one.

She turned to face Rolant. He was leaning back against the same oaken table where they'd composed their letter to the King, his eyes unfathomable over the rim of his cup.

He was dressed splendidly, for once not in the blue colours that she'd noticed he favoured. A long, dark brown tunic trimmed with gold thread at neck, hem and cuffs graced his body, and a leather belt, skilfully tooled, circled his lean hips. Fine hose of tan wool covered his legs, and his soft leather shoes shone as black as his hair.

Gwennan cleared her throat. 'The words you spoke to me...the other day in the hall...'

Mercifully, he spared her the agony of repeating them, though his face dulled in a flush. 'I meant them, Gwennan. You have no need to worry on that point.'

'Then where...where will you sleep?'

In answer, he put his cup down and strode into the sleeping area. Dragging the pallet which his body servant Berian normally slept on into the living area, he pointed down at it.

'Here—with your permission.'

He didn't need to ask her permission, and they both knew that. Gwennan bit her lip as she remembered the other thing he'd said up on the parapet. That if she needed him she only had to call. That he wouldn't trespass unless she invited him.

The room seemed suddenly much smaller as Rolant went to the door and shot the bolt across. He hesitated before turning back, shrugging his broad shoulders.

'In case anyone be so drunk as to fall into the wrong room!' he said, on a strange sort of laugh.

It was a jest, and yet it was not. If anyone should enter, either out of mischief or mistake, the shame for Rolant were he to be discovered sleeping on a pallet and not in their marriage bed would equal only the ridicule he would face from all in the *llys*.

Even if he never bedded her again, a husband was expected to do his duty by his wife on this night at least.

Gwennan turned away and, doing her best not to run, went into the sleeping area, drawing the curtain quickly behind her again. Her hands were shaking, yet there was no need to be nervous, was there? He'd said he would leave her be. And it seemed he'd meant it.

She stood and looked down at the gown that still clothed her. She could always sleep fully clothed, of course, as she'd done many times out on the hills, under the stars, when she was a fugitive.

But she wasn't a fugitive now. She was a bride. And it was a warm night and she was already burning up... as if a fever raged through her veins.

Gwennan sat on the edge of the bed and one by one took the flowers from her hair, dropping them into the rushes on the floor, which had been strewed with fresh and fragrant herbs. She removed her shoes and *socasau* and, after rolling them up, placed them neatly under the bed. Then she dropped her hands uselessly into her lap.

Now what?

She couldn't call for Nest. Her maid was a bride herself tonight, and probably already making her way with Ywain to a far more welcoming bed.

Perhaps even now she was laughing and tumbling into it, into her new husband's arms, her body willing and ready for love, her heart filled to the brim with joy. So different from the shy and scarred girl she'd taken into her service not two months ago.

But then Nest loved Ywain, and love was the greatest healer of all—or so they said. Strong enough to bring hearts out of the darkness and into the light if those hearts were brave enough.

Hers clearly wasn't.

'Do you need any assistance, Gwennan?'

Gwennan jumped off the bed as Rolant's voice pierced the curtain, half expecting to see his head poking through the material, so close had his voice been.

'What? No, no…' she replied, too quickly, holding her palms up to ward him off and resisting the urge to tug the thick hangings even closer together. 'W-why do you ask that?'

There was a little pause. 'I have three sisters, Gwennan. And, while I am not an expert on the clothing of women, I can recognise which gowns require help in the putting on and putting off and which do not.'

Was that a note of indulgence and humour beneath his words? This dress had been made especially for her first wedding, with intricate lacing that did up at the back, from her tailbone to the nape of her neck. Impossible for the wearer either to get into it or out of without help.

'Mayhap I could ask your mother to come and help you out of it?'

Gwennan's hands flew to her cheeks. Oh, the shame! Whose foolish idea had it been to hold both weddings on the same day and deprive her of her maid? Rolant's, of course—though surely he hadn't had any foresight of this situation…or had he?

She stared at the curtain as if she might see through

it and find the answer written on his face. But even as she looked she didn't need an answer—because she knew already that, whatever else might happen, Rolant would keep his word.

He wouldn't come unless she called him...

Gwennan drew the curtain aside with a smart swish and snatched a breath at discovering how close he was actually standing.

'No, don't send for my mother.' Her voice was too thin, too high, but at least it wasn't trembling—unlike her knees. 'It is only a matter of undoing the lacing at the back of the dress...which I cannot reach, naturally. The rest I can take care of myself.'

He bowed his head. 'Of course.'

She'd intended to move out into the living area for the task of unlacing to be completed as quickly as possible. But before she could take a step he was through the curtain. All at once the private little space seemed filled to the walls—she, the bed, the dress and him all somehow pushed together.

He had already removed his tunic and stood in only his hose and white linen shirt. Below the neckline the strong line of his throat flexed and glowed like bronze. Their eyes met and held, his steady, yet gleaming with a strange intensity, while hers, she knew, were as wide and as wild as a hart cornered by the hunter.

Breath and words deserted her, and she realised she was twisting her hands together in front of her. Unlocking them, Gwennan lifted one to her hair, the gesture as revealing as it was defensive. She watched his gaze follow it, linger a moment, then return to hers.

'Shall I begin?'

She nodded, and a heartbeat later he was standing

behind her, his fingers at the nape of her neck, his body warm and almost touching hers. Her skin quivered as he swept her hair to one side. She hadn't realised until then how long it had grown over this last month, and how it now hung half a handspan below her shoulders.

Rolant's mouth came close to her ear—too close. 'Your hair is longer than it was. In this light, and against the colour of this dress, it is…'

He didn't finish, but began to undo the lacing of her dress, his fingers brushing lightly against her flesh through the thin shift she wore below. And as he worked his way downwards Gwennan's mortification grew.

And, worse than the mortification, her nerves began to flutter, as if her senses were responding instinctively to his touch, the pores of her skin opening as the material parted.

'What…what are their names?' she asked, clutching at conversation to hide that mortification. 'Your sisters?'

'Marguerite, Isabelle and Marie.'

The cool air from the open window without and his warm breath as he spoke mingled into a delicious caress on her bare neck and almost naked shoulders.

'Are you close to them?'

She sensed, not saw, the sadness in the shake of his head.

'I haven't seen them for a long time but, yes…we were very close. All of us.'

Remembering the story of his brother's death brought sadness to her too, but it didn't expel the exquisite ache that had possessed her, pulling at her whole being from her head to her toes.

'You must miss them very much,' Gwennan said instead, knowing his response long before it came, many heavy heartbeats later.

'Yes.'

She longed to turn around and look into his face, and yet she didn't. She yearned to speak more, and yet she couldn't. More than anything, she craved to touch him as he was touching her, but she dared not.

She wanted to call him to her, bid him stay, but she wouldn't.

Then his work was done. His lips pressed lightly upon her shoulder, barely there, yet as keen as a cut, and then were swiftly gone. The curtain swished as he passed through and drew it across again. And then it was too late for wanting or longing, craving or calling.

Gwennan placed her fingertips on the place where his lips had alighted, so briefly, so chastely. Just like the kiss that had sealed their union before the altar earlier. A kiss goodnight, nothing more, since he clearly neither wanted nor intended to come any closer to her than that.

Because what husband would not insist on his dues, at least on his wedding night, unless it was no hardship for him to abstain?

'Where is Gwennan?'

The following morning, Rolant bowed to the Queen Angharad, who was walking, as she always did, on Meuryn's arm across the bailey—a daily constitutional that, slowly but surely, was bringing her vitality back to her.

And not just vitality but beauty too was returning— Gwennan's beauty—since it was the sort that was eternal. And now it bloomed again like a rose after a long and harsh winter, under the attentions of this fierce warrior who appeared to be deeply in love with her.

'She rode out, my lord Rolant, an hour since.' Even as he spoke the man's eyes flickered only briefly to him, then went back to the face of the woman on his arm. But at least Meuryn too was less hostile these days, their relations moving slowly from tolerant to almost cordial. Love, it seemed, could work miracles.

Except in his case!

'Did she go alone? In which direction?'

'Towards the river. I advised her to take Nest and Ywain, or some other escort, but she said she needed solitude.'

'Lord Rolant.'

Angharad addressed him, her tone far kinder than on the day she'd returned with her dead husband. Now there was something akin to affection in the eyes that shone brightly into his.

'You will have discovered long since that Gwennan is too strong-willed for her own good at times, so perhaps if you went to look for her...?'

Rolant took the hint and, bowing quickly, turned away and made haste for the stables. He saddled his bay himself, and was out through the gates almost before the guard had time to open them fully.

He set his horse into a smart trot down the hill, not unduly worried, but nevertheless uneasy. Not a good omen, the day after a man's marriage, that his wife had disappeared!

He was at the river in no time, for it bounded the village in a loop, and then threaded its course to the sea to the west. Stopping to ask one of the villagers in halting

Welsh, he learned that Gwennan had ridden eastwards a while since.

Rolant followed the riverbank towards the rising sun. The autumn morning was clear…it was a warm and pleasant day for a ride under different circumstances. But now his heart was pounding, his palms on the reins moist with sweat, and he pushed his gelding into a gallop.

As he sped on, he recognised the valley around him. The hills were not as green now as then, and the leaves were tinged with autumn colours, but he knew the landscape all the same. It was where Giles de Fresnay had died—where Gwennan had pitched him out of the saddle and escaped him.

It seemed far more peaceful now and yet at the same time a sense of foreboding drummed in his ears, louder even than his horse's hooves. And then Rolant pulled up sharp as, rounding a curve in the river, he spied the grey stallion tethered to the low-hanging branch of an oak tree.

The next moment he saw Gwennan, kneeling on the bank, staring down at the water below. She'd heard his headlong approach, of course, and turned in alarm. A flush swept her cheeks and she turned quickly away again.

Rolant dismounted and tethered his gelding. Then he paused, wiped his hands on his tunic, then ran them through his windswept hair. Now he was here, both his haste and his foreboding seemed foolish. Worse, he'd been told she wanted solitude, and here was he, intruding when he'd promised her he never would.

And yet…something had made it imperative that he come. So, since it would be even more foolish to mount and ride away without a word of explanation, he went over to Gwennan and squatted down beside her.

'What are you doing here?' he asked, softly.

'Nothing. Thinking.'

Her profile was pale despite the sun and the sparkling reflection of the water on her skin.

'About the last time we rode through this valley, when you unhorsed me as ably as any knight might do?'

She shook her head without meeting his eyes. 'That was a mean trick.'

'But an effective device, and one I've used myself from time to time.'

Rolant smiled, but she didn't return it and his heart froze. Did she long to escape him now, as she had on that long-ago summer's day?

'Then what *are* you thinking about, Gwennan, that you need to do it here, so far from home?'

Reaching into the grass, she pulled a green blade and began to twist the stem. 'I needed to...'

'Be alone?'

She nodded, her eyes staring intently down at her fingers as they tore the blade of grass in half, then in half again. 'Yes.'

'Do you want me to go?' he asked, dreading the answer.

There was a pause. Then she sighed. 'No.'

She wore a coif today, as befitted a married woman, and her hair was completely hidden. That, however, exposed her slender neck, pale as milk, the skin so soft that he wanted to touch it as he had touched it last night, and not just her neck but all of her.

'Then would you like to talk? Or would you rather me be silent?'

She turned her head and looked at him at last, and Rolant felt his gut twist far more violently than that blade of grass between her fingers.

'I think perhaps I *need* to talk.'

This time it wasn't his stomach but his heart that turned over, although he steeled his face to show nothing. Just as he'd schooled it the previous night, in their chamber, when he'd unlaced her dress. And before that when he'd kissed her at the altar, making her his wife, his lady.

Heaven knew how he'd restrained himself on both occasions. But he'd given her his word, his promise, and he would never break that—no matter how much agony it caused his flesh.

'Then talk, Gwennan. I am listening.'

Gwennan plucked another blade of grass, twisted the stem, and stared down at her reflection in the river. The water was shallow after many days without rain, and gurgled musically over the pebbles on its bottom. And she saw an image there that no mirror could ever have shown her.

A woman with short hair, a sulky mouth and a brow furrowed with ill-temper, dressed in a gown but still hiding beneath it. A wife who yet wasn't a wife.

As if trying to see too, Rolant leaned closer, his reflection almost touching hers in the water. The flooded ford at the Dyfi flashed into her mind, where he'd hauled her onto Tarian's back and carried her across. *Forwyn Fair!* A lifetime seemed to have slipped away since he'd taken her captive.

Had he laughed at her too, then, as the Earl had done in Shrewsbury? Was he still laughing behind that easy, good-humoured mouth? Had he condemned her too, just as the Bishop of Chester had? Was that truly why he found it easy to lie on a pallet instead of with her?

Upstream, an otter or some other river creature splashed and dived. Gwennan shuddered as the disturbance on the water stirred her feelings even more violently.

'I need to speak about us...about me.'

'Speak on.'

His gentle prodding was like a hand reaching inside her. His hand did actually reach out—to delve into the water and pluck out a smooth blue-grey pebble. He weighed it in his palm.

'If something is worrying you, Gwennan, I want to know about it.'

'I... I am afraid.'

The breath left her lungs in one go. She'd said it. It was out and she couldn't take it back. Now all that was needed was his response. And it came soon enough, as the pebble dropped from his hand and plopped back into the river.

'If any other woman said that to me I might believe her. But I have discovered you are afraid of nothing and of no one.'

Gwennan watched their reflections, shimmering and then growing still again in the water. Too still, too clear, too revealing.

His, in profile now as he looked at her, was noble, handsome, strong, honourable, brave—that of a man of his word. A man who had pledged himself her protector, a man who defended her honour, who would fight for her as he'd done at the bridge in Shrewsbury.

And her reflection...? Oh, how she wished it were as

clear as his! If it were, she wouldn't have to tell him—he might see it for himself.

'Simply because I can wield a sword,' Gwennan said at last, 'and face my enemies without fear, it doesn't mean that I'm not a coward inside.'

The sun beat down on the back of her neck, and the buzzing of a bumblebee nearby added to the drowsy peace of the morning, mocking the war that raged inside her heart.

'I think everyone knows fear sometimes…perhaps all the time.' His words were as soft as a breath on her cheek. 'Doing what has to be done despite that fear is what matters.'

'As you did what had to be done when you married me?'

He smiled. 'That had a certain amount of fear attached, I admit, but I have faced far worse ordeals. And so have you—have you not?'

Gwennan's heart constricted and she folded her hands tightly in her lap. 'Yes, I have.'

The bumblebee buzzed closer, hovering from flower to flower along the riverbank. Gathering as much late-summer nectar as it could before the autumn came. Enough to sustain it through the winter, to nourish the new bees that would emerge to a new life next spring.

'It takes a good deal of courage to admit to fear, Gwennan.'

Rolant's hand moved to cover hers…warm, strong, steadfast and unafraid. Exactly like he was.

'So what is it that frightens you?'

And because—unlike those bees—it was her new life that frightened her, Gwennan's courage fled and she lied.

'I am afraid that you have been laughing at me, like the Earl did. Condemning me for the clothes I wore, like the Bishop did.' She turned her head and met his eyes. '*Have* you, Rolant? *Do* you?'

His response was instant—in his words and on his face. 'No, I never have and never will.' Then his dazzling smile came again. 'Though I must confess that I prefer you in a gown.'

Gwennan felt herself start to drown in those green-gold eyes that shone so bright as sun and river lit them. It would be as easy as floating to lean into him now. To banish fear and let those arms enfold her, melt into the beauty and the strength of him and offer him her lips.

But what if he didn't take them? What if those arms didn't close about her as she longed for them to do? What if, despite those few fleeting, feather-soft kisses he'd bestowed so casually upon her mouth and on her skin the day of their wedding, he didn't want her as she wanted him?

And suddenly that was the most fearful thing of all— so fearful that, like every other fear she'd ever known, Gwennan knew she had to confront it.

And—leaping to her feet—confront it she did.

'Kiss me, Rolant.'

Rolant's breath left him, and for a moment he doubted his own ears. But she was staring down at him intently, her eyes imploring, her lips already parted, expecting, waiting.

He'd seen Gwennan in many guises. In her tunic and the woollen leggings they called *socasau* here. In this same kirtle—the one she'd worn before the King—and in the red gown he'd unlaced last night. But he'd never seen her quite like this. He'd never seen her afraid.

But he saw fear now. Not the fear that sharpened all eyes before a battle, or the fear that met danger head-on, but the glazed, inner fear that lurked in the dread of something unseen, unknown.

'Kiss me!'

The demand was more urgent a second time, coming out through trembling lips on a breath that quivered too.

Rolant got to his feet. Was she testing him? Testing his word because she didn't believe it?

'You want me to kiss you?' he asked tentatively.

'We are man and wife, are we not?' Her brow creased and the fear in her eyes flared brighter. 'Yes! I want you to kiss me.'

Carefully, he reached out and closed his fingers about her wrist, where the long sleeve clung. Drawing her to him, he traced the forefinger of his other hand along her jaw, smooth and delicate and tense.

She was tense all over. He felt it in the way she forced herself to stillness, saw it in the panic of her eyes. He'd seen animals adopt that stance in the hunt, so still they blended into the landscape, hoping the hounds would never scent them.

But Rolant did as he was bid, since he could do no other, test or no. Tilting her chin up with his finger, he touched his lips lightly to hers. But, as light as it was, a shock of desire shot through him. His body jolted and at once, though without haste, he drew his head back.

Her eyes had closed as their mouths met, and now her lashes fluttered open. His body jolted a second time and so did his heart, violently inside him.

'Like that?' he asked, relieved that there was no jolt in his voice, or hardly any.

She nodded, but the expression in her eyes didn't match her words. 'Yes, just like that.'

The flush on her cheeks flamed, then faded. She looked down and away, and even though he'd done exactly as she'd bade him, if it really had been a test, Rolant sensed that he'd failed.

'Then I will always kiss you like that—unless you bid me otherwise, Gwennan.'

Neither of them moved for a moment. Through the stillness came a multitude of sounds and scents. A blackbird singing in some bushes, the leap of a fish midstream, the scent of honeysuckle on the air.

And above all his promise, like a silent echo, so easy to make yet so hard to keep. Even now, with the words hardly cold on his lips, Rolant wanted to break that vow. To pull her into her arms and kiss her as he really wanted to, in the way she clearly didn't want at all.

Yet did her blood not flow like his did? Alive and fervent? Did she not have needs that craved fulfilment, as he did? Did her heart not beat as his was hammering now? So hard it was a wonder his ribs didn't shatter?

If it did, it didn't beat for him.

She turned abruptly and walked to where their horses waited. Rolant followed, and as he stooped and linked his hands for her foot, and lifted her up into the saddle, it was his turn to feel fear.

Fear of failing to keep his promise should his body master his resolve.

Fear that he might one night weaken and so break the thin thread of trust between them.

Fear that if he did attempt to sever the thread that tied her to the past—as his bonds had once tied her to a cartwheel—she might hate him more than ever and for all eternity.

Chapter Sixteen

Three long nights later, Rolant was in dire fear of not just breaking his promise but of losing his wits completely.

His mind had taken to living in the realm of dreams and his body in the world of fantasy, where it lay alongside Gwennan's in that comfortable bed at night. While his loins boiled in fiery torment night *and* day.

Had he really thought it would be possible to lie on this infernal pallet and listen to Gwennan sleep? To hear the rustle of the coverings as she turned over onto one side or the other? To listen to her sometimes murmur through a dream or give a sigh or a cough?

Rolant rolled over onto his back and gritted his teeth, expelling a deep breath between them. If it wouldn't bring shame on them both he'd decamp to the strong room, barred windows and all!

'Rolant? Are you awake?'

Gwennan's voice came quietly through the curtain and he turned his head, half expecting—hoping?—to see her appear through its thick folds.

'Yes,' he replied. 'Is anything amiss?'

'No, nothing is wrong. I just wanted… I was just wondering about what you said.'

'What did I say?' he asked lightly, his heart missing a beat.

'You said I only had to call and you would come.'

Rolant balled his hands beneath his blanket and stared upwards into the darkness. The fire in the hearth was down to embers now, and it cast dim patterns around the room. But the fire inside him flared right up to the rafters.

'That is what I said.'

He waited. She hadn't asked once these past nights. She hadn't spoken at all after the curtain was drawn between them and the candles were doused. Would she ask tonight?

The silence stretched out and he thought she must have gone back to sleep. He was about to try doing the same thing when her voice came again.

'Do you remember the day we crossed the Dyfi ford?'

Rolant put his hands behind his head and smiled into the darkness. 'When you told me you'd happily see me go under the water but would never let Tarian drown?'

A little sound, halfway between a choke and a giggle, came from beyond the curtain. 'Tarian was Rhys's horse.'

He looked across to the table where the sword rested. It was hidden in the dark, of course, but he didn't need to see it. Every intricate carving, every gleaming inch of steel, was etched into his memory as indelibly as if she'd cleaved it right into his skull.

'Yes, I know.'

Rolant turned his eyes upwards to the roof again.

Even before Robert of Rhuddlan had recognised the stallion, her care of Tarian had told him that. Just as her possessive passion for the sword had shown him her undying love for the former owner of both.

There was a rustle of bedclothes and suddenly her voice was nearer. 'I lied to you the day after our wedding...by the river. That is, I didn't tell you the true cause of my fear.'

'Didn't you?' Every nerve in his body tightened. 'Do you want to tell me now?'

Lifting himself up on one elbow, Rolant stared hard at the curtain, less than a yard or so away from where he lay. By stretching out his arm he could sweep it aside, but he didn't. He wouldn't—not until she asked him to.

'Do you, Gwennan?' he pressed, praying for her to speak.

But, even so, he wasn't prepared for the words that came a moment later.

'It's the loss that frightens me.'

Before his eyes the curtain changed from black to a dim murky green, a slight movement of its heavy folds implying that she knelt just beyond it.

'What loss?' he asked.

'Any loss...all losses. First Caradog and Cadell, my brothers. Then Rhys. Then my parents were imprisoned and I lost my home. And finally, when my father came back as he did...'

He needed to see her face, but all he could do was grope blindly for the right words to say. 'Loss is a part of life, Gwennan. However painful, however hard to bear, it is inevitable. All we can do is try and live with it...accept it as the will of God.'

'Do you think your brother John's loss was inevitable?' The curtain moved again. 'Have you accepted the loss of your family—of Adeliza—as the will of God?'

Rolant's blood froze. She might as well have reached out from behind that heavy curtain and plunged a dagger into his chest, so sharp and unexpected was the pain that suddenly lanced through him.

Hauling himself up from the pallet, he crossed the room and lit a candle from the dying glow of the fire. Then he poured a cup of ale from the pitcher on the table, and sat down heavily upon a stool.

The cup was almost drained when the curtain parted and Gwennan stepped through it, blinking as the light hit her eyes. She wore a shift of pale saffron, and her feet were bare as they crossed the floor.

Drawing a stool forward, she sat opposite him, her hair falling forward and her eyes unrelenting as they searched his. 'Have you, Rolant?' she asked again. 'Tell me truly.'

Rolant shook his head. She'd admitted to her fears and he could do nothing less. Pouring another cup of ale, he filled a cup for her and pushed it across the table, noting the shaking of his hand.

'No, Gwennan, I have not.' There was a tremor in his voice too, but he didn't try to disguise it. The time for guise was done. 'Often we make things happen— good things and bad things. We cause pain to ourselves and to others without even realising it.'

Her gaze went to the sword and she ran her fingers over the scabbard. 'And we live with the consequences of our acts?' She looked back at him. 'Like a penance?'

Rolant nodded, and suddenly the sight of her hand resting on the weapon seemed to cut through the last remaining plates of armour that covered his heart. The final piece of his confession came gushing out, thicker and faster than blood from a wound.

'Once I asked for death because I was too much of a coward to face life. I got down on my knees and begged my father to kill me, because I couldn't live with the guilt of John's death.'

Gwennan's lashes flickered and he knew she was thinking back to the day she'd made him kneel in the dirt.

'But my father was wiser than me, and braver, because he knew that life goes on—no matter how much you wish it wouldn't. No matter how grievous a mistake you've made. How much you'd give to go back and change it.'

In the candlelight, her eyes were like dark bronze as they delved into his. 'But we can't go back, can we, Rolant? None of us can.'

Rolant shook his head. 'No, there is no going back, only forward, with faith and with courage. I know that now.'

She leaned forward, the shift opening a little to reveal the creamy skin of her throat and the swell of her breasts.

'But that's what frightens me, Rolant. I don't have enough courage or enough faith. I'm too much of a coward to bear any more losses.'

Rolant placed his hand over hers, finding it as cold as ice. 'Gwennan, you have the King's protection. You have your lands back, your mother is returned safe, and you are more secure now than before. What is there to fear?'

Gwennan shook her head. Didn't he realise what she was trying to say? After winning all those things, the loss of them would be hard, but she'd be able to bear it. But after finding love again, how could she ever survive if she lost it again? If she lost him?

She stared into his face, saw the strength in the strong bones, the wide, sensual curve of his mouth, the vivid eyes so full of vitality. 'You don't understand what I'm trying to tell you, do you? And I don't know how to make it clear.'

He put his cup down and then suddenly he was on his knees before her. The night shirt he wore hung loose from his shoulders, open at the throat to reveal his breastbone, the rise and fall of his chest, muscle rippling below bronzed skin.

'Then try to make me understand, Gwennan, for pity's sake!'

A lump rose into Gwennan's throat. He'd gone down on his knees before of his own accord. In the forest to dry her wet feet. And she'd tried to kick him away. A lifetime seemed to have passed since then, but even so her cheeks flamed at the memory of her ingratitude.

Now he was on his knees before her once again. But how could she tell him that she'd lost her heart to him? That he'd consumed her soul until she'd disappeared into him? That he was now a piece of her that she couldn't live without?

The green-gold eyes, locked imploringly on hers, burned inside her, demanding and deserving of the truth. And, at last, she gave it him.

'I am afraid that…if I let myself love you, I will lose you.'

Gwennan struggled to interpret the reaction on his face. It wasn't anger, or pain, or fury, nor disbelief or even disagreement. It was an expression she'd never seen before, and it alarmed her so much that she leapt to her feet.

But Rolant leapt too, so quickly that the gasp that broke from her died on her lips. And then his hands were around her upper arms, pulling her close and holding her away at the same time.

'You are afraid of loving me?'

His fingers tightened, digging into her flesh until she almost winced.

'God's blood, Gwennan!' His curse was a soft one. 'And all this time…!' A laugh broke from him—a strange, half-strangled sound. 'I believed no one could ever win your love because it still belonged to Rhys.' His gaze narrowed, grew sober. 'Does it, Gwennan?'

Gwennan shook her head. 'I will always keep a candle alight for him in the church. And I'll honour his memory for ever. But…it is *you* my heart craves, Rolant. *You*…no one else.'

His palms lifted to cup her face, tender and strong at the same time. 'Then let me get this clear, so there is no possibility that I am in reality still lying on that cursed pallet and this is all a dream.'

His fingers threaded into the hair at her temples. Gwennan tried to pull away but, gentle though his hold was, she was held firm. There was no escape and no hiding any more.

'Are you saying that you *might* love me if you weren't afraid of losing me?'

'Y-yes.' Her voice began to crack. 'And…if I *were* to lose you, I don't think I could survive…not a second time.'

He looked down into her eyes, his own dark with sincerity. 'Gwennan, listen to me. I loved John deeply,

and even though he's dead he lives on in my heart. I
love my parents and my sisters, even though we are es-
tranged. And I live in hope that the rift will be healed
one day. Do you know why I live in hope now? Why I
want to live at all?'

Gwennan shook her head, her limbs feeling so weak
that if he removed his hands she might well slump to
the floor.

'Because I have learned here—from *you*, Gwennan—that a family can surmount anything if its strength
is built on love, as yours is. It can survive all losses,
even the greatest of fears, if it is sustained by love.'

She felt tears sting behind her eyes and, wrenching
herself free, spun away to conceal them. Beneath her
feet the rushes felt cold, and the darkness she stared
into was like the ice that covered the water in winter.

'Oh, Rolant…'

Behind her stood the light and life of spring, if only
she was brave enough to look—to see it, to grasp it.
If she found the courage and the faith to let her heart
emerge from its hiding place and relinquish all disguise
and all defence.

But if *his* heart didn't respond—didn't even want to
see hers—what would she do without her inner sword
and her shield? How could she protect herself?

Then Rolant came up behind her. A soft sigh touched
the back of her neck and warmth spread all the way
through her as his arms enfolded her.

'Don't close your ears, Gwennan. I haven't finished.
There is more to say yet, before I'm absolved completely—or damned for all eternity.' He bent his head
and whispered in her ear. 'I love you, Gwennan, and
have done since the moment I picked you up and threw

you into that cart. Since I ruffled your hair and you looked at me as if you wanted to kill me.'

Gwennan bit back a sob as shock and disbelief and joy surged through her. She twisted in his arms, looked up into his face, saw a passion burning in his eyes that stole her breath away.

'You love me? But…what about when I pitched you out of the saddle? When I hit you with that rock? When I made you kneel in the dirt and kiss the sword? How *could* you love me when I did all that?'

His smile stretched wide and beautiful. 'Granted, there were times when my love was sorely tested…but nothing could stop me loving you and nothing ever will.'

Her heart was beating so fast she could barely breathe. Was this truly happening? Was he really looking down at her with love in his eyes? Yet his chest rose and fell even faster than hers did and his breath fanned her face, hot and ardent.

Gwennan placed her palm over his heart. It was beating hard and fast as well—too quickly for her to count. But was it real? Lasting, safe and true?

He seemed to see inside her to where the fear still lurked.

'And my love is yours for ever, if there is room in your heart for it, Gwennan.' He put his hand over her breast, where her heart thundered. 'If we live in here, and for each other, there is no loss to fear. Because love never truly dies.'

She swallowed, the beauty of his words, the sure and unshakeable truth of them, vanquishing fear at last. It wasn't fear or doubt that turned her legs to water and made her lips tremble, but something far stronger.

'Kiss me, Rolant.'

His gaze narrowed but his eyes twinkled a dazzling gold-green behind the long lashes. 'Like I did on our wedding day, perchance? And by the river?'

She shook her head. 'No, anything but like that!'

Taking hold of his shirt, she pulled him to her. His arms went about her waist, and when his mouth took hers it certainly *wasn't* the chaste kiss of their wedding ceremony, nor the one by the river.

Gwennan leaned into him, her lips parting, giving him entry. She drank in the taste of him as his tongue swept hers, melted into the body that pressed against hers, hard with passion.

And when his head lifted, a long moment later, fear had vanished for ever. 'I love you too, Rolant,' she whispered. 'So very much.'

His eyes flared, darkened, and then a wry grimace pulled at his mouth. 'Then do you think you might ask me now, Gwennan? Please do, for the love of God!'

She nodded breathlessly, her heart full of his beauty and her body on fire. 'Come to our bed and make me yours, Rolant.'

Rolant didn't wait to be asked twice. He picked Gwennan up and carried her over to the bed. Kneeling, he laid her down, as gently as he could, since his arms were shaking and the blood was coursing through in his veins as the last shreds of his self-control withered.

She pulled him down with her, her arms entwined around his neck, her fingers in his hair, their mouths meeting again. He allowed himself a moment, no more, because he wanted to savour this, not devour it like a man starved too long presented at last with an unimaginable feast.

The saffron shift fell loosely over her body, like a summer flower meadow. Her hair splayed in a vibrant fall of silken autumn on the pillow behind her head. A lump of humility rose into his throat, vanquishing lust for a moment, and he stilled and just gazed down at her.

'What is it?'

Her eyes were glazed with need, yet a shadow of doubt sounded in her question and in the crease of her brow.

He smiled and touched her face. 'Nothing is the matter, sweeting. Nothing at all.'

Her skin was soft, warm, glowing with the love she'd confessed. Love for him! He trailed his hand down her throat, his fingers caressing her skin, rejoicing in the beat of her pulse below. Then he peeled her shift down over her shoulders, partly exposing her glorious body.

'I thought you beautiful in a gown, Gwennan. You are even more so out of one!'

His eyes took in that beauty. The pale skin, the small round breasts, their tips erect and ardent, waiting for his touch. He bent his head and sucked one of the hard peaks into his mouth, swirling his tongue, nipping softly with his teeth, and she arched beneath him with a gasp.

Rolant smoothed his hand down over her ribs, her belly, to the soft curls between her thighs. Without him asking with words her legs parted and she gasped and arched again.

His loins screamed at him to take her, but he tightened his restraint and, kneeling up again, stroked his hand down her slender leg, her calf, her ankle. Cupping the foot that had once kicked out at him, he bent and kissed the toes, one by one. Then he trailed his fingers up the other leg, to tease the inside of her thighs again.

She arched once more as he delved there, at the sweetest part of her, and her gasp this time was accusing and complaining. 'R-Rolant, you are torturing me!'

Rolant chuckled. It was torturing him too, this honeyed teasing, this blissful reawakening of his heart and not just his body. 'That is my intention, Gwennan Fwyn, since you have done the same to me, many times over, this last month.'

'Oh? Such as when?'

'When you sat me as far away from you as possible at table. When you banished me to the strong room. When you bade me kiss you so chastely, like a brother. Need I say more?'

An instant later she was on her knees too, her hands fisting in his linen shirt. 'I see. So this is revenge, is it?'

He nodded. 'But of the very sweetest kind, my love, as you deserve.'

'We shall see about that.'

The next moment she was hauling his shirt over his head, *her* eyes devouring *him* now. She put her hands on his shoulders, exploring them from his collarbone to the blades of his back. Her fingers traced the old scar at the base of his neck, and then she placed her lips there and kissed it.

Then her hands moved down his body, over his chest and ribs, his stomach, to where his manhood pulsed and ached. She brushed lightly down the length of him, and with a groan he grabbed her wrists.

'If you do that, sweeting, this night will be over much too soon. And I want it to last as long as possible, so that I can show you how much I love you'

Rolant slipped the shift all the way down her body. It pooled like a bed of buttercups around her where she knelt, like a warm, golden living statue rising up out of the earth.

'Gwennan… I must tell you that I haven't lain with a woman…'

His voice faltered and her eyes searched his, then widened with incredulity. 'You are not a virgin?'

Rolant smiled, the whispered slurs of his former comrades rising up and then fading away into obscurity. Drawing her down beside him, he leaned on his elbow and looked down into her face. 'No, but it has been a very long time. I fear I may be out of practice!'

She giggled. 'I am no virgin either…as you know.' Her fingers lifted to trace his mouth. 'But at this moment everything is new, because you make it so, Rolant. And I am glad of that.'

Rolant took her lips then, softly at first, then deeply, his tongue tasting hers, their breathing quick and insistent. His hands touched all of her—her face, her throat, her breasts, her belly. Only when she was quivering like a bow in his hands, all her senses pulled taut, ready for release, did he stroke his way between her parted thighs once more.

She was warm and moist, like nectar, and he played and teased, stirring her passion until she was on the brink of release. Her gasping breaths, her soft moans, the honeyed glaze of her eyes guided him. When the time was ripe, he thrust inside her in one smooth movement, laying his body down upon hers so that they were skin to skin, heart to heart.

Their joining was perfect, as if all this time, his body, his soul, his love had been waiting for this moment, for this woman. They moved together as if each had become part of the other, their mouths clinging in kisses and sweet moans of ecstasy.

When she reached fulfilment, crying his name, Rolant felt his own release surge to the heavens. And afterwards a peace such as he'd never known settled over his soul and filled his heart. A peace that he knew would never be shattered as long as he lived.

Daylight broke with a burst of sunlight on the crest of the mountain and the song of a thrush outside the window. Gwennan's eyes flew open and fell into Rolant's. He was leaning up on one elbow, staring down at her, his face holding an expression of warmth, of wonder, of contentment…and of love.

'Good morn.'

He touched her cheek, brushing away some strands of hair from her eyes, before bending his mouth to take hers. A light kiss but not a chaste one.

'Good morn,' she replied, her heart picking up where it had finished last night—in the throes of a completion and a joy that she'd never expected to know again. A new and different joy. Because no man was the same as another, and no new love was the same as an old love.

And this glorious morning not even a shadow of fear remained to spoil either joy or love. The past had faded and settled peacefully, at rest at last.

Gwennan touched her fingertips to the scar on his cheek. He smiled into her eyes, their minds meeting in perfect tune, as their bodies had done. Then, taking a strand of her hair, he began to curl it around his forefinger.

'I had begun to think I was destined to sleep on that accursed pallet for the rest of my days, Gwennan Fwyn.'

He began to sing, his voice deep and rich, drowning out the birdsong outside the window. *'Gentle Gwennan, lovely maid. Dear heart, pure beauty...'*

The song had her bolting upright. 'How...? When did you learn that?'

His gaze twinkled. 'I asked Ywain the meaning of his song the night you sent him with the balm for my cheek.'

'And he told you? *Y cnaf!*'

'You mustn't blame him.' Rolant drew her back down into his arms. 'The wretch was so enamoured of Nest that he would have given me the keys to the door if I'd asked him, and a horse to ride away on.'

'And if he had would you have gone?'

He shook his head. 'No. I knew even then that my place was here, at your side, and always would be... Gwennan Fwyn.'

Gwennan felt her eyes fill and his gaze sobered, his face clouding with contrition as he brushed away the tear that fell onto her cheek.

'I won't call you that again if you don't wish it, my love.'

'Do you not know that women can cry with joy as well as with sorrow?' She smiled and placed her hand over his heart. 'And although that name might be fitting now, I have another one you might prefer—given what we did last night!'

'Oh?' His brow lifted and his eyes gleamed darker still, contrition gone, passion reigning.

The sun slanting in through the window touched his face, lighting the green-gold depths until she wanted to melt into them. 'Then, pray, enlighten me!'

The last piece of the past settled gently into the earth, and with a giggle she whispered in his ear.

'Gwennan Wyllt?' His face creased and his laughter filled the room. 'Should I go and ask Ywain the meaning this very moment, or are you going to tell me?'

Gwennan threaded her hands into his hair, pulled his head down until their mouths touched. She felt his body harden, his breath quicken, his heart start to thunder, as did hers.

'Kiss me, Rolant, and I'll *show* you what it means!'

And as he kissed her, deep and long, and then possessed her all over again, body, heart and soul, she knew she would be whatever he wanted her to be.

Gentle Gwennan or Wild Gwennan—as long as she was his Gwennan and he her Rolant.

Epilogue

❦

January 1092

Gwennan and Rolant sat on either side of a blazing hearth, wrapped in furs. It was a bitterly cold night, and life at Carn Egryn had slowed down with the coming of snow. The new year had been welcomed and celebrated, with everyone hoping for a year of peace ahead—many years of peace, if God were merciful.

And that morning, despite the snow, a messenger had come with two letters. They lay now on the table, opened and read, their contents surely a sign that the coming year would indeed be a good one.

Rolant broke the long and thoughtful silence that had fallen between them, as each was lost in the significance of those letters.

'I shall press the King to set a suitable amount of compensation, Gwennan. Your father deserves no less and the Earl can well afford to pay.'

Gwennan looked from the fire into his face. Her husband grew more handsome day by day, if that were possible. His eyes still shone like Talyllyn Lake under the summer sun, even though they were in the depths of a harsh winter.

She smiled, despite the shadow of sorrow that settled briefly over her soul. Money would not make up for her father's loss, but it would help in so many other ways.

'I imagine the King's decision in our favour will have spoiled the festive season at Rhuddlan this year!'

Rolant laughed, the sound warming her blood, stirring the love in her heart that seemed to grow day by day too, until she felt she would burst with it.

'And your own news, Rolant... I hope that makes your festive season even happier?'

He nodded. 'To be reconciled with my family makes my world complete. My home is here, Gwennan, and always will be, but one day you and I will have an estate in Normandy too. Mayhap next Christmas—if this peace prevails... God willing—we might visit my parents and sisters? Celebrate the festivities with them, if you would like it?'

'Perhaps a better question would be do you think they will like *me*?'

He smiled. 'They will love you, *f'anwylyd*, as I do.'

Gwennan snuggled further into the warm furs, her whole being bathed in contentment. 'Meuryn once said that you'd never master our language, but it seems you are determined to prove him wrong.'

'I have made a wager with Ywain that when your uncle and your mother return from visiting her family on Ynys Môn I shall welcome them in fluent Welsh.'

'Then I predict that you'll win that wager, like everything else you set your aim on.'

As he'd won her heart, and the hearts of her people—even her irascible uncle—over the last months.

As if in confirmation, footsteps echoed in the passageway without and two voices were softly heard—a man and a woman. The muffled words ceased and the notes of a love song drifted quietly on the air. Ywain was singing to Nest. The singing died away after a few lines and there was silence—the bursting silence of love—then came laughter and the feet passed on.

Gwennan met Rolant's eyes and they both smiled, reading each other's thoughts. Carn Egryn had become a place of love now, and the wrongdoings of the past, although never forgotten, had been replaced by happiness. Ywain was a healer in more than just herbs and balms—he was a healer of Nest's heart and womb too. The first was whole again and the other fruitful, not barren, as her maid had once feared.

'So, shall we visit Normandy next Christmas, my love?' Rolant leaned forward and took her hand. 'Or would you prefer to invite my family here?'

Gwennan felt as if her heart would burst with joy. Because Nest was not the only woman possessed of a fruitful womb. And Rolant had provided the perfect opportunity for her to share some news of her own.

'Under the circumstances, I think they had better come here.'

His brows lifted. 'Circumstances?'

She nodded. 'But when you write to invite them don't tell your parents that they will soon be grandparents. Let us keep that as a surprise for them!'

His eyes flared wide, bright and green and vivid in the firelight. The next instant he was on his knees in front of her, furs and all. 'Gwennan...are you saying you are with child?'

Gwennan touched his cheek where the scar she'd inflicted lay, almost invisible but always there. Healed, forgiven, and remembered not as a token of her former hatred but of the love that had come instead.

'That is indeed what I am saying, *'nghariad gŵr*. You are going to be a father come Michaelmas.'

He pulled her out of the chair and into his arms and they knelt together before the fire. He kissed her hair, her forehead, her lips, and then his hands cradled her face with such tenderness that she wanted to weep with love of him.

'A year ago I'd never met you. I knew only of your existence—the stubborn renegade Welsh Princess who refused to yield. And now...' He shook his head and his voice broke. 'There is one thing, at least, for which we must thank Robert of Rhuddlan.'

Gwennan blinked, then stared astonished into her husband's eyes. 'And what would *that* be, pray?'

'That he sent *me* here, and none other, to bring you to heel.'

She giggled, wrapped her arms around his neck, and steeled her tone to a mock reprimand. 'And is that what you think you've done? Brought me to heel... *Norman*?'

He chuckled. 'I think rather it is the other way around... *Arglwyddes*...my love.'

Her heart swelled as he took her mouth, his kiss kindling her passion, as his kisses always did. And when his lips left hers again Gwennan whispered into his ear. He might not have conquered her in the way he'd set out to do, but he'd captured her heart and would hold it for ever.

'Take me to bed, Rolant...and make me yours.'

* * * * *

*If you enjoyed this story, make sure
to pick up Lissa Morgan's debut*

The Welsh Lord's Convenient Bride

Historical Note

Following the Norman Conquest of England in 1066, William Rufus, like his father before him, endowed his barons with lands along the Welsh border. These powerful men had licence to conquer as much of Wales as they could from their Marcher strongholds of Chester, Shrewsbury and Hereford.

Hugh d'Avranches, Earl of Chester—called The Wolf or The Fat—and his bellicose cousin Robert of Rhuddlan had taken possession of most of the North Wales coastal strip by the late eleventh century. Although they probably didn't encroach as far as the Dysynni Valley, further south beyond the Cadair Idris mountains, they doubtless would have done so in time.

However, with the escape of Gruffudd ap Cynan from Chester around 1093 the tide turned. Robert of Rhuddlan was killed that year, after recklessly taking on a combined Welsh and Norse raid near his castle of Deganwy. Over the next decade the Normans were driven out of North Wales, not to recover it again until the final conquest by Edward I in 1282-3.

My heroine is inspired by Gruffudd ap Cynan's

daughter, Gwenllian, who did indeed wield a sword and fought bravely alongside her husband to defend their homeland of Deheubarth. She perished in battle with the Normans in 1136, and her husband, Gruffudd ap Rhys, died the following year. But their sons carried on the fight.

It isn't known whether Gwenllian donned men's clothing as she waged war against her enemy, and it would have been unusual for women to flout the rules of Medieval law and the Church in such a way.

But, as Gwennan says to Rolant... How can a woman ride and fight in skirts?

COMING NEXT MONTH FROM

HARLEQUIN
HISTORICAL

All available in print and ebook via Reader Service and online

HIS INHERITED DUCHESS (Victorian)
Daring Rogues • by Bronwyn Scott

With his promotion to duke, carefree Logan must bear the responsibility of a new household...and its widowed duchess, Olivia. Unraveling Olivia is a challenge Logan never anticipated...but cannot resist!

A SEASON OF FLIRTATION (1830s)
by Julia Justiss

When Laura offers to tutor her friend in flirtation, she doesn't expect that she'll have to put her own lessons to use—on one Miles Rochdale no less!

MARRIAGE DEAL WITH THE EARL (Regency)
by Liz Tyner

A convenient marriage to long-term friend Quinton seems the only solution to her late husband's debt, but Susanna's not prepared when buried feelings start to resurface!

THE MAKING OF HIS MARCHIONESS (Victorian)
by Lauri Robinson

After Clara finds refuge in the Marquess of Clairmount's estate, her attraction to the marquess is bittersweet, as this Cinderella knows she doesn't belong in his aristocratic world...

BEGUILING HER ENEMY WARRIOR (Viking)
Shieldmaiden Sisters • by Lucy Morris

Captured by a Welsh prince intent on revenge against her family, Helga must keep her wits about her. Easier said than done when she desires him rather than fears him!

CONVENIENTLY WED TO THE LAIRD (Georgian)
by Jeanine Englert

Ewan and Catriona have one rule in their arrangement—they mustn't fall in love. Yet faced with Catriona's bravery, can Ewan resist the one rule he must not break?

YOU CAN FIND MORE INFORMATION ON UPCOMING HARLEQUIN TITLES, FREE EXCERPTS AND MORE AT HARLEQUIN.COM.

HHCNM1222